Kate Mears

A HOUSE IN THE COUNTRY

Persephone Book N° 31
Published by Persephone Books Ltd 2002
Reprinted 2005 and 2010

First published 1944 by Hodder & Stoughton
© The Estate of Jocelyn Playfair
Preface © Ruth Gorb 2002

Endpapers taken from a 1942 Jacqmar scarf
reproduced by kind permission of the owner.

Typeset in ITC Baskerville by Keystroke,
Wolverhampton

Printed and bound in Germany by
GGP Media GmbH, Poessneck

on Munken Premium (FSC approved)

ISBN 978-1-903155-202

Persephone Books Ltd
59 Lamb's Conduit Street
London WC1N 3NB
020 7242 9292

www. persephonebooks.co.uk

A HOUSE IN THE COUNTRY

by

JOCELYN PLAYFAIR

with a new preface by

RUTH GORB

PERSEPHONE BOOKS
LONDON

PREFACE

Throughout the 1950s a woman in her middle years could be seen riding her out-sized bright yellow bicycle through the streets of South Kensington. She could have been, more often than not, on her way to the Institut Français to study Proust. She was striking, with her cropped hair and trousers, and her name was Jocelyn Playfair.

A well-known, somewhat eccentric figure in the London of her day, her name is virtually unknown today. But between the years 1939 and 1952 she produced ten novels, ranging from murder mysteries to romance. They were well-received by reviewers, including luminaries such as C.P. Snow, and by readers – one of her books, *The Fire and the Rose*, was reprinted only two months after it was published in 1948.

There is a certain neatness about her output: she started to write as the Second World War was imminent, and she stopped in 1952, as life returned to normal – a direct result, it is easy to say, of the boredom, loneliness and frustration experienced by so many women during the war years. But for Jocelyn Playfair that very loneliness was an opportunity to think, to ponder huge questions such as the validity of war, the quality of human kindness, the conflict between love and duty, and between tradition and the need to look to the future. These questions, all of them as important today as they were then, are at the heart of this, her best novel, *A House in the Country* (1944).

The title is misleadingly cosy, and so is an outline of the plot: a valiant gentlewoman struggles with the inconveniences of running a large country-house in wartime, and dreams of the man she loves. And yes, Cressida is stunningly beautiful and Charles is the romantic figure of all women's dreams. But to say any of this is to underestimate Jocelyn Playfair's thoughtfulness and intelligence; she had things to say, and she said them in a setting that she knew well – a setting that we in turn know well from the work of Mollie Panter-Downes and Jan Struther, and none the worse for that.

Jocelyn Playfair's life appeared to be archetypal English upper middle-class: she was an army daughter who believed that it was her proper place to be a good army wife (which in the fullness of time she was) and that she should be looked after by servants. Look into her background, though, and a less conventional picture emerges. Her father, Noel Malan, was a Lieutenant-Colonel, but he was also a talented artist and a member of the Younghusband expedition to Tibet. Her mother, Christine, was a gentle soul, a talented violinist, and both she and her husband were descended from the highly artistic French Huguenot Malan family who had emigrated to England in the mid-nineteenth century.

These artistic roots took time to manifest themselves in Jocelyn. She was far from academic, left school as soon as was decently possible, and preferred horses to dolls. As a young woman she did what was expected of her and in 1930 married Ian Playfair, an army officer in the Royal Engineers as her father had been. She and her husband, who was later to be a much-decorated Major-General, spent most of the 1930s on postings abroad, first in Singapore and then in Quetta, India, now Pakistan. She had two sons, John, born in 1931, and Guy, born in 1935 – the very year when Quetta experienced an earthquake in which some thirty thousand people died. Jocelyn Playfair and her little boys were, understandably, sent home to grandparents and safety in St John's Wood.

It is possible that the leisured life of a pre-war army wife (not entirely to her liking – it annoyed her that the cook did not even allow her into her own kitchen) gave her the first opportunity to write. But the outbreak of war changed everything for her as it did for everyone. Ian Playfair spent the war serving in South-East Asia, while she stayed in England with the children, moving no less than seventeen times to country cottages and houses of varying degrees of discomfort in Wiltshire and Gloucestershire.

She did her bit for the war effort, working as a nurse and in a munitions factory, and for one happy period as the cook in her boys' boarding school in Salisbury; she was an excellent cook and her sons' popularity shot up overnight. She took in paying guests, and was one of the first of her kind to realise that one could do without servants, and that without servants it was really rather more convenient to eat in the kitchen: 'How quaint and amusing . . .' says Cressida's deeply shocked aunt, Miss Ambleside, in *A House in the Country* as Cressida serves tea at the large scrubbed kitchen table, and bravely goes on to add, 'I find this most original. Somehow one never visualises meals in the kitchen.' Cressida points out that it saves her eight hundred and thirty-five hours of work a year, the army wife Madge Rimmington-Clarke says it's a relief not to have the servants' squeaky shoes as a dining-room background noise, but Miss Ambleside remains unconvinced.

For most of the war years, however, Jocelyn Playfair led an isolated life. Her husband was abroad, her sons were at boarding school, and she had never been very good at organising a social life, nor did she care for it; her friends were few, but close. It was then that she started to write in earnest. The first two books were crime novels. The first, *Murder Without Mystery* (1939), was rejected the first time round, then accepted by Hodder & Stoughton who thereafter published all her books.

The 1940s were immensely productive; Jocelyn Playfair, working on an old black Remington typewriter that her son Guy still has, produced almost a novel a year, and seemed at first to be all set to join the ranks of the lady thriller writers she so enjoyed reading herself. By some quirk of coincidence her second book, *Eastern Weekend* (1940), had virtually the same plot as Agatha Christie's *Then There Were None* [original title *Ten Little Niggers*] which was published at the same time as her book but which she could not possibly have read.

But as the war dragged on she became more reflective. She was passionately left-wing; collective farms, she was apt to say, were the answer to England's social problems. She developed a hatred of what she saw as the Conservative toff culture and of snobbery – witness Cressida's fury with the tweedy Mrs Brandon in *A House in the Country* who refused to have private soldiers billeted on her for fear of what their boots would do to her stair carpet: 'Did Mrs Brandon, she wondered, suppose that the boots of sergeants were more delicately constructed . . . or would she perhaps prefer the boots of the German army?'

The action of the book takes place at the time of the Fall of Tobruk in June 1942, one of the worst disasters of the War, which threatened to drive the Allies out of Egypt and after which 30,000 British soldiers were taken prisoner. This debacle caused dismay and trepidation in Britain and accelerated radical thinking; soon afterwards the new 'Common Wealth Party' was formed, led by Sir Richard Acland. He believed that service to others, not private gain, should be the mainspring of social action, and the Common Wealth movement proposed that all property beyond what was necessary for personal use should be taken into common ownership. In 1943 Acland made over his hereditary estates in Somerset to the National Trust.

Through Cressida one sees a Jocelyn Playfair whose growing radicalism would not have fitted easily into the county set, even in wartime. She was a thinking, admittedly intolerant woman with strong ideas who liked to impress those ideas upon other people. The move to London after the war meant that she would soon stop writing, but that her delight in intellectual conversation could blossom – one of her great joys was arguing with her writer son, Guy, and her scientist son, John.

Together with John and his Corsican wife, in the 1950s Jocelyn Playfair moved to a large house in Ovington Square,

Kensington. The house had been abandoned after being bombed during the war, but if there was one thing Mrs Playfair loved it was a challenge, and she rose magnificently to a crisis: on one memorable occasion the roof fell in, the house flooded, and the mopping up operation was undertaken with enthusiasm that verged upon glee.

The years in Ovington Square, with John and his wife Line upstairs and Jocelyn Playfair in the garden flat, were happy and liberating. Once again there was a series of lodgers, at one time a Polish family whom Jocelyn Playfair taught English, at another the comedian Peter Cook – Jonathan Miller and Dudley Moore used to join him in his rooms at Ovington Square for rehearsals of their inspired lunatic performances.

There was also a great deal of family closeness: Jocelyn Playfair was devoted to her sons, and welcomed her daughter-in-law into the fold in her own inimitable fashion – the fact that Line never once resented being taught the ways of English customs and behaviour by her mother-in-law is a credit to the essential niceness of both women. It was, in fact, Line who visited her mother-in-law almost every day when in the end the older woman lived in a residential home.

As Line, John and Guy talk about their mother, a picture emerges of a stylish, brisk, unconventional woman of remarkable talents and paradoxes. Loyal and loving towards her army husband (although he, too, defied the stereotype by writing humorous pieces for Punch and composing pop dance music), she was also a maverick and a bohemian. She went in for carrot juice and yoga, before such things were fashionable and rather at odds with her heavy smoking – she favoured Passing Cloud cigarettes, oval-cylindrical in shape and in a pink packet. She loved jazz, and she wore trousers much of the time before it was usual in woman of her class – as does Cressida in *A House in the Country*. If she had innate chic, it was very much in her own style. She stunned the other guests at Line and John's wedding in Corsica with her glittering fake diamond dog collar. She would make all her own clothes, on one occasion designing a long tweed house-coat embroidered in brilliant colours. She made dramatically beautiful jewellery, was a skilled carpenter and wood-carver, loved to unravel jerseys and re-knit them into something multi-coloured, lovely, and totally original, she would take a wilderness and turn it into a garden – one manifestation after another of the Huguenot craftsmanship that was in her blood.

As she grew older she became more outrageous and swung dramatically to the right. She talked disparagingly of the Labour Prime Minister, 'that dreadful little man, Wilson', was apt to pronounce that 'what the world needs is another war', and actually professed a grudging admiration for Mrs Thatcher. She became interested in comparative religion and psychical research, and was increasingly impatient with the ageing process. 'What they should do with old people,' she would say, 'is line them up and shoot them.'

Her mind (and her tongue) remained lively, and the imagination that had produced her novels was channelled into new interests and combative conversation. And it was a fertile imagination: her plots were not drawn from her own life, and her romantic heroes (who, rather strangely, were often called Charles) were, apparently, delightful invention. The only time she used a real-life incident was in the novel *A Man Called Miranda* (1949), in which a woman meets a man from her past on the night train to Lausanne, with romantic consequences. In 1947 Jocelyn Playfair did in fact travel by train to Lausanne to fetch her son Guy from school; but she was there only briefly and her son is sure she did not have time for the adventures depicted in the book.

In *A House in the Country*, though, there can be little doubt that she was expressing her own strongly held views and feelings through the voices of the fictional Cressida and Charles. And they were views that were significantly ahead of her time. She wrote the book in a period when the war effort was all, and the plucky little Mrs Miniver figure had no doubt about what England was fighting for. But for Charles this was the big, all-embracing question: 'Why am I fighting? . . . Fighting for my country, fighting because it's my job, because I obey orders, because I hate the Germans, because I'm frightened, because everyone else is fighting . . . How many men would give that last answer, and yet of how many was it not probably true?'

Cressida sees war as having reached 'such a peak of insensate fury that it could lead nowhere but to ultimate chaos.' And in confusion and depair she sees the place of her own helpless, tiny self in this terrible scheme of things: she hears that a thousand British bombers had flown over a German city the previous night; she thinks of the cabbages in neat rows in her kitchen garden, and a pie she left in the oven and must hurry to take out, and a thousand bombers going out in a night. . . The beauty of small, domestic things survives in the setting of a world being torn apart, and she cannot see the sense of any of it.

Jocelyn Playfair pulls no punches in *A House in the Country*, and Cressida's is not a sanitised war. Charles survives an appalling fourteen days in an open lifeboat after his ship is torpedoed. Tori, the Central European refugee who lives briefly in Cressida's house, and who loves her, has seen unspeakable horror in his native country. Six bombs are dropped one night on Cressida's quiet village, and there is heartbreak as her gardener scrabbles in the wreckage for his dead wife. Yet somehow life goes on, and the cabbages stand in rows . . .

This conflict between the contentment of the garden, cooking and home, and the cataclysmic events outside form a leitmotif to the book. And Brede Manor, the Georgian house that belongs to Charles and which he has left in Cressida's keeping for the duration of the war, is a symbol of all that is good and beautiful, and under threat. Adrift at sea, Charles has a vision: 'It was a picture of Germans in uniform clattering up and down the staircase at Brede, of Germans armoured vehicles roaring through the gates of Brede, those gates whose gossamer loveliness should open upon nothing but sacred peace.' Ever since he can remember he has thought it the most lovely house in the world, but the war has made him see that he has been possessed by it. To Cressida, though, it has been made lovelier by being a haven for people made homeless by the war. The kitchen is the heart of that haven, and as she riddles the Aga and cooks the porridge and plans what vegetables to have for lunch, she creates her own peace. Jocelyn Playfair, constantly on the move during the war, surely saw Brede Manor as the embodiment of all the stability and beauty she yearned for.

A House in the Country was published in April 1944; the war was far from over when it was written, yet it has an elegaic quality. It is both thoughtful and moving, and one is left with a sense of regret that the author wrote no more when she passed her forties; what, one wonders, would she have made of the turbulent years of so-called peace?

She lived until the great age of ninety-two. When she could no longer manage alone, her son John arranged for her to go to a nursing home near where he lived in Chiswick. She was very happy there, but became solitary, asking nothing more than to sit quietly in the garden and to look at old family photographs with her daughter-in-law. She died when she had had enough of life, and just before she died she described a dream she had: it was, she said, like a Douanier Rousseau painting, with naked people and clear, pure colours. 'This,' she said, 'is what it must be like on the other side.'

Ruth Gorb
London, 2001

A HOUSE IN THE COUNTRY

CHAPTER ONE

'Well, the Government damn well ought to –'

Charles Valery interrupted. He knew the rest of the sentence would annoy him.

'Hold on,' he said, 'who is –'

A long time afterwards he remembered the noise and the ship's wild leap that had sent him skating across the deck and slapped him against an iron derrick so violently that his arms had been flung round it as if they had been wet coat sleeves blown by opposing gales. He remembered, in time, the scream of tearing metal and the hard roar of fire, and he was never able to forget Harcourt's face, floating bodiless in a sea of flame, so distorted that it was difficult to recognise. He could not remember any of his own sensations; if it had not been for Harcourt's face the whole affair would have been like a memory of a well-produced film of a ship being torpedoed, except that he didn't think about torpedoes at the time, or very much about ships. He thought about Harcourt's face and was grateful when a sheet of flame as bright as glass hid it from him.

He did not remember unwrapping his arms from the derrick; in fact he did not remember moving at all, and as he was the sole survivor of the *Alice Corrie*, 5,700 tons of lost shipping, no one ever knew that he had forced a way through the fire, groping for Harcourt's anguished face. He had never liked Harcourt very much.

By sunrise the convoy was fifty miles from the place where the *Alice Corrie* had gone down, and even by daylight it would have been difficult to see that the single lifeboat still floating on a patch of slightly oily sea contained two bodies.

CHAPTER TWO

By the time John Greenacre had walked a quarter of a mile up the drive of Brede Manor he was in a panic. He tried to concentrate on a vision of Felicity with her flaming red hair and green eyes, and the wonderful clothes she wore, and her tormenting figure. He reminded himself for the hundredth time that she was going to marry him. Round a curve in the drive he came upon a view of the house. He stopped dead. This really was impossible. He could not walk up to that magnificent Georgian façade, the mere sight of which evoked visions of butlers, hunt balls and prize carnations grown in mid-winter. The lawn that lay between himself and the house looked as wide as a good-sized lake. John stuffed his hands into the scratchy pockets of his battledress and thought with increased fervour of Felicity.

This is hell, he also thought. It's all very well for cads like Chris Hemmingway who seem to be able to treat all women as if they were barmaids and make them like it. I'm getting out of this.

He half turned away from the view of the house. As he did so the sun caught every pane in the high, evenly spaced windows of the lovely front and spread warmth over the old red bricks, so that the house glowed like a jewel against the dark trees behind. John Greenacre felt like a fly under the eyes of at least a dozen spiders. Someone would have seen him by now, out of one of those endless windows. He squared his shoulders. He was going to marry Felicity. He marched on with great determination and a sinking heart.

High, white painted doors under an Adam portico were wide open. Feeling more than ever like a fly under observation, John rang the bell. It seemed to him that he waited hours, trying not to stare into the vast cool hall, so disconcertingly exposed before his eyes. To take his mind off the size of the hall he looked back at the immense lawns. The sight of a flourishing crop of daisies comforted him a very little, but the sound of footsteps in the house made him jump, his nervousness in full control once more. Oh, well, he assured himself, probably some quite harmless old trout owns all this.

A figure stood between the open doors. John Greenacre became aware of shining pale hair, long fingers with varnished nails on the doorknob, and grey flannel trousers with an oil mark on one leg, a combination that somehow produced an impression of terrifying smartness. Oh, God, he thought, this is the end.

'Oh – um –' he began, and cursed himself because he knew he was blushing.

'I'm Mrs Chance,' a voice said, 'are you looking for rooms?'

Out of sheer relief John Greenacre laughed.

'How did you know?' he said, and almost ceased to be nervous.

Cressida Chance smiled. The outer ends of her eyebrows flew upwards like delicate antennæ. John Greenacre was sufficiently recovered to notice that she had a wide, lovely mouth and eyes as friendly as those of a nice dog. He took in very shortly the fact that she was startlingly beautiful.

'We get about fifty a week,' she said. 'Come in.'

'How awful for you,' John said, 'I mean it must be pretty grim.'

'No worse than vacuum cleaners. I used to get landed with dozens.'

John found himself sitting on a large leather sofa, being amiably sniffed by two Dalmatian dogs.

'This is marvellous,' he said. 'I was feeling frightful, walking in here like this.'

'I can imagine it,' Cressida said, thinking that it was lucky he didn't know how little imagination had been necessary.

'I've been to four other houses in the village and this was a last despairing effort.' John blushed, more vividly than before. 'I mean – I didn't mean that!'

Mrs Chance laughed again. 'Did they make you feel you smelt?'

'Practically, yes.' John hurried on gratefully, 'There was one house, the one on the corner, with green shutters and pretty well strangled with honeysuckle, where I got an outsize rocket.' Oh, Lord, he thought, they're probably her best friends.

'I know them. They're reduced to three maids, so of course paying guests are quite too much trouble. We haven't got any servants, thank God, can your wife work?'

John had not yet encountered Mrs Chance's habit of running a question on to the end of a sentence about something else. He jumped slightly.

'Oh, yes, rather!' he said with unnatural enthusiasm, and then checked himself. 'At least – well – well I – I think so.' He could not remember ever having seen Felicity do anything that could be called work, but of course she would be able to. She was wonderful, perfect, and could do anything. And hearing her called 'your wife' . . . his heart quickened. 'You see we – we're getting married next week,' he ended, hoping he hadn't given a cue for coy observations.

'Oh, I see,' Cressida went on calmly. 'Well, we'd better discuss rooms. I'll show you what there is.'

A telephone bell rang at the far end of the hall. Mrs Chance left John and answered it.

'Yes,' she said. 'Yes. Hold on a minute.' She disappeared through a door and John heard her calling someone. 'Mary. It's for you.' She came back into the hall, followed by another woman whose hands were fluttering a little, although her plain, pleasant face was quite calm. She hurried to the telephone. Cressida Chance came back to John.

'Let's go upstairs,' she said, as if the other little scene had not interrupted the conversation.

The staircase, railed with delicately wrought iron, rose in a gracious curve to a railed gallery. The woman below could be heard at the telephone.

'Yes, yes,' she was saying, quite quietly, but with unmistakable urgency. 'Oh, yes, thanks.' The bell clinked as she put down the telephone.

Cressida Chance ran downstairs, leaving John in the gallery. He stared down a wide corridor that ended in a window which, though he knew nothing about architecture, seemed to him remarkably beautiful. In a moment Mrs Chance was back.

'I'm sorry,' she said. 'I just had to see. Her husband's in Tobruk. It was a cable from him. This is one of the rooms no one's in at the moment.' She opened a door.

From the far end of the corridor a man appeared. He was small and dark, and had a lined, ugly face, like a monkey. He also had so much personality that it did not matter what he looked like.

'Cressida,' he said, giving the name an exaggerated beauty by his strong foreign accent. 'Cressida. You are more beautiful and clever every day, and you will, though it is three o'clock, give me some lunch.'

'It's a quarter to four, Tori,' Cressida answered calmly. 'But there's some food in the bottom oven which you may take out and eat.'

'You know that without you I shall not,' the little man said. 'I bring it to your feet.'

'No good, Tori, I'm busy. And walking all over the house, anyway,' Cressida remarked.

'Ah! Then am I bored and shall not eat,' Tori said, and walked purposefully downstairs and in the direction of the kitchen.

John Greenacre looked past Mrs Chance through the door she had opened. He saw what seemed a huge expanse of grey carpet, very thick, yellow silk curtains at least twelve feet long, and a pair of divan beds whose luxuriously rounded forms suggested almost indecent comfort. A small boy in dirty blue dungarees lay on his stomach in a shaft of sunlight on the grey carpet. There was a wooden cage, about six inches from his face, with the door open. Mrs Chance appeared to be unmoved by this sight.

'John darling, don't you think it's a bit stuffy of you to stay in here?' she said. 'This is one of the rooms you could have,' she went on without a pause.

John Greenacre, a little dazed by so much luxury, hesitated, and the small boy spoke first.

'I'll go in the garden if you insist,' he announced. 'The children are a nuisance in the nursery. Ajax won't come out unless we have perfect quiet.' He stood up, shut the cage doors carefully, picked it up and left the room, flashing a smile of such dazzling charm at John Greenacre that the young man was stricken with a silence even deeper than before.

'But you'd better look at some others too,' Cressida went on. 'Although this is much the warmest in the winter if you should happen to stay so long.'

It'll be five guineas a head, John Greenacre thought miserably. I'll have to get out of this somehow.

He was led to another room, and then to a third. He managed to answer when he was spoken to, and at the end of ten minutes was beginning to feel so much at home that he had to concentrate, with an effort, on the thought of five guineas a head, so that he should not find himself committed to bringing his Felicity to a house whose loveliness was for him overshadowed by the hideous spectre of far more money than he was ever likely to possess.

From the window of the third room there was a view of some stables, and a paddock with a few show ring jumps visible at one end. John began to talk about horses, feeling the meshes of his desire to live in this house tightening with every word. Cressida Chance saw him look at the stables.

'The stables are rather misleading,' she said, 'but there are still two horses. The – the owner of the house used to race a lot.' If they're going to live here they'll have to know, she reminded herself. 'The house belongs to Charles Valery,' she added casually, thinking: It ought to be quite easy by now, I've told dozens of people; anyhow, this boy's so young he won't know.

John Greenacre's interest, however, quickened visibly. Oh, God, Cressida thought.

'Not *the* Charles Valery?' Greenacre asked eagerly. 'The chap that won the National in '36 I think it was? I was there. It was terrific. The finish –'

'Yes, that's the one,' Cressida told him. 'Well look, when were you thinking of coming?' Stop him asking any more questions.

John Greenacre's mind came back with a jolt to the question of money, which had become every moment more difficult to mention. Damn, he thought, damn.

'Well I –' he began, and blushed for the first time in half an hour.

'It'll work out at roughly four guineas,' Cressida said, 'in case you'd like to know the worst.'

John made a painfully simple calculation. His pay was under thirty pounds a month; four eights were thirty-two. . . .

'Not each, you know, altogether,' Cressida finished, taking care that this time he should not see her smile. He had a quite remarkably transparent mind, she thought, amused, and at the same time full of pity for him.

Half an hour later John Greenacre walked down the drive. This time he was so happy that it was likely he would begin to sing at any moment. He was a young man with very simple emotions, and giving them expression came as naturally to him as breathing.

We'll be married in a week, he thought. In one week. By Gad, Valery rode a damn good race . . . a good day that had been, luck not getting caught by anyone from the college . . . that wizard room with the yellow curtains, Felicity would love it . . . sixteen guineas a month left quite a bit over . . . wizard life . . . horses . . . sun was grand. . . .

John Greenacre broke into song. By the time he reached the gates his pace had made him sweat, but he did not slow down.

CHAPTER THREE

Cressida Chance, alone in the kitchen, slammed the oven door, filled a kettle and put it on the boiling-plate of the stove, scattered cups and saucers and plates on the big table at one side of the room and fetched bread and butter and honey from the larder. She did all this at great speed but, except for the slam of the oven door, scarcely any sound. She moved with quite astonishing rapidity, yet her movements were not jerky or violent; they were, rather, casual and sometimes almost lackadaisical. It always seemed mere luck that the things she arranged on the table should land neatly in the right places. She glanced at the heat indicator on the cooker. It showed well below the proper mark.

Tori again, Cressida thought, well, they can't have scones.

Evidently Tori had eaten all the food she had left for him. He had washed his dishes and put everything tidily away, so that, probably, no one but himself would be able to find any of them. But he had not managed to shut the door of the oven which would, therefore, not get hot for an hour at least. Tori tried very hard, and even if he had not it was impossible to get angry with him. But it was a pity about the oven. Charles used to say that Tori was brilliant in every way but would go through life losing keys. Charles –

Cressida swung away from the cooker to the window, from which there was a view of half an acre of cabbages with the stables in the distance.

Oh, God, why did that young man have to have seen Charles on that day of all others? He ought to have been too young to be at any race meeting, and why choose that one, that one day when it had all started; or not started exactly but reached a stage at which it couldn't be stopped? As clearly as if it had been last week every detail of that day flashed through Cressida's mind.

The long drive with Simon . . . Simon as nervous as one of his own horses, talking, talking as if he would never stop . . . meeting Charles outside a stand, already wearing his pale-green jacket and silly papery little boots . . . Simon in a desperate, irritable hurry, rushing off to change although there was plenty of time . . . Charles talking a little, but mostly just standing by her, watching the people, very quiet and calm, lighting a cigarette for her so that, for a second, she saw his hand shaking. . . .

Cressida tried to count the cabbages, but it was no good.

. . . Charles and Simon going off at last to mount . . . Simon still talking, with his arm on Charles's shoulder . . . Cressida trying to watch the race with only a normal display of excitement . . . putting up and removing her field glasses at the right moments . . . glancing at her card from time to time; as if it was necessary. The flashing chestnut and Charles's apple-green jacket were never hard to distinguish . . . Simon in

scarlet and black, leading the field almost the whole way . . .
Charles and Simon taking the last fence together, the last of
those sickening moments which she thought she must faint
over . . . the nightmare of riderless horses and glare and great
black barriers over . . . the mass sighs and gasps of the crowd
swelling to the roar that would greet the winner, roaring in
Cressida's ears already . . . the bright chestnut's last lovely
leap and sudden spring forward, as if he had only that
moment realised he was racing . . . Gold Mohur wins! . . . he
wins . . . Gold Mohur! Gold Mohur . . . ! Charles winning by
two lengths. . . .

Masses of people crowding round Charles after the race
. . . Simon there too, grinning and slapping Charles on the
back, but with his sulky mouth quivering at the corners,
the beginning of one of his ugly moods too easy for Cressida
to foresee. Simon Chance, handsome, petted, fascinating
and spoilt, beaten again and working up a sulk . . . Charles
very pale and obviously exhausted, but perfectly calm,
with his eyelids half lowered as if the light hurt his eyes . . .
Charles looking at Cressida for a second, just long enough
for her to see in his eyes a small boy sick, nearly mad, with
excitement . . . Cressida, feeling almost sick herself, with the
longing to get him away from the crowds and the chatter
and excitement . . . staying and chattering like everyone else,
watching the lines in Charles's thin face grow deeper and
the set of his mouth tighter, knowing his knee had begun to
hurt. . . .

The kettle began to sing on the cooker but memory would
not be stopped.

. . . Dinner in that hotel with Charles and Simon and some other dim people who didn't matter . . . Simon drinking steadily all the evening, Charles looking as if it was long past his bedtime . . . dinner dragging on and on, everyone being so cheerful and 'amusing' . . . Simon going off at last, with two other men, in the direction of the bar, leaving her for a minute with Charles, who said, 'I'm sorry, Cressida,' as if he was apologising for winning the race. . . .

The kettle was boiling vigorously. Cressida made the tea. Oh, God, oh, God, she thought.

She could hear several people talking in the hall, their voices growing louder.

In a minute that Yates woman will come in and apologise for not being in time to make the tea. Charles, Charles. . . .

'Oh, Mrs Chance. I'm sorry. I'd've got tea . . .'

Wonder how much longer they're staying . . . if she says that every day. . . .

'Well, I was here, doing nothing. Please don't worry.'

Doing nothing. Doing nothing but dream about something that was nothing to do with life any more.

'The honey's at your end, Jim. . . .'

Tea went on. Mary Handley told everyone about her cable from Tobruk. Mrs Yates told everyone about her baby's bad night. Jim Rimmington-Clarke told everyone that Sunday was the only day of the week he got a decent cup of tea. His wife said how hard he worked, but of course it was an interesting job. He tried to look overworked and interesting, but entirely failed to do either. Mrs Yates said of course her Willy never got back to tea, but then the aerodrome was so far

14

away. Everyone knew this and the conversation looked like petering out.

Tori came in. In spite of his fragile body his vitality was so intense that he could overshadow anyone else in the room. When he arrived in the kitchen, Jim Rimmington-Clarke, who could reasonably be called, and often was, a fine figure of a man, became almost invisible.

'I am late,' Tori announced unnecessarily. 'I come only to drink . . .'

Cressida smiled at him. With Tori in the room it was impossible to be bored. He acted like a catalyst on even the most ponderous party.

'. . . and to talk,' he went on, inviting with one of his wicked monkey grins the attention of the whole table.

He was well aware that everyone except Cressida was in some degree afraid of him. The fact amused him. He, a little beetle of a man, outcast from his own ruined country, was yet able to afflict with nervousness all these large brave English; these English whose size and bravery were even now in the process of delivering the world from the larger and most terrible evil; whose grip had all but succeeded in crushing out all bravery. With his amusement, however, went a sufficient admiration and gratitude. One could never again, he admitted, laugh at the English in the old careless manner, with laughter that was a mixture of patronage, envy, irritation, and only a little genuine amusement. The English might be, no doubt were, stupid, smug, overbearing, boring and unimaginative; but in the face of disaster they were valiant. Their sudden startling courage was no mere spark kindled in emergency. It was steady and enduring. It burned like a flame, parting the smoke and darkness of a wrecked continent. Tori could become at times extremely eloquent on the subject of the English. In the meantime he would preserve a little of his own self-respect by laughing at his power over the company in which he found himself.

He sat down in an empty chair next to Jim Rimmington-Clarke, who was trying to look as though he did not think of Tori as one more of these foreigners the country's swarming with. His efforts were not very successful, but it scarcely mattered, because no one was looking at him.

'Have you been working, Mr Tori?' Mrs Yates asked him. She never tried to call him by his surname and always meant to ask him if he minded. But she had never achieved the question. It wasn't, she found, easy to speak to him at all, but of course one had to try, because it would never do to be rude to a foreigner.

'I have written,' he answered her, 'for four hours. It is, perhaps, too much, and I am now stupid.'

Mrs Yates laughed in a politely unbelieving manner and hoped someone else would continue the conversation.

'The young man,' Tori asked of Cressida, 'he is to live here also?'

Cressida told them about the young man, realising for the first time that she had not asked him his name.

'Ah, so!' Tori said with relish. 'He will bring a beautiful bride, and we shall all grow romantic and dream of love.'

Mrs Yates blushed and was furious with herself. But really he had a rather odd way of saying the word love. Jim

16

Rimmington-Clarke guffawed and wondered if perhaps he should have done so more quietly.

There were times, Cressida thought, when it was difficult to laugh at Tori.

. . . In that moment when Charles and Simon had taken the last fence together, dangerously close, she had known for certain . . . it was Charles she had watched, Charles for whom the sob in her throat had broken, unheard in the roar of the crowd. . . .

Oh, damn and blast that wretched youth, she thought, it's time I forgot all that.

The sound of a motor-bicycle passed across the windows.

'How early,' Mrs Yates said brightly. 'It must be Willy. Fancy him getting in for tea.'

She spoke in what Cressida thought of as a cosy domestic voice. Well, she was right. Life was cosy and domestic for some people, boring and domestic for others, or just domestic. Emotion on the scale of the Grand National did not come into it any more.

'Well, exercise I suppose,' Jim Rimmington-Clarke said, and heaved himself out of his chair. His wife followed him, and as soon as they were out of the room Flying Officer Yates appeared, very red in the face and breathing noisily.

He was a ponderous young man of thirty-six who did everything with a sort of suppressed urgency, as if he was always afraid of being late. Cressida was the only person in the house, perhaps excepting his wife, who did not think him rather ridiculous. She had been unable to avoid seeing how bewildered he was. She could see him as the hard-working, reliable mainstay of some city office staff, catching with un-failing regularity the eight-forty to town from his comfortable suburban residence, returning thither by the six-ten with equally comfortable certainty, delighted to face a quiet evening with his wife and the football pools and the wireless, and being good-natured and facetious about the baby.

Now, snatched out of his natural surroundings, he was doing a probably more boring office job than his normal one; he was living and working among, but not with, dashing young men whose minds and outlook were so different from his that they might have spoken different languages for all the companionship they could give him; he was filling in forms in triplicate, while young men with the same romantic title risked their lives in the most spectacular manner, making adventure as common as a game of golf. Flying Officers soared into the sky in their pyjamas and shot down German aeroplanes before breakfast, but Flying Officer Yates went to his office at half-past eight and began to fill in forms, and answer the telephone. He wore, unsuitably and uneasily, a uniform that had become throughout the world a symbol of incredible courage, ringed with glamour, and he was, quite simply, thoroughly bewildered by it all.

'Hullo, Willy, how early you are,' Cressida greeted him. She called him by his Christian name in an attempt, which she knew was useless, to make him feel at home. Poor Flying Officer Yates would never feel at home until he escaped from his uniform and from the false character he tried so patheti-cally to assume. He regarded Cressida as a phenomenon quite outside his experience. Her appearance terrified him, her kindness charmed; her house, which he had only dared to approach because he thought it looked big enough to be a hotel, overpowered him; her disregard of convention astonished him. In all he found himself in a gallery of incomprehensible contradictions quite beyond classification.

'Oh, Mrs Chance. I hope it's O.K. I mean I'd've phoned . . .'

Cressida did her best with him, but his ears were still pink by the time he had finished his tea and departed with his wife.

'That young man, I am sorry for him,' Tori remarked. 'He does not swim in his own water.' Although Tori was perhaps not more than two years the senior, it seemed quite natural that he should call Flying Officer Yates a young man. If he lived to be ninety, Flying Officer Yates would never be more than half Tori's mental age.

Cressida laughed. 'I believe you're quite sentimental, Tori, under all the glitter.'

Tori shrugged his thin shoulders. 'I can see,' he said, 'I can see very well. And I shall tell you something else that I can see. A lovely thing. Your kindness, Cressida. You are more kind than anyone I have seen who is so beautiful as well.' Tori's voice was no longer flippant. 'You must never lose that gift of kindness, Cressida. It is of so great a value.'

'I don't know,' Cressida said, a little wearily. 'It means you have to be nice to a lot of bloodily boring people.'

'Perhaps yes,' Tori said. 'But as well one can be grateful to those who do what you would call the bloodily boring jobs.'

Mary Handley, who was unobtrusively finishing the washing-up, said suddenly, 'Well, I think it's very satisfactory when people like those Yates's find each other.'

19

'Dull plus dull adds up to a happy marriage,' Cressida said, her tone of voice saving the remark from bitterness. 'Sorry if that sounds cynical,' she added.

'But it is true,' Tori said. 'It is indeed most true. Ah, no, you shall allow me to continue!' He waved aside an impending interruption from both women. 'I do not, of course, say that it is only the dull who marry with happiness. I am not able,' he went on with deliberate pompousness, 'to make a remark so foolish. But I would say that for the dull it is easier to be happy. Those who are dull are safe! It is not for them that there comes the battering at the gates! Ah! You can see it often, the woman who does not attract men, she will be a very good wife and it will be quite easy for her. But a woman who is beautiful, who is alive with charm' – Tori produced an explosive sound that might or might not have been a word – 'she will not find it so easy! To say no and no and no, it will become a bore, intolerable, impossible even.'

'You're a cynical little rat, Tori,' Cressida said, 'and sometimes I hate you, but I expect you're right. I hope you marry a hag with large teeth and no eyebrows!'

Tori grinned. 'I marry no one,' he said cheerfully. 'It is too difficult a matter. A plain woman – bah! I should be safe, yes, but so bored! A beautiful woman, it is conceivable' – he shrugged his shoulders, clearly suggesting impossibility – 'but just conceivable that she will find, in time, another man more interesting than I. So! I do not marry. It is simple.'

'Too bad, Tori,' Cressida said. 'You must find yourself a beautiful dull woman and be happy! There are lots of them,' she added.

Tori's hands, shoulders and eyebrows shot upwards together. 'Ah, but how right you are!' he exclaimed. 'A beautiful woman with no brain. What a terrible trap, what a pit of danger from which the good God will deliver me because I will help!'

Cressida, with one of her swift, quiet movements, fetched something from the larder and put it in the oven.

'Well, well,' she said, 'I'll laugh at your wedding, Tori dear.'

'If it is also yours,' Tori replied cheerfully. 'If not, there will be no wedding. So! I am safe. It is well.' He left the kitchen, whistling happily. The sound of his whistling retreated, becoming more cheerful and shriller.

'He's one of those people one doesn't know whether to be sorry for or not,' Mary Handley said. 'I mean, being a refugee and all that, one's automatically full of sympathy. But with him you can't tell whether he needs it or not.'

'I know,' Cressida answered. 'I used to wonder if he was nobly rising above it all the time, or whether he just stays up naturally.'

'He's a funny person,' Mary went on. 'I often wonder what on earth he does, shut up in his room for so many hours a day.'

'He's – writing a book, you know,' Cressida replied, with the barest perceptible hesitation. 'He – he says it's to make money so that he can keep himself instead of – letting himself be kept. He lost everything, you know. He had a sort of castle and lots of land and so on. He used to stay here sometimes, before the war, when – when the Valerys lived here. He's a friend of Charles's, and so he came here when he got to

England, because it was somewhere he knew. He didn't know – Charles wasn't still here, or that it was let to me, but of course I had to make him stay. It was fairly difficult. He's frightfully proud, though you might not think so.'

'Lucky he came up against you in that case,' Mary remarked. 'I can't imagine many people who could talk him round, even if they tried, which everyone certainly wouldn't.'

Cressida said nothing for a moment, then she suddenly began, 'That's what's so frightful about us. The English I mean. Everyone realises more or less how – ghastly it is for the people who've lost absolutely everything. I don't suppose there's anyone in the country who doesn't talk about how sad, and dreadful, and horrifying and all that it is, but if it comes to a practical thing like having them in your house, there are still millions of people who are damnably good at thinking up reasons why of course they can't. I know I'm lucky and Tori's one of the world's star turns, but – well, some of the people I've had here have been grimmish!' She paused for a moment and added, 'You know old Jim thinks Tori's a lazy slug and ought to have a man's job. At least he hasn't actually said so to me, I rather wish he would! Well, he just doesn't know! Tori was so damn nearly dead when he got to England that it's a miracle he can even walk. He was in a concentration camp. He – told me a bit and – well, it was the sort of thing you read about and feel sick, and imagine must be overwritten propaganda or something, because it's so much too appalling to be true.'

Mary shuddered. 'I know,' she said. 'Sometimes I feel the war's just something one's read about and – had nightmares over.'

'And yet you look out of the windows and there are the cabbages,' Cressida said.

She took a pot off the cooker and put it in the oven.

'Well, that'll do for the moment. I'm going out.'

'I'm finishing some letters,' Mary said, and went out of the kitchen.

Sometimes it was easier, she found, not to talk to anyone who made you say the things you really felt. It was difficult, these days, not to collapse and cry when you heard your own voice saying your thoughts. But with half her mind she wanted nothing so much as to stay and talk to Cressida until she did achieve the release of tears.

CHAPTER FOUR

As always, the moment Cressida crossed the threshold, the dogs appeared from apparently nowhere, their extreme *empressement* obviously assumed partly out of excitement, and partly to give an impression of not having been on one of the spare beds. She petted them absently for a second or two, producing, had anyone been there to see, a picture of strong contrasts. The Dalmatians, like china mantelpiece ornaments, fitted the mellow front of the house, which seemed, in some lights, to exist solely for the purpose of serving as a copy for a coloured engraving. Cressida's old flannel trousers and her carelessly flung back shining hair should have been, but for some reason were not, out of the picture. Her beauty and that of the house had something in common, some effortless tranquillity which united them so that exterior details lost their disruptive power.

Cressida walked over the daisy-spattered lawns, wrestling with a strong sense of guilt. The grass seemed to have grown three inches in the last two days, she thought. Two days since she had nerved herself to tell Northeast, the gardener, that the lawn must not be mown again. The lawns of Brede Manor had been the pride of a Northeast for perhaps two hundred years. Cressida could remember old Valery, Charles's father, telling her of the disapproval caused by the purchase of a motor-mower. The disapproval of Northeast on that occasion must have been as nothing in comparison with his feelings twenty years later when the mention of hay must have seemed to him to herald the crack of doom. Perhaps he had then felt something less than hatred for the motor-mower. Cressida had used all her charm and eloquence to soften the blow, but had been too well aware of the insufficiency of both. But it had had to be done. With two horses and twelve miles to the nearest town, two acres of grass could not be kept mown, apart from the necessity of producing hay for the horses. She had tried to comfort the old man's heart by pointing out the preferability of hay to ploughing, though she realised that one was as bad as the other to a man who could not live to see the ruined lawns regain a perfection that had lasted two centuries.

Cressida hurried into the woods at the end of the discomforting lawns. It was better in there, the woods were unchanged and dim, and still seemed to wrap one in an underwater atmosphere of green warmth, scattered with dusty stars of sunlight that had eaten through the thick, delicately patterned ceiling. Deep in the woods there was a clearing, where the sky was a piece of bright colour, like a silken tent stretched across the gap in the trees. A tiny aeroplane, looking no bigger than a dragon-fly, dangled from a tail of fiercely white smoke tapered to a needle point at its lower end, blown at the other by some current of air too gentle to reach the earth, into curves and drifts like the light brushstrokes of an artist painting delicately upon blue silk. Cressida lay down in a drift of last year's beech leaves and gave herself the pleasure of indulging in absurdly poetical and flowery thoughts which she knew were neither intelligent nor original, but were none the less satisfying. Having persuaded the dogs that she was neither dead nor in need of their attentions, so that they gave up their attempts to lick her face so suddenly within their reach, she watched the aeroplane and allowed its bird-like quality to enchant her. She followed the delicate evolutions of its smoke-trail until her eyes closed against its blinding whiteness. She even permitted romantic impulses connected with gallantry, and daring and blue-eyed young men, to rise in her to such an extent that it seemed she must rush immediately into the bloodiest possible battle in order to restore herself to calm. Suddenly she laughed aloud and sat up. She was getting, she realised, into one of her most unmanageable moods, a state of mind such as a certain patriotic and well-produced film she had lately seen had evoked, when she had felt that nothing short of walking under the nearest bomb would release the emotion pent within. It was a distinct handicap, she decided, to be so excessively impressionable, and was in any case not suitable to her age. After that film, for instance, it had been an effort to face the daylight when she knew it must be obvious that she had cried for at least an hour. The traces of tears, sentimentally described by inaccurate novelists as being touching and even love-inspiring, were in reality discouraging to even the most dewy beauty, and when one was thirty-seven . . . .

Cressida called the dogs in what she considered a healthily sporting tone of voice and continued her walk.

In a queer detached way she felt happy. For the moment it was enough that she was alive and that it was a lovely evening, and that somewhere Charles existed. She was not, as so many people tragically were, left with the impulse of love on her hands. Better to have loved – oh, much better, incomparably better. Absurd how true all those trite old sayings were. And yet they meant nothing unless you learnt their truth from experience.

At the end of the wood she came upon the road that would lead her home by way of the village and the front gates. She decided to leave the woods so that the evening sunlight would not die unnoticed. She passed the squat Norman church, very composed and stolid, with its brood of tomb-stones cosily lapped in long grass. It had a comfortable, comforting appearance. Cressida thought, as she often had before, that it seemed to take faith as a matter of course rather than to demand it as more ambitious churches did, with their urgent spires and outflung buttresses that looked sometimes as though they would lift a whole building to heaven. The little church of St Mary-in-the-Meadow, Brede Somervel, with Brede Somervel carefully blacked out of the notice-board against invaders, lay quietly beyond the narrow, slow stream that ran with the road through and beyond the village until it joined a larger stream important enough to be called 'fishing'.

'. . . as the year advances, German cities, harbours and centres of . . .' Cressida heard in the clear, reassuring tones bred by the B.B.C., and from the next cottage but one,

'. . . ordeal the like of which has never been experienced by any country in continuity . . .' This cottage window was open and the words followed her down the road, '. . . severity or magnitude. Mr Churchill went on to say . . .'

Cressida could no longer hear the words that had gone already twice round the world that day, telling the people of the world that a thousand British bombers had flown over a German city. A thousand bombers. And yet she was hurrying a little because of the pie she had left in the oven and must shortly remove. Yes, there are the cabbages, she thought, in neat rows, and a pie in the oven, and a thousand bombers going out in a night; five or six thousand highly trained young men with nervous, useful fingers, good at mending wireless sets, playing the piano, tinkering with cars and leaking roofs, doing endless fiddling, invaluable jobs. . . .

She increased her speed. At the end of the tiny village street she narrowly avoided a head-on crash with a short, massive woman in good tweeds and a wool hair-net who was striding in the opposite direction, her eyes so full of purpose that they nearly missed Cressida's lightly moving figure altogether. Once observed, however, Cressida was brought up all standing, as it were, by a direct attack.

'Mrs Chance, it's quite outrageous,' the tweeded woman began, speaking as if she wished to impress a large audience fifty feet away, and as if she considered each member of it solely responsible for the current outrage.

Opening B, Cressida thought in parenthesis. Opening A with Mrs Brandon consisted of the words, 'My dear! Have you heard . . .?'

'I'm going to see Major Carstairs immediately,' Mrs Brandon continued. 'It's quite absurd . . . four private soldiers . . . with their army boots . . . one's stair-carpets . . .'

Cressida, had she given her full attention to Mrs Brandon's remarks, would perhaps not have missed the connecting clauses between the major points of the speech, but even so the gist of it was fairly clear.

'. . . shall tell him that perhaps a sergeant . . .' The tirade battered its way past Cressida's unlistening ears.

Did Mrs Brandon, she wondered, suppose that the boots of sergeants were more delicately constructed, or would she accept the private soldiers without their boots, or would she perhaps prefer the boots of the German Army?

It would have been pleasant to have uttered these questions aloud. But with Mrs Brandon one must be content to remain a victim. One must not aggravate the spate by argument. Cressida made instead a firm statement to the effect that she was sorry to be in a hurry at the moment and strode swiftly on. Poor Major Carstairs, she thought, I must ring him up and mention the attics.

A hundred yards down the road she passed Mrs Brandon's 'converted' cottage. Its conversion had not been very skilfully effected. It looked, Cressida thought, like a rather plain cake iced with cheap and nasty sugar. It was aggressively clean and roses were severely trained in neat lines against it. Four private soldiers were just what it needed, and their boots.

A little farther on she reached another cottage, or rather pair of cottages, now used together as one house. Their stone walls had scarcely been touched, and the house looked what it was, unassuming, charming, homelike, and so suited to its surroundings that it might almost have grown there. A white-haired man was digging in a part of the garden which ran parallel to the road. He straightened himself with an obvious effort and hailed Cressida. Walking in a manner that betrayed his rheumatism, he reached the low fence and leaned over it.

Cressida paused. 'I'm sure you oughtn't to stop,' she said, 'you make me feel terribly guilty.' She decided to talk for at least ten minutes, because it was clear that Colonel Wintringham-Masters needed a rest. He looked overtired and much more than the sixty-five he actually was.

'Oh, you mustn't let that worry you,' the Colonel said cheerfully, 'got to pack up anyhow, getting down to the drill hall at seven. Exercise you know, chaps all mad keen. Don't mind telling you I'm getting past staying out all night, all right for the youngsters. All the same, last time we had an all-night show it was young Joe Pinhorn went to sleep! Gave the old hands a laugh, but it's youngsters that need the sleep after all. Doesn't matter so much if old crocks wear out what's left of them!'

Cressida led him on to tell her about his Home Guard activities and about the results of his labours in the garden, and about the latest exploits of the bees, the hens and the pig he was fattening for the local farmer. Eventually he said it was time he got into uniform and she left him. Talking to him had been a pleasant corrective to listening to Mrs Brandon, but she could never meet Colonel Wintringham-Masters without getting what she called a rush of sentiment to the heart. It was so easy to imagine the feelings of a man who had commanded his regiment in action in the last war and was now obliged to content himself with exercises and digging potatoes and helping his wife with the washing-up. War was bearable, even at times exciting and enjoyable, for people who were young and lucky enough to come in for spells of action between the long periods of intolerable boredom that seemed to stand out as typical of the latest form of war. People in cities had the acutely engrossing, if only occasional, crisis of an air raid to mitigate the boredom of being continually prepared for one. But old people in quiet unraided country had nothing but endless 'jobs', endlessly dull and incredibly tiring. For men like Colonel Wintringham-Masters the war was a trial of no mean severity. So far he had surmounted it magnificently. Cressida had never seen him other than cheerful; he could talk about his trivial and numerous minor activities with so much animation that dullness was never even suggested; he could, and did, inspire the men of the local Home Guard with the most impassioned enthusiasm. Seeing him reminded Cressida of a Home Guard parade recently held in a neighbouring and slightly larger village. She would never forget the sight of all those white-haired men, roughened and aged beyond their years, as countrymen often were, some of them so bent that the inadequacy of battledress was painfully obvious, marching with pink-faced immature boys, self-conscious as children playing at soldiers. The vigour and enthusiasm of the whole performance had been infinitely touching and had precipitated Cressida's impressionability to a most trying degree. The remark of an old village woman that 'them parryshooties wud'n be no wuss'n all them wild lads shooting off their guns up t' meadows' had lightened the atmosphere considerably. It was true, probably, that excitable boys, and men whose sight wasn't what it was, loosed on the country-side in charge of lethal weapons, might add to the dangers of an invasion. But that did not alter the fact that a parade of the Home Guard was a sufficiently moving spectacle.

Old people, Cressida thought. People who are too old to see the new world, if it ever comes. People whose old age is ruined, from whom peace has been taken for ever because they may not live to see it come. Sad old age. And yet – yet these very people, who are old now, who are sad and old and have nothing to look forward to, these people were not old after the last war. They fought the last war and won it, and then threw away the vision of peace that had never been allowed to materialise. Men who are fighting now were children, babies, after the last war. They had no responsibilities, no power. It's the men who are old now who had the chance of saving peace, and made a terrible failure of it. Perhaps a sad old age is a mild punishment for such an act of blindness. Some of these people who are now old and sad have had twenty years since the last war, twenty years of comfort and selfish, irresponsible life. Some of the people who are being killed every day now have had no life at all.

Cressida reached her own gates and turned in. Two Army lorries tore past as she did so. For a moment it looked as though at least one of the Dalmatians must be under their immense wheels. Cressida clenched her teeth and did not shout at the dogs. They needed all their attention for their own methods of escape. As usual both achieved this satisfactory and unlikely manœuvre in a flurry of eel-like curves, their black spots dancing crazily, and their tails appearing triumphant from under the very noses of the lorries. As always on such occasions Cressida had a sickening vision of John on his ridiculous bicycle. Well, he's got to grow up in that kind of world, she told herself, but the vision remained.

In the hall she found letters. Evidently someone had been down for the second post. Two bills, an appeal from a hospital, and a letter from an aunt in London, which Cressida recognised without enthusiasm. She had two aunts of whom she was extremely fond. It was always the third one who wrote. She opened and read the letter, and said, 'Hell!'

Madge Rimmington-Clarke was in the hall. 'What's bitten you?' she asked.

'It's Aunt Jessie,' Cressida said. 'She wants to come down "just for a day or two in the country . . . so lovely at this time of year . . ." and can I meet her, "if not just order a taxi for me, dear, and I'll find my way . . ."' Cressida stuffed the letter into her trouser pocket.

'My God, these people,' she said. 'She knows we're twelve miles out, but she probably thinks we still have at least two cars. She's got a house of her own in the country, but she lets it because it's so boring being away from London. She uses taxis all day long to get to the sort of committee meetings that'll get her picture in the *Tatler*, in her new hat and all her rings, and now she wants to come and have a look at what I'm doing, because she thinks it'll amuse her and give her something to giggle about with the old harpies she uses as friends.' Cressida took a deep breath and became calmer. 'And yet she's kind, you know. She's amiable to everyone and has masses of people in the house always, or she did before the war; she takes them to hotels now, what she calls saving labour, dear, this wretched rationing. On a price basis she probably gets through fifteen meat rations in a week, and it's not that she has to eat in hotels, she just does it for fun. I suppose you just can't make people like that think.' Cressida gazed into space for a moment. 'Oh, well, she'll have to come,' she said at last.

'Can't you say you've got a house full of lunatics and the children have smallpox?' Madge suggested.

Cressida shrugged her shoulders. Her delicate eyebrows rose with them.

'I've used up all those,' she said, 'in the last ten years. I can't make it convincing any more.'

'When's she descending?' Madge asked.

'On the fourth, and this is – oh, hell, it's the day after tomorrow. The horses can't go to Wichlesbury again before they're shod, and Garton can't do them tomorrow I know. I'll have to ring up some taxis and argue about the ten-mile limit and feel like the black market.'

For the next ten minutes Cressida sat at the telephone, saying, 'Yes, I see,' and 'of course not,' and 'all right,' to several different numbers. At last she finished.

'I've got one to come as far as Chilbury. I suppose I can take Beltane three miles in the dog-cart and meet her. As long as she doesn't have a damn great trunk. Beltane shies like a stag, which won't add to her fun, poor dear. Isn't it extraordinary,' she added after a pause, 'what a lot of trouble one takes over things one doesn't want to do when the things one does just don't get done?'

'Life is like that,' Madge said heartily, 'and never forget, my dear, how lucky you are to have such a nice house in the country for your relations to come and stay at!'

CHAPTER FIVE

Miss Jessica Ambleside settled herself in her first-class carriage and sighed for a variety of reasons. It was nice to have caught the train comfortably, there was forty minutes to spare, not any too much really, these days one felt trains might go off at almost any moment without warning. Though, of course, the railways were wonderful, or so one always heard. The country would be charming. Dear Cressida's house was always so comfortable, and such good hot water, or else, of course, one would have gone to the Gethrins' instead. But they had had such a bad cook last time. One had had a poor dinner at the Imperial Palace last night, mustn't go there again; poor Cissie Hartley, she'd lost all her looks. One had forgotten to book a hair-do for the tenth, such a bore, must remember to write, one couldn't rely on last-minute appointments nowadays. Really, they might turn on the lights, waiting in the station where it was too dark to read was so trying. One was depressed enough without having to sit in the dark for forty minutes. But perhaps it was as well not to be able to read *The Times*, so depressing the news from the Middle East. Dear Cressida, she would have made arrangements for a taxi, no doubt; such a long journey, and then having to drive ten miles, or was it more? How much more pleasant to have gone, as one normally did, in the Daimler. Hiscocks was such a good driver, so wasted in an Army lorry, great heavy, ugly things; Hiscocks had always been accustomed to such good cars. The station seemed full of troops, such a pity they were allowed to travel so much; even in first-class carriages one wasn't always sure of being comfortable, and they really shouldn't let them carry those very awkward tin mugs, very annoying losing one of those silver buttons off one's new coat, so hard to match anything these days, shouldn't be surprised if it was one of those tin mugs. . . .

A man in uniform, and a woman, entered the carriage. For a moment they stood looking at the seat cushion an inch above Miss Ambleside's head. Then their eyes ran along the rack on which two large suitcases in white leather and a hat-box *en suite* were perched, a gas-mask in a green patent-leather case filling the small space left by the boxes. On the seat beside Miss Ambleside were three illustrated papers and a very large pigskin handbag.

Quite a nice-looking couple, Miss Ambleside thought, very lucky; all that gold on his hat, must be a General of some sort, very young looking.

Damn the old trout, the General thought, spreading herself all over the carriage. But his courage was not quite equal to suggesting any compression of the old trout's possessions. The General was a mild man and afraid of all women over forty. He did, however, manage to shuffle Miss Ambleside's gas-mask and hat-box on to the adjacent suitcase so that his own considerable possessions should not occupy the whole of the rack opposite.

Three other people appeared in the doorway. How tiresome, we're going to be quite full, Miss Ambleside thought. Still, perhaps the troops would avoid the General.

By the time the train started the troops were in possession of the corridor. Miss Ambleside could see the bottom of a tin mug pressed against the glass next to her. Very tiresome, and so embarrassing, one really couldn't –

For an hour the journey was uneventful and the train did not stop. It reached the outskirts of a country town. It slowed down and the view from the window became a row of forage caps, rifle-barrels, tin hats in nets, and shiny yellow oil-skin bundles with unmanageable corners. When it actually stopped, the view was slightly altered, in that the forage caps were of an unfamiliar shape, though still of military cut. This sea surged and broke into units of troops with the very evident intention of boarding the train.

Well, with the General – But Miss Ambleside's thoughts were disrupted. She had reckoned without the American Army.

'Pardon me, lady . . . keep it going, boys . . . sorry, mam . . . pass right along . . . pardon me, lady . . . say, buddy, you going . . .?'

In the face of invasion on such a scale Miss Ambleside's faith in the General was shaken. Under the impact of these lusty, carefree voices, endowed by nature with the power to carry across the prairies, or merely be heard above the Chicago traffic, Miss Ambleside found it impossible to state that this was a first-class carriage. She was defeated. The General was defeated without a struggle. The rest of the journey for Miss Ambleside consisted of a vast slab of khaki, swaying from side to side, about a foot from her face. She was conscious, if only by suggestion, of large boots that threatened at every lurch of the train to crush her elegant feet to powder.

It was a long journey and Miss Ambleside became uncomfortable. But even if she could have forced herself past the initial barrier of the United States Army there would still be that terrible struggle with all the tin mugs – so Miss Ambleside resigned herself to discomfort, and her misery increased steadily.

The train stopped once more before reaching Wichlesbury. The General and his wife struggled out of the carriage, helped with vigour and enthusiasm by the Army. The compartment was, however, not appreciably emptier for the departure. Several units of the American Army seemed to materialise from somewhere to take what might have been a few vacant cubic feet of space. The movement and squeezing entailed in the redisposition of troops caused Miss Ambleside acute discomfort.

By the time the train drew in to Wichlesbury station she had reached, or so she thought, the limit of her endurance. She saw, as through a haze, the dreaded sea of khaki and netted tin hats heaving on the platform. She pushed with savage energy and very little effect at the khaki slab blocking any forward movement on her part.

'Hey, buddy, cain't you see the lady's shifting?' she heard a clear voice say. The mass before her face retreated. Miss Ambleside managed to stand. Her luggage loomed in sight. Oh, dear, supposing the train started. . . . Perhaps subconsciously she made vague gestures towards her boxes. The packed carriage became in an instant a hive of furious activity. The prairie-conquering, traffic-quelling voices rose to a volume hitherto unsurpassed. Miss Ambleside found herself on the platform, her knees shaking, her ears singing. Her immaculate suitcases landed beside her with the velocity of lethal projectiles. All her cut-glass bottles . . . the Lalique powder-bowl. . . .

But Miss Ambleside was past caring. She glanced wildly round. Her gas-mask arrived suddenly, apparently of its own volition, with ferocious force, so that she failed to catch it, and the shiny green leather fell on the dusty platform. The train steamed out of the station. The army on the platform was undiminished. Either it was the same army or else an army had left the train and another one embarked. Miss Ambleside neither knew nor cared. A porter . . . the word 'Ladies'. . . .

Miss Ambleside forgot her luggage. The fact that rings worth several hundred pounds were in her suitcase was as nothing to her. She threaded her way unsteadily through the troops. This time no tin mugs deterred her.

For the sum of a penny Miss Ambleside regained her poise. She began to think intelligibly about porters. She remembered her rings. She caught sight of a man in a dirty tweed coat and flannel trousers hanging vaguely about in the neighbourhood of her little pile of luggage. She looked anxiously about her. There was no sign anywhere of the safe dark blue uniforms associated with railway-stations, nothing but a khaki sea, still static on the platform. The man in the tweed coat, seeing an owner for the expensive-looking luggage, produced a piece of rope.

'See you outside,' he said, and vanished, the white suitcases humped upon his back.

Miss Ambleside experienced real anxiety about her rings. Such a very odd-looking man . . . in this crowd one never knew . . . if the taxi hadn't come. . . . All the worries of a journey beset Miss Ambleside, exaggerated to nightmare proportions by her own helplessness. She suffered from the emotional disturbance of the very rich who suddenly find themselves in a dilemma from which money has no power to deliver them. It took so long to get even as far as the barrier. So many soldiers . . . and the ticket collector seemed to be reading every word on all the tickets . . . one was continually pushed from behind and jostled on all sides . . . it seemed to have become terribly hot. . . .

Miss Ambleside peered past as many of the soldiers as she could, searching for a glimpse of the odd man with her luggage. A rifle-barrel flashed past her eyes, within an inch of them, it seemed. Miss Ambleside blinked. Her line of sight cleared for a moment.

Is Your Journey Really Necessary? she read in large flowing black letters directly before her eyes.

It was the last straw. Miss Ambleside felt the tears welling in her eyes. It was too much. After all one had been through . . . it was the final insult . . . to be expected to be amused at these facetious posters. . . .

Eventually Miss Ambleside passed the barrier. Outside the station the first object that caught her eye, and the eyes of the troops to a man, was a girl of such dazzling appearance that Miss Ambleside was dazzled, in spite of her preoccupation with the odd man and her suitcases. The girl had magnificent auburn hair, twice as much of it as any normal woman, it seemed, waving lavishly to her shoulders. She wore, quite reasonably, no hat, and an exceedingly well-cut grey flannel suit. Her shoes and lips were artistically matched, and on closer inspection it was seen that her finger-nails completed the colour scheme. Miss Ambleside, even in moments of agitation, had an eye for clothes. The girl's white *piqué* shirt was clever, she noticed, that collar, one must remember. . . .

'Are you Miss Ambleside or something? I'm sharing your taxi. I'm Felicity Brent.'

Miss Ambleside's newly regained poise was not yet quite equal to the assimilation of these statements, which followed each other in quick succession and an entirely toneless voice. It took some seconds even to realise that the spectacular young woman with the hair had spoken to her. Miss Ambleside was not accustomed to being made to feel flustered and did not appreciate the sensation. She made a great effort to pull herself together.

'Yes, I am Miss Ambleside,' she said. And not 'something', her tones suggested. 'My niece ordered me a taxi,' she ended with increased severity.

Gradually, with her own words, a background to the girl began to be visible. Miss Ambleside saw that a small private car with a woman driver stood at the kerb. On its luggage grid she saw, with extreme relief, her own white suitcases.

'I know,' the girl went on. 'I phoned her last night. She told me to look out for you.'

Miss Ambleside was made aware of the odd-looking man. The sight of her luggage had comforted her so much that she gave him half a crown and a vague smile.

'Is – this er –' Miss Ambleside began. Her idea of a taxi was either the London variety or a large luxurious car to seat at least seven.

'Yes, it seems to be the taxi,' the girl said, rather as if she shared Miss Ambleside's view on that point if no other. 'I suppose we'd better get in.' The old hen seemed to be going to dither on the pavement indefinitely, she thought.

'Brede Manor, you know,' Miss Ambleside remarked to the driver, as if she wished to point out that the taxi was, or had originally been hers.

'Have to drop you at Chilbury,' the woman in the driving-seat said cheerfully. 'Ten-mile limit, see?'

'Oh,' Miss Ambleside said doubtfully, 'oh, really. Well – well, how much farther is the manor?'

'Couldn't say. Maybe a couple of miles, like,' the unmoved driver replied. 'Maybe the lady'll meet you,' she added by way of consolation, seeing Miss Ambleside's face.

Two miles, with all those suitcases. . . .

'I'll sit in front,' Miss Brent stated, and did so without delay. She had, as no doubt she realised, chosen rightly. The car was almost in the class of those known as occasional fours, except that there were doors to the back seat. At least three-quarters of this seat was piled with luggage as handsome as, but larger than Miss Ambleside's own. The poor lady's morale was not up to the effort of complaining or suggesting that the sylph in front should change places with her. She contracted her generous figure into the inadequate space and the car started. Round every corner Miss Brent's luggage slid into Miss Ambleside's ribs. Miss Brent herself seemed to be in a conversational mood. She flung remarks over her shoulder from time to time, which entailed an effort on Miss Ambleside's part to lean forward and catch their drift. The stability of the luggage was affected by these movements as well as by the swaying of the car.

'What's it like at Brede?' Miss Brent wanted to know. 'I'm going there for a bit next week,' she added by way of explanation. 'My boyfriend's taken rooms, but I'm going to look them over before we're stuck. You can't trust men.' Her last remark was made apparently for Miss Ambleside's information rather than as an observation between two who knew.

'Oh – er, really,' was the best Miss Ambleside could do in reply. She could not have said herself which of Miss Brent's remarks she was answering. 'It's a very beautiful house,' she added, in an attempt to regain control of the conversation. 'Georgian, you know, quite lovely.'

'Oh, God,' Miss Brent remarked flatly, 'all passages, I suppose, and the bath'll be cold.'

Miss Ambleside bridled. A rush of affection for, and pride in, Cressida overcame her.

'I have never,' she stated loudly, 'had hotter baths than my niece provides.'

'Has she always let rooms?' the young woman, as Miss Ambleside had begun angrily to classify her, went on undaunted.

'My niece,' she said sternly, 'does not let rooms. She is kind enough to allow people to stay in her house because the war has filled the country with people who have nowhere to live.' And no right to exist, her tone suggested.

After this reprimand she wrapped herself in an impenetrable mantle of apparent deafness and did not reply to any further remarks. Really, the young woman was intolerable, she thought. For the first time she began to be glad of the ten-mile limit. Even if she had to walk the last two miles, she decided, she would walk alone.

It began, quite lightly at first, to rain.

CHAPTER SIX

The rain increased to a considerable shower.

Oh, Lord, Cressida thought, that's torn it. She spread rugs over the unprotected seats of the dog-cart with one hand and made encouraging sounds to the huge chestnut she was driving. The horse was already doing a smacking twelve miles an hour, but he pricked his ears and showed every inclination to move faster.

Poor Aunt Jessie, Cressida thought. She'll be in what the smart woman is wearing for travel these days, probably a rather good hat, and I'll get her umbrella in the eye all the way home. Well, she needn't have come, dammit.

She arrived in the tiny village where the taxi was to deposit her aunt, and drove under the arched courtyard entrance the local inn luckily possessed. She remained in the dog-cart because the taxi might arrive at any moment, so it was not worth getting out. The landlord, a friend of hers, appeared and talked to her for a few minutes and was assured that it wasn't necessary for anyone to be found to hold the horse, not that there was anyone to find these days. Lucky thing, the landlord considered, that some ladies could look out for themselves; made things a lot easier, and it was a pity there weren't more like Mrs Chance. She wasn't one of those rough sort of ladies, either; the sort that seemed to be trying to show you all the time how well they could get on by themselves. The landlord knew one or two of those. Come into the bar and shout for drinks like men, and kind of swagger about in trousers; Mrs Chance wore trousers too, of course, but she had a sort of natural way of doing it so that you didn't notice. Ladies were doing all kinds of good work, he wouldn't deny, but there were some that had a very annoying way of showing it.

Cressida wondered how her aunt was getting on with the voice that had rung up the night before and announced that its owner was coming down to leave some luggage, and would like to stay a few nights. Cressida, after that telephone call, did not think that she was going to like Felicity Brent.

The landlord returned to his duties. The rain was a little less, Cressida noticed. She heard a car approaching. It stopped at the inn. Cressida backed Beltane out of the archway and got her first sight of Felicity Brent's dazzling hair. For several moments she did not notice her aunt, wedged in with the luggage at the back. She climbed down from her high seat and hitched the horse to a post. She took her eyes off Felicity Brent's hair and concentrated her attention on getting her aunt out of the car.

'Dear Cressida, how nice . . . such a journey . . . oh, dear, the rain . . . my dear, the train . . .' Miss Ambleside found herself staring into the face of an enormous horse with, she thought, a very alarming expression in its eyes. Oh, dear, were they to go in that . . .?

'Would you like to wait till it stops?' Cressida was asking her aunt.

Felicity Brent was still in the car and did not look like moving.

'Oh, no, dear.' No indeed, much better to go on; anything rather than wait in the company of that young woman.

Miss Ambleside paid for the taxi, feeling that somehow she restored her status by so doing, though twenty-two shillings seemed a great deal, and she supposed one tipped the driver even if she was a woman. The arrangement seemed to suit Miss Brent, who, when the tipping was over, slipped easily out of the car and stood looking blankly at nothing.

Cressida glanced at the luggage. Miss Ambleside's suit-cases were very wet.

'We'll have to leave some of this,' she said, 'the carrier can bring it later on. I'll go and fix it.'

She went into the inn. Miss Ambleside, Miss Brent and the horse remained in the rain, wrapped in their own thoughts and oblivious of one another. The taxi-driver began to unload the car without help.

Cressida reappeared. It was time she tried to thaw out the red-haired wench, she supposed.

'D'you mind hopping up behind?' she asked amiably, 'and I'll hand you the suitcases if you'll say which you'd like now.' If you can speak, she added mentally.

Felicity Brent, without enthusiasm, did climb into the back seat of the dog-cart and did receive the two boxes she had indicated as essential to her immediate needs, but she did not speak. Cressida slid her aunt's smaller luggage under the front seat. Miss Ambleside was with difficulty hoisted into the cart and the party set off. Fortunately the rain was now considerably less, though it spotted Miss Brent's light flannel suit pretty freely.

Beltane, turned for home, put forth his best speed, which was considerable. It was all Cressida could do to hold him. Miss Ambleside was very much alarmed, but the fact that she was now in the most comfortable, or least uncomfortable seat, and the red-haired little horror perched at the back, made up for a good deal. The rain trickled down the back of Felicity Brent's neck. Miss Ambleside put up her umbrella. The rain, splashing off it, poured more freely in the same direction.

If Beltane shies, Cressida thought, that girl will fall out. Felicity was sitting huddled together, holding with both hands the turned-up collar of her coat.

'I should hold on,' Cressida called back to her, 'in case the horse shies,' she added, not without malice. Anyhow, I've warned the creature, she thought.

The rain stopped but Miss Ambleside did not put down her umbrella. One was dreadfully exposed, she felt, in these old-fashioned contraptions, and the umbrella was quite a comfort.

'There's Tarring Beacon, you remember, Aunt Jessie?' Cressida said.

They were driving along an open part of the road and there was a view of meadows falling to the river, with a mound beyond rising like a miniature mountain. Behind it there was a very faint splash of rainbow, like a many-coloured blush on the elephant-grey cloud. One ray of sunlight pierced the clouds as they passed and lay like a sword along the smooth summit of the beacon, turning the grass to a copper green, brilliant as a colour in a fairy-tale. A flight of white birds, magically silvered by the shaft of sun, flew low and swift, it seemed into the sun itself. Cressida's heart seemed to fly with them.

'Lovely,' she murmured inadvertently.

Miss Ambleside gazed at the spokes of her umbrella.

'Yes, dear,' she said.

Felicity Brent clung to the back of her seat very awkwardly. She wished the woman would keep her eyes on that damned horse instead of raving about the scenery.

The dog-cart bowled past a large house with bright green shutters and a blaze of roses in the garden which ran by the road. The house had an air of almost blatant prosperity. The grass had evidently been mown with a motor-mower.

Cressida turned to Felicity.

'That's where' – she remembered she still did not know the name of the rather nice young man who was going to marry this girl – 'your fiancé' – she had to make do with – 'says he got a terrific rocket.' Perhaps the girl would be human if one mentioned the youth.

Beltane swung round a fairly sharp corner. The dog-cart swayed.

'Oh,' Felicity remarked flatly.

It may be partly fright, Cressida reminded herself. She probably wishes I'd attend to driving. For the next few minutes she had to. The inevitable army lorry was careering down the lane towards them. Fortunately the driver, who was country bred, saw trouble looming with that horse. He slowed to a crawl. Beltane's ears quivered and stiffened. He blew loudly through large open nostrils. Miss Ambleside felt that her umbrella was quite inadequate to break a fall from this distance. Felicity felt sick. Cressida pursued her usual course for such occasions, a combination of violent language and gentle movement which never failed. The lorry was passed without disaster. Beltane leaped forward as if he had acquired extra speed from the menace behind him. In another moment they had turned in at the lovely wrought-iron gates of Brede Manor and were approaching the house.

Felicity Brent, having her back to it, missed the first view of the Manor. Until the dog-cart stopped she looked at nothing, and did not realise she had reached her destination. Perhaps the sight of the house, so suddenly at her elbow, was the more startling. Felicity was impressed. She disliked being impressed, and made up her mind that nothing would induce her to show it. Her manners, if such a negation of behaviour could be called manners, became more distant than ever. She got stiffly down from her seat and walked into the house. There was a ghost of an excuse for doing so, because it was again very lightly raining, but she gave the impression that she would have behaved in the same way anyhow.

Cressida got down and hitched Beltane to a post. She hauled out Miss Brent's large suitcases and left them neatly together in the middle of the drive, in the rain. She then conveyed Miss Ambleside and her luggage into the house. Felicity was standing in the hall, staring as usual at nothing.

Why Felicity, of all names? Cressida thought, and said, 'Do you mind waiting here for a minute while I get rid of the horse, Aunt Jessie?' She deposited her aunt on a sofa. 'He'll get in a fuss if I leave him, and it's Springett's day off. Your suitcases are outside,' she said sweetly in passing Felicity's unresponsive presence. 'I'm afraid they may be a bit wet.'

In spite of her apparent blindness Miss Brent had not missed seeing Cressida carry in her aunt's luggage. She realised now that she was being told to fetch her own. She did so, discovering for the first time how heavy her suitcases were. She and Miss Ambleside then ignored each other as thoroughly as if only one of them had existed. Miss Ambleside soothed her sorely tried feelings with the balm of having a niece with such a particularly lovely house. Miss Brent wondered how, without losing what she considered her sophistication, she could modify her offhand behaviour. It was a pretty reasonable house, she admitted to herself, and would probably do quite well for a bit. She did not, however, admit to herself something she was more than half aware of; that in Mrs Chance she had come up against someone who would always get the better of her, and with whom it would be as well not to fall out. If she had thought about it she would not have realised that the reason for Cressida's undoubted supremacy was her complete lack of interest in it.

While the two ladies were thus occupied, if such a word could be used for total inaction, John Chance came down the stairs, saw them, and continued to descend without a second's pause. He walked up to Miss Ambleside.

'How do you do?' he said, using his flashing smile with the usual effect.

Miss Ambleside's heart was warmed. She gushed. It was her normal reaction to inner warmth. John endured her endearments with grave politeness, but he did not smile a second time.

'I came,' he said, 'to tell Mummie the fish hasn't come. We missed the bus because I cut my knee.'

Miss Ambleside, who did not see their relevance, was a little slow in answering his remarks. The small boy took her silence to mean the usual lack of interest shown by grown-ups in matters of importance. If you said something thoroughly babyish, John found, grown-ups seemed amused and said how clever you were. But a perfectly sensible statement of fact seemed to leave them quite cold. He transferred his attention to Felicity.

'Would you like to sit down?' he asked, using the smile again.

Felicity, in the face of his perfect composure, found herself quite unable to think of anything to say. Being at a loss she fell back on the offhand manner long practice had made easy for her.

'No, thanks,' she said, paying high tribute, for her, to the small boy's dazzling charm, and smiling for a second herself.

'Most people prefer to,' John remarked politely and left her. 'I must find Mummie now,' he added to the room in general.

Miss Ambleside told him that his mother had taken the horse to the stables.

'Then I shall go and help her,' he announced, and left the hall by the front door.

'What a darling,' Miss Ambleside said, 'I haven't seen him for two years.'

In the enchantment cast over her by the small boy's charm she forgot that she had spoken in a most amiable manner to the intolerable young woman whose presence she had intended to ignore.

'So very like his father,' she went on, and sighed heavily. 'Tragic, absolutely tragic,' she finished before she realised what she was saying.

Even Felicity Brent could not repress curiosity at such a remark.

'Oh, what happened?' she asked with rather more animation than she had hitherto shown.

Miss Ambleside collected her wits. How very careless, she told herself, to have said such a thing.

'One doesn't speak of it,' she said firmly, and retreated into a forbidding silence.

Felicity shrugged her shoulders slightly. The gesture was lost upon Miss Ambleside, who was carefully looking the other way. Unwillingly Felicity became aware of a growing interest in this family. Mrs Chance, she admitted, did look rather the sort of woman things happened to. To Felicity, things happening meant chiefly one thing only. She decided that it might be worth trying to get to know Mrs Chance. And the father of that child, she added mentally, must have been a peculiarly good-looking man.

By all this thought Felicity was sufficiently roused to look round the hall. She knew nothing, nor did she care, about furniture, as long as it was luxurious, clever, and, if possible, amusing. She did not notice the Adam mantelpiece or the superb pair of Chippendale chairs for which the owners of Brede had for some years been invited to name the price. She did not know that the Chinese carpet was almost a museum piece, or that the great tooled-leather sofa on which Miss Ambleside sat was reputed to have belonged to the mistress of an unspecified king, one of the Georges it was assumed. The lovely curve of the staircase and its delicate wrought-iron handrail were just the stairs to her. But the combined result of all this effortless perfection had its effect, even upon her unappreciative mind. The one individual object she actually noticed was an immense jar of flowers, arranged with the care and attention to detail of a master painter's still life. That, she thought, was very clever, in fact definitely good. With electric light at the bottom of the vase, and a mirror underneath the table, it might even be amusing as well. Felicity's praise could go no further.

Miss Ambleside began to think hopefully about tea. She watched the hands of the grandfather clock, which marked the comfortable hour of four twenty-six.

A powerful roar of heavy machinery broke into her pleasant, if mildly anxious mood. Felicity, who was nearest the door, saw an armoured car drive past the opening, brake suddenly and turn back till it stopped opposite the doorway, which was filled in the next instant by the tall figure of a man in battledress and a plum-coloured beret. With the removal of the beret, hair of the same startling fairness as Cressida's shone in the light behind. Felicity cursed inwardly because she had wasted time standing about instead of doing her face.

After that awful drive, she thought, one simply wasn't in form for this. She contemplated the possibility of retreat up the stairs, but decided that it was too late and that it would be a poor start. It just would, she thought sourly, have to be the handsomest young man one had ever seen, when one was feeling particularly jaded and unequal.

'Hullo,' the young man said, 'is – er – Oh, hullo, Aunt Jessie!'

Miss Ambleside peered at the towering figure between herself and the light.

'Why, Rudolph!' she exclaimed, 'but how nice! I didn't know you were here.'

'Well, I'm not actually. I'm moving from A to B, and thought I'd take in Cres in passing. Have you' – his eyes wandered over the luggage with which the hall seemed to be filled – 'arrived, or are you leaving?'

'Dolphin! My dear rabbit!' Cressida had come in behind him. For a moment she stood with her arm through his, forgetting her guests. Together they made a picture that was quite overpowering, almost too Nordic to be real.

'Tell me one thing,' Cressida said after a minute, 'do we have the convoy in too?'

Her question drew attention to activity outside the door. A dull, heavy rumble of machinery troubled the air. Felicity, who felt out of it and was restless, moved so that she could see out of the door. There was a long line of armoured vehicles of various kinds extending down the drive.

'Well, no,' she heard the Nordic vision say, 'we've got everything. Might like the odd kettle of water or so.'

'Better have the bath,' Cressida remarked, glancing out of the door in her turn. 'Oh, poor Aunt Jessie, you must be dying for tea. Dolphin, you're in the nick of time to carry up all this. Miss Brent,' she added a little stiffly, 'this is my brother, Major Standing.'

She did not pause for Miss Brent to have an innings. She was too well used to the reactions of young women to her brother's appearance, and they nearly always led to complications and wasted time. Besides, this wench was engaged, and she was damn well going to remember it, Cressida decided severely. Also she was a damn little this and that and would get no change out of Dolphin anyhow.

The rumble outside diminished gradually as the convoy settled itself in a neat line against the park railings. Rudolph Standing picked up all Miss Ambleside's luggage, contriving to make it look like a cluster of handbags, and followed his sister and aunt upstairs. Felicity, feeling ineffective, trailed behind the party. Halfway up the stairs she realised that it would have been much better to have waited for the young man to come back and fetch her own suitcases. She was losing her grip, she told herself, and something would have to be done about it.

Having settled her aunt, Cressida led Felicity into the grey and yellow bedroom and, with sufficiently polite remarks, left her there. She joined her brother outside and went down with him. At the bottom of the stairs they met John.

The little boy stood, without a word, watching every step his uncle took. The descent of some Norse god could not have been more raptly attended. The expression in John Chance's eyes left nothing for words to do.

'Have you seen all the lorries and things outside?' Cressida asked him.

'Yes, thank you,' John said. 'They're armoured cars, you know, and one of the drivers gave me some stamps.' His eyes never left the figure of his uncle. They rested on the flying horse and the word above it. 'Airborne,' he murmured, half to himself, dwelling on the word lovingly. 'I like that.' Suddenly his dazzling smile broke out. 'Uncle Dolphin, you're a flying fish!' he said, and fled up the stairs chuckling with laughter, ducking under his uncle's hands.

'This the glamour baby's baggage?' Dolphin asked without interest.

Cressida nodded, wishing that Felicity had heard him. Standing went upstairs once more loaded with suitcases.

Felicity, who had had time to study her face and decide that it wasn't too frightful considering, was not accustomed to young men who put down her luggage and left her with a grin and a just sufficiently polite remark, but without a second glance. She even got the unlikely impression that she was only just visible. She had never met anyone, certainly not a man, who looked at her without appearing to see her. She was disconcerted.

Rudolph Standing, unconcerned with what effect he had had on the glamour baby, found his sister boiling kettles in the kitchen.

'I've only got half an hour,' he said. 'Wish I could have stayed a bit longer. I say, rather a bore having Aunt J. on you. What caused her this time?'

'Oh, just a rural urge,' Cressida said. 'I gather she had a

hellish journey, poor old dear. How are you, Dolphin? How's
– everything?'

For a second or two her brother did not answer. Then he
said, 'Oh, all right,' in the tone of voice that showed he meant
the opposite.

Cressida glanced at the back of his handsome head,
silhouetted in the window. He had square, broad shoulders,
and stood with the same easy grace as his sister did. Although
his figure was disposed in such slack lines, Cressida could
tell that he was not at rest. Something about him, or perhaps
it was Cressida's inside knowledge, gave away the fact that
his nerves were under continual strain and that his casual
manner was an effort.

'Do I ask where you're going?' Cressida said, because she
had to make him talk somehow, and he hated direct questions
about the only subject he really would want to talk about.
Cressida knew that he needed to be started, and that that one
subject would emerge from almost any conversation.

'Place to place,' her brother said. Then, after a slight
pause, 'I was in town last night.'

Here it was already, Cressida thought, and said, 'Did you
see Rilla?'

'Yes,' Standing said shortly.

'How was she?' What a damn silly question, but there
wasn't anything else to ask.

'All right.' Dolphin did not move so much as a hair.

Cressida's heart ached with pity. Blast the creature, she
thought. Why the *hell* should Dolphin have come up against
probably the only woman in the world who could torture him

like this. He could have had anyone else he wanted, absolutely anyone. Women fell for Dolphin as inevitably as the sun rose in the morning, sometimes with a horrifying lack of restraint in spite of the total absence of any encouragement from him. But he had to break his heart over this one woman, whose voice was more important to her than anything else in the world.

Cressida, whose sympathies were all one way, had to recognise the importance of Rilla Hamar's voice. She knew that the reputation of being one of the finest living singers of the world was justified. One could not imagine her becoming an army officer's wife. But marrying Dolphin did not, somehow, seem to imply becoming an army officer's wife. Cressida pushed the kettles about viciously, wishing there was anything to say that could be of the slightest use.

'Was she singing last night? I never seem to see the paper,' she said, as if she was just making conversation.

'*Figaro*,' Dolphin answered. 'I managed to get there just before the lights went out.'

His perfectly ordinary words brought an agonisingly vivid picture to Cressida's mind. She could see Dolphin looming above all the people in the stalls, his fair hair white under the lights, everyone watching him, wondering who this magnificent young man was. Dolphin would be looking at no one, or, if he had to recognise someone he knew, he would look at them with that dreadful blind stare that made his automatic smile heart-breaking. She could imagine him as the lights went out, watching the curtain, watching the lighted stage, watching and watching until he could relax for a few moments, released by Rilla Hamar's voice.

'We had supper at the flat,' Dolphin went on suddenly.

Her flat, Cressida knew that meant.

'She – she wanted me to stay.' He did not seem to be going on, although the sense of an unfinished sentence hung uncomfortably in the air.

'Well, why didn't you?' Cressida asked abruptly, knowing he hadn't.

Her brother moved for the first time since the conversation had started. He swung round and laughed with a slight sign of real amusement.

'Same as ever, Cres,' he said, 'always four sentences ahead and knowing all the answers. Oh, well, there's always the war to fall back on.'

So that was that, Cressida thought. Still, as he said, there was always the war. Funny how often lately it had occurred to her that there was something to be said for the war. It was frightening to consider how enormous personal worries and tragedies would look without the infinitely more immense background of the war to dwarf them into insignificance. Cressida shied away from further consideration of personal tragedies and made the tea.

She went in search of her aunt, who would not, she knew, think of looking in so unlikely a place as the kitchen for her tea. She met Miss Ambleside on the stairs.

'Tea's in the kitchen,' Cressida said, ' I hope you won't mind.' It did not matter, she had long ago decided, whether her visitors minded the kitchen or not. But one went on asking them, just the same; one of those pointless questions that were supposed to denote good manners. Still, there was even less point in looking or sounding rude.

'The kitchen!' Miss Ambleside echoed. 'How quaint and amusing, Cressida dear.'

How odd, you mean, Cressida thought. But she said, 'It's easier, you see, and most people seem to bear it pretty well.'

The kitchen was entered by Miss Ambleside. She stood just inside the door, waiting, Cressida guessed, to see what she could smell. Actually the more noticeable smell in the room came from a large bowl of carnations on the window-sill, over which a light breeze was blowing. The rest of the party appeared in due course and introductions were made. Miss Ambleside, her society manner very well in hand, turned to her neighbour at the large, scrubbed deal table.

'I find this most original,' she said. 'Somehow one never visualises meals in one's kitchen.'

'I'm all for it myself,' Madge Rimmington-Clarke said heartily. 'Food's hotter, y'know, and seems to be more of it!'

'Well, yes, perhaps,' Miss Ambleside compromised with, 'but I feel one would miss all one's nice things so terribly.'

'Nice things are all right if there's someone to clean 'em,' Madge went on. 'I can't stand polishin' tables myself.'

'I rather like polishing,' Mary Handley said, 'but it's carrying trays of ullage I loathe. Here you can at least drop things straight in the sink.'

'Yes,' Mrs Yates broke in, glad of a conversation she could for once really take part in. 'Yes, I do think washing-up is *so* much less nasty if you don't have piles of dirty things arriving on a tray. I mean a tidy stack *in* the sink is so different somehow.'

'And I like my second helpin' hot,' Madge continued,

'which they aren't in most dinin'-rooms, unless you have the servants runnin' backwards and forwards all the time, and that's so fidgetin' for 'em, poor dears, and generally hellish noisy as well. Their shoes squeak and they do so *breathe*!'

Everyone laughed mildly, and Madge went on, 'Of course I'm not pretendin' I've ever had a smart set-up of domestics. I've just suffered from what you get in the Army, and God help me from ever havin' any more of them!'

'Well, I don't want to sound snobbish,' Mary Handley said, 'but through no fault of my own I was brought up by an uncle with a footman behind every chair. I once poured my soup into the flower bowl just to see if that would shake the butler. It didn't. After that I got so jittery I couldn't eat without looking behind me first!'

'Well, it's nice to know,' Madge said, 'that the upper classes suffer too!'

'Speaking as a cook,' Cressida said, 'I can only tell you meals in the kitchen make a difference of eight hundred and thirty-five hours of work a year! At least something like that. I did work it out once.'

'Well,' Miss Ambleside said, a little breathlessly, 'I must say you all have quite unanswerable reasons, but I don't know, I'm sure. I'm too old, I expect, for all these new ideas.' She contrived to convey disapproval of kitchens in spite of what anyone might say.

'As visiting member of the Brains Trust,' Dolphin said, 'I will air my views unasked. I like kitchens. I agree about tray carrying and hot second helpings. And the kitchen atmosphere's friendly for some reason or other.'

Tori sat up, his eyes twinkling.

'It is my experience,' he said, 'that in the kitchen you make friends; in the drawing-room you make conversation.'

'Knocked it off as usual, Tori,' Dolphin said. 'Too right, as they say down under.'

'But,' Tori continued, turning to Miss Ambleside with what would have been a bow from the waist had he not been seated, 'I must agree with you when you speak of beautiful furniture. Who does not enjoy food upon shining tables with glass full of light and silver – Ah!' he expanded his shoulders and waved his thin hands lavishly, 'the sensation to the fingers of a well-polished silver spoon!'

Miss Ambleside beamed. A nice little man, she decided. She had not caught his name but must remember to find out.

'I see *you* understand what I mean,' she said in gratified tones.

Next time she'll leave out the last three words, Cressida thought, and then it'll be just a wallow of understanding. She grinned at Tori, who would, she knew, be thinking much the same thing.

Tori, however, had not finished.

'But,' he said dramatically, 'what shall happen when the tables no longer shine, when those who clean them are taken from you and there is no time to sit and polish spoons?' He uttered a very Central European sound of a gloomy nature. 'Then how terrible to see the table dull, to see, perhaps scratches, to know you cannot preserve the beauty you enjoy, because there is not time in the day for so much. No, no,' he went on, 'that shall not happen, that must not. Silver and shining mahogany and bright glass must remain in memory beautiful, and not be seen in actuality smeared and unkept. I like better to have this table' – he smote the deal with vigour – 'which is so clean, and to see my good food *en casserole*, rather than to have it made lordly and perhaps cold in a silver dish not well cleaned!'

Miss Ambleside joined in the laugh, but she would not admit defeat.

'But I must own,' she said, 'that I could never admire a sink!'

Tori, equally undefeated, answered her. He sugared his reply with one of his most disarming smiles.

'I,' he said, 'can find it pleasant to see something which is right in the surroundings. I do not admire the sink, because the sink does not call for admiration. It has, however, a certain beauty, because it is an object designed for a necessary purpose which it fulfils. It would be senseless, and I should find it most irritating, to have a sink dressed up to be pretty!'

'Like those terrible kitchens they have on the films,' Cressida said, 'all hard and shiny, like laboratories.'

Tori bowed to her. 'So!' he said, 'That is true. If a kitchen is not homely it has lost its soul! As for beautiful furniture,' he went on, 'I have for it a very great love and admiration. But something I cannot admire is the mahogany unclean, and dishes of earthenware placed upon it. No! You shall have one thing or the other, as you say. The silver and elegance in the dining-room, or the homely and useful in the kitchen. You shall not make of these things a mixture. Ah, horrible!'

'Thank you, Tori,' Cressida said, 'you've summed it up perfectly.'

'I say,' Madge remarked, 'hasn't the bride shown up?'

'My God,' Cressida said mildly, 'I'll have to fetch it.'

'But you will allow me!' Tori was on his feet. 'And I must go to work at the same time. I will send to you the beautiful bride.'

Cressida grinned at him. 'All right,' she said, 'and don't say I didn't warn you.'

Almost before Tori had left the kitchen the front-door bell rang above the heads of the party at tea.

'My turn,' Dolphin said, and went to answer it.

In a few seconds John Greenacre, obviously palpitating with excitement, joined the party.

CHAPTER SEVEN

The last of the armoured cars crawled round the curve of the drive in the direction of the gates. Cressida watched them until there was nothing to see, only a dull regular rumble, like a menace retreating into silence. She was thinking about her brother at the head of that long rumbling column, driving stolidly for miles, trying to concentrate on the importance of a journey which seemed to have no particular reason, trying to find all the petty details of routine sufficiently absorbing to keep out thought. Funny, she thought inconsequently, that all those powerful vehicles should be so imposing when going slowly. If one met a convoy on the road, hurtling along at an alarming speed, the lorries, or whatnot, seemed merely noisy and a nuisance. But there was something terrifying about their slow progress, a suggestion of enormous and lethal power only just held in check. Her thoughts ended, as they had begun, with her brother. Poor Dolphin. Poor, darling Dolphin; one more nice, unhappy human being trying to lose his personal trouble in the war. So much easier for the lucky ones who happened to be actually fighting. They would be too excited, or too frightened, or both, to worry much about their own sorrows. People talked a lot about the various hells of war; the dust and heat in the desert, the steam and exhaustion of the tropics, the icy terror of the sea, the nerve-shattering clash of actual battle anywhere. But there was another sort of hell; the hell of impatience. Living in England, surrounded by normal people, living near-normal lives, trying to do a job that seemed to have no end and no purpose, a life of exercises and long journeys in lorries from one English village to another, without even an air raid to give reality to what felt like merely an irritating and prolonged succession of manœuvres. Much better, she thought, to be right away from England, where the spectre of pre-war life was not always hovering in the background, constantly reminding one of normality, making it impossible to cut oneself off and become really a part of the machine humanity had to become in order to fight this latest form of war. Coming to tea, as Dolphin had, in the middle of a journey, could not be really a pleasure or a relaxation. It was simply one more glance back to life, when glancing back might be fatal. People who looked back, one was always being told, were caught out in the end, from Lot's wife onwards.

Cressida put her hands in her trouser pockets and turned back into the house. And yet, she thought obstinately, yet perhaps the ability to remember, to keep a vision of the past, was the one way to preserve sanity. In the end perhaps it would be the machine that broke down, while weak and wishfully thoughtful and retrospective human nature would hang on somehow and conquer mechanisation.

In the hall Cressida met her aunt, coming downstairs in the dignified, comfortable manner of one who has washed her hands after tea and would now like to look at the garden.

'It's cleared up so nicely, Cressida dear,' Miss Ambleside began, 'that I really think I must just peep at your delightful garden. I remember how lovely it always was. When one's in town so much a garden is so restful.'

I ought to show her round, Cressida thought, and said, 'Yes, do, Aunt Jessie. I must do a thing or two, and then I'll come and look for you.'

'Do, dear. I'm sure you ought to get out more. You look so pale, you know. I don't expect to find pale people in the country!'

There seemed to be no particular answer to this remark, and Cressida did not invent one. She smiled vaguely at her aunt and thought about the fish which had not come. Cressida had heard the full story of the missing of the bus owing to John having fallen down and cut his knee halfway down the drive, which meant old Nannie hustling him back to the house to have it thoroughly washed, and then having to look for the iodine, which one of the paying guests had put back in some place where it never was kept, and how the bus would never have been missed if some people would put things in their right places, and what things were coming to if your house wasn't your own, Nannie didn't know, she was sure. Dear Nannie, Cressida thought with affection, it was nice to be sure she would put John first if the heavens were falling, but perhaps he wouldn't have got blood-poisoning in a quarter of an hour. . . . Oh, well, thoughts like that wouldn't fetch the fish. Nannie was seventy and couldn't help being a fusser.

Cressida made the necessary calculation as to where the fish would have been to, and when the bus in which it had travelled so extensively would pass through the village again. She had just reached a decision on this point when she encountered Felicity Brent and her young man, who was clearly in a hopeless state of bewildered love and would not be the person to send in search of the fish. Felicity passed Cressida without speaking. The young man, with an obvious effort, made some attempt at a perfectly unintelligible, but doubtless polite remark, and followed his mannerless and beautiful young woman into the garden. Mary would go, Cressida thought, but finding her might entail missing the bus again. Old Madge was almost certainly having her exercise, probably five miles away by now. Mrs Yates would be feeding the baby, John was having his bath. Poor old Tori would go in a flash, but Tori mustn't be made use of too often. It was too easy to make a slave of anyone so anxious to be one. Cressida realised she would have to go herself. It generally came to that in the end.

On her return, with the very damp and smelling parcel, which had been to a village fifteen miles away and back, Cressida met Miss Ambleside, who had just completed her peep at the garden and was preparing to go in and have a nice hot bath before changing for dinner. She managed to keep Cressida in conversation for quite a time. Cressida heard a good deal about the meals her aunt had eaten at various of the more expensive London restaurants, and about the people in whose more or less exalted company she had eaten, the activities of the relations of these people, and the thoughts of their friends in high places regarding the conduct of the war and the hypothetical intentions of Hitler; the conversation, or rather the monologue, continued on the dinginess of London, the crowded tubes, the iniquities of shops where after hours of waiting one could buy only one pot of face-cream at a time, so that one had to wait more hours in another shop to get another pot, and, of course, the difficulty of giving one's friends a meal!

Odd, Cressida thought, how everyone talks about the difficulties of giving people meals, but no one thinks much of taking them. In the end she was driven to waving the fishy package under her aunt's nose and telling her firmly that it contained the dinner she would not get if she talked any more. Feeling she had narrowly escaped being rude, she reached the kitchen at last, having finally told her aunt that dressing for dinner was not expected.

'Of course, I understand, dear,' Miss Ambleside had said. 'I've only brought an old rag, something light, you know, travelling as one does in suitcases.'

Cressida had just finished her cooking when Tori appeared in the kitchen with a bottle of whisky. Cressida had long ago decided that she could afford no drinks except beer.

'Oh, Tori, you're wonderful. How did you know it was an answer to prayer?'

'It is simple,' Tori said, 'I have heard you talking with your aunt. I have waited long enough so that you shall prepare beautiful food, and here am I!'

'You're wrong if you heard me talking,' Cressida said, smiling at him.

'Ah, so! I have heard you listen then.'

'More like it,' Cressida said. She took a cigarette, which Tori lighted for her. It warmed the heart, she thought, to know that Tori had done so much thinking about her. In spite of the flippant way he spoke, she knew that he meant what he said. After a minute she went on, 'You know, Tori, when I meet people like Aunt Jessie I get – positively frightened.'

Tori looked as though he would leap to her rescue. She waved her hand at him in a calming manner and continued.

'I mean, I can't help thinking something quite frightful will have to happen to us, the English, because there are still so many people who simply don't notice the war, except as a sort of boring obstruction to their own comfort. It's people of Aunt Jessie's age and type who are the worst I think. Heaps of them have sons and relations to worry about, and, of course, they do worry and go through the tortures of the damned about them, but for themselves, personally, the war seems to mean practically nothing. They don't see why they shouldn't wangle petrol and hoard biscuits and run the central heating and have three lights in the drawing-room and hot baths up to their necks, in fact go on as nearly as possible in the way they've been used to. When you think of the rest of Europe – I suppose I oughtn't to say things like this to you, Tori, about my own country, but – well, it's just to you that I've got to say them. I'm apologising to you, I suppose! Tell me honestly, Tori, doesn't it make you feel madly angry?'

Tori thought for a few moments. Then he said, 'Yes, Cressida. I will tell you, because you speak honestly and I must do so also.' His face had become, if possible, more lined than ever. For almost the first time since she had known him

Cressida thought he really looked like a man who had been through horrors. 'When first I arrived in England –' he went on.

He's remembering, Cressida thought, perhaps I ought not to let him.

'I – could not understand, I could not believe in such – such – I cannot tell what to call it. Unawareness, perhaps, if you have such a word. To come from – from my country' – with every word his face became more haggard and his eyes no longer twinkled – 'where – where the things you read of, you English read of in your papers and shudder and cannot believe, happen to one's friends, one's own family. And things no newspaper could print – happen in actual life – and truth, truth is more terrible than any dream, any nightmare' – Tori put his thin fingers over his eyes, but Cressida knew he could not shut out horror that way – 'and to be free from pain for one instant is to become afraid, but afraid to madness, of the next touch –'

Cressida moved involuntarily towards him and put her hands on his. He faced her then and smiled.

'Ah, Cressida, thank you,' he said quietly, 'your hands have healed the memory of my fear. I was foolish to remember – so much.'

'Tori, don't go on. I'm sorry. I don't know how I could have –'

He interrupted her vigorously. 'Ah, it is for nothing for you to be sorry! It is not good to forget, or to try to pretend to forget. I would remember, rather, remember everything so that this – this sanity, this normality that is so strong in England shall not seem to be the only truth! I would prefer to feel again as I did when I first came to this safety, that it was a dream, that I must wake soon, that I dare not continue to dream too long.'

'That's it,' Cressida interrupted in her turn, 'it is like a dream. It's like a dream that seems to be about ordinary things but – but has a sort of background of – panic. You feel that at any moment, round any corner, there's a nightmare waiting, and no one knows about it. I've sometimes had a dream that I'm shouting at someone as loud as I can and no sound comes out and I get frantic and nearly burst, and still there isn't a sound. And I don't even know what it is I'm trying to shout!' She laughed, quite without mirth. 'Silly, isn't it? But that's what I sometimes feel about – some of these people we were talking about. I feel they are being screamed at, loud enough for anyone to hear, but they simply don't. Then, of course, one stops being frightened and gets madly angry.' She stopped and finished her whisky.

Tori refilled her glass. He was now perfectly calm.

'I was angry too,' he said quietly, 'at first. But – you can learn to understand.'

'Tori, how do you bear it?' Cressida asked urgently. 'I've never felt I could let you talk about it before, but I must now. How can you go on – laughing it off and – not hating us?'

Tori took her free hand and kissed it lightly, but without a sign of a flourish.

'Because I am sorry,' he said gently. ' I am sorry for these people of whom you speak, because they are afraid to look at truth. They do not want to know that they have been wrong all their lives.'

'I see,' Cressida said after a pause. 'Yes, I see. I suppose I can sympathise with that sort of fear. But – well, it isn't all fear, Tori, a lot of what I mean is simply selfishness, and you can't sympathise with that. People have wrapped themselves up in comfort and got so used to it that they really feel it's their right, and are quite hurt if anyone suggests they're being selfish.'

'They know, all the same,' Tori said. 'In their hearts they know, and that is why they are afraid. And why they talk so much!' he added lightly.

Cressida snorted. 'The thoroughly guilty pay the highest lawyer's fees. Same idea, I suppose?'

'Certainly,' Tori agreed. 'The guilty man must have defences, but the man who knows that he is right has faith. He does not need to talk.'

'I suppose one might be the same,' Cressida said slowly. 'It's pretty damnable having to admit that one is wrong!'

'Ah, no!' Tori exclaimed with vigour, 'I would rather die knowing that I had been honest if it should be for only one hour.'

'Of course you're right,' Cressida said, 'but I can't help thinking that there's more to it than just being wrong. I mean – Well, take people like the Greersons, you know who I mean, the house with all the green paint.'

'Ah, yes,' Tori murmured, 'the Rose Villa.'

Cressida smiled. 'Actually it's called Hartley Priors, but the idea's the same. Anyhow, as I was saying, the Greersons. They're what everyone would call nice people. They go to the right schools, have good manners, answer nicely when spoken to, and have nice dinner-parties, or they did before the war. They shoot and fish and do all the right things in quite a nice genuine sort of way. But it doesn't strike them that they're at all lucky, that they can only afford to hunt because they've inherited enough money and not because they've worked for it. If they had to live on what they've earned they'd just about have enough to eat and not much over! They've got all the comfort they want, and if anyone like that harmless Green-acre boy asks them for a room, they behave like tigers. They treat these pathetic people like impertinent – well – almost criminals! I argued about paying guests once with Mrs Greerson. She said she thought it was quite outrageous the way all these young people seemed to think they could go round the country living in other people's houses and making nuisances of themselves. I was so angry I got a bit dramatic and said did she suppose these nice, shy young men liked walking up to private houses and asking for rooms, and being made to feel like commercial travellers or even confidence men, and did she realise that it might be the only chance some wretched couple might have of living together. I'm afraid I even said it might be the last few weeks of any of their lives. Mrs G. looked as if she thought I'd said something indecent. She even smiled in a pitying sort of way for which I'd like to have strangled her! I could almost hear her thinking, "Dear, dear, poor thing, a little overwrought, talking such nonsense," and so on. Well, I gave it up, and now we just bow and remark on the weather. But what's the matter with a person like that? Is it really possible for convention to get such a hold that it becomes natural?'

'I think so,' Tori said. 'I think a great many of those you call the nice people are clothed with a kind of dress, a suit of convention which they have worn always, so long that it has come to be to them as part of their body. So well has it come to fit that they can forget that they have not been born with it upon them. They can truly forget that they have been given at birth a skin! Some, perhaps, are aware of that skin. It is tender and they keep it covered, they are afraid to be exposed. But others, I think, have forgotten all except the suit of convention and the warm covering of habit.' He paused for a moment. Then he went on, 'Yes, it is those who have forgotten who are now so afraid. To say "forget" is to use a relative term only. Little things may be in truth forgotten, but I think it is not possible really to forget what is in your heart, even if it be so covered and buried that it is easy to imagine it does not exist. This is a war that shall tear away all coverings, and perhaps – perhaps it is possible that to everyone will come that realisation. And then, how fearful, how terrible to find that you have forgotten the skin that wraps your bones! To find that you do not know what it is like, this skin, or if it is strong enough to bear the rays of daylight which must reach it sooner or later.'

Cressida said nothing for a few moments. Tori poured her another drink.

'You mean,' she said at last, 'that all these people simply don't know themselves at all?'

'Yes,' Tori answered, 'that is what I mean. These people who seem to us so wrong, so selfish, are strangers to themselves. They see what they have made in their own image by their own will, but they do not see themselves! And so must they be even more strange to us. How is it possible to know a man who does not know himself?'

'Well, Tori, I can't think of an answer. But what's to be done about it? Is one supposed to ignore these wrapped-up creatures until the awful moment comes when they are forcibly stripped? Not that I want to run around telling people to look into their souls or anything embarrassing like that, but it seems a bit grim to – well, not to prod them now and again!'

'I think it is perhaps no use to – prod, Cressida. You cannot give that which a man refuses to take.'

'A simple, painful truth, my dear!' Cressida agreed warmly. 'I can't think of anything that hurts more than having something flung back in your face.'

'To you I think that cannot happen,' Tori said gently. His meaning was evident.

'But it has,' Cressida said, and laughed rather bitterly. 'I've never mentioned it because it still makes me blush, but I'll tell you. I had some people here who were fearfully hard up, or, anyhow, so they said pretty often! I tore up their cheque after the first month. I hoped they wouldn't notice. Well, they did. They didn't say anything, they just left, in the ordinary way, I thought. Then I got a letter, enclosing another cheque and – saying would I please refrain from handing out charity.' Cressida laughed again, a little more cheerfully. 'I suppose it was absurd and I was in the wrong and all that, but – I felt like hell, and angry and miserable and thoroughly nervous. I was terrified of ever meeting them again.'

Tori looked at her, his eyes very serious and revealing.

'To me, Cressida,' he said quietly, 'it is terrible that anyone can be who does not see the cruelty of refusing a kindness from you.'

'Thank you, Tori,' Cressida said, 'no one's ever said a nicer thing to me.'

She turned away and became engrossed in the Aga. Tori sometimes managed to make it very difficult not to cry.

CHAPTER EIGHT

Dinner was ready and Cressida rang a bell, first in the passage outside the kitchen, and then out of the window. Within a few seconds Miss Ambleside, wearing her old rag that had clearly cost thirty guineas and looked it, appeared in the door of the kitchen, trying, Cressida felt, not to look as though she thought that perhaps dinner might have been in the dining-room. She sat down at the deal table, which had been scrubbed till it was as white as a cloth. Miss Ambleside contrived to settle herself with a social flourish that almost transformed the table, in imagination, to mahogany. Three very fine rings flashed as she straightened her knives and forks with little dignified pats. Felicity Brent swept into the kitchen next. She was looking more glamorous than ever in a jade-green housecoat whose skirts swung widely from a tiny waist. Madge Rimmington-Clarke, fresh from a five-mile walk, clattered in in nailed shoes and very old tweeds, accompanied by the Colonel, who was still in uniform but did his best to rectify the fact by removing his coat and dining in his braces. Flying Officer Yates did not follow the example of the Army. Every button, and his belt, remained neatly fastened. Last of the party came John Greenacre, very pink and recently washed. At first blinded by the dazzling appearance of his beloved, and also partly by Miss Ambleside's diamonds, he fidgeted nervously with the collar of his battledress and wished that he had had time to change into service-dress. The sight of the Colonel's braces reassured him, however, and he began to look a little happier.

Cressida introduced him to such of the men who had not been at tea.

'. . . and Count Kristori Czepanskow-Ansdalt,' she ended with the slight relish inseparable from the successful handling of Tori's full name.

Felicity Brent's green eyes grew larger with every syllable of it. She favoured Tori with a sweep of her long lashes, which could not have failed in effect had he not been looking the other way.

Tori chose to devote himself with assiduity to Miss Ambleside, who was suitably gratified and beamed upon him with rather more than normal amiability. She felt that, with a little practice in private in the pronunciation of his name, she would be very pleased to have this amusing little man at her dinner-table at some future date, and not in the kitchen. He would look distinguished, she decided, in any company, no matter how exalted.

The meal proceeded. When her fish was finished Miss Ambleside sat back in her Windsor chair and almost forgot herself sufficiently to sigh with comfortable repletion. It was a long time, she felt, since she had been so thoroughly satisfied by any one dish of food.

'How good that was,' she said warmly. 'How well you cook,

Cressida dear. I'm sure it will be quite a pity when you don't have to do it any more.'

'I'm so glad you liked it, Aunt Jessie,' Cressida said, 'it only got here in the nick of time. Food does a lot of wandering around in buses these days.'

'Well, that makes it all the more a credit to you, dear. Really, you must invite me to stay with you again before your cook comes back!' Miss Ambleside was very lively and arch.

Cressida laughed. 'She won't come back,' she said, 'so you can always be sure of my cooking. I'm quite determined never to have any more servants.'

Miss Ambleside was staggered and showed it.

'Dear me,' she exclaimed, with all the vigour of a much more violent phrase, 'no servants! Why, Cressida, what a quaint idea. But you're not serious!'

'I certainly am,' Cressida said firmly. 'I feel I've only discovered how to live since the servant question's stopped being a question.'

'I absolutely agree,' Mary Handley said, 'except that I rather hate housework. But one could have a daily who would vanish at eleven.'

'I'd give in as far as that,' Cressida said, 'at least in a house this size. But not another inch.'

'But surely you would find it a terrible tie?' Miss Ambleside objected.

She seemed quite as genuinely concerned about the matter as if Cressida had announced her intention of doing something utterly outrageous, if not actually dangerous to life itself.

'When you wanted to go out, for instance?' she pursued anxiously.

'I'd go,' Cressida said. 'I do now, you know, occasionally, and the house doesn't come apart.' She flashed a smile at her aunt, thus removing any suggestion that she had been impertinent.

'Well, I expect you'll change your mind. After the war, I mean, when one'll be able to get about again and take up all the interesting things that are so impossible now.' Miss Ambleside finished her sentence with the air of one who has had the last word.

This was too much for Cressida. Her aunt's bland assumption that she didn't know what she was talking about would have been a challenge to defend her point of view without the added irritation of Miss Ambleside's obvious intention not to try to understand it. Her aunt's reference to interesting things was the final straw. Cressida knew too well what things Miss Ambleside found interesting.

'I don't think so,' she said, trying to begin, at any rate, in as mild a manner as possible. 'I expect it's my low origins,' she went on lightly, 'but I could never again bear anyone else messing about in my kitchen! And it really isn't a tie, Aunt Jessie. I feel I'm free for the first time in my life.'

Miss Ambleside smiled unbelievingly. She contrived to imply that, of course, her niece was behaving very bravely and taking her hardships in the right spirit. She could have chosen no surer way to spur Cressida to speech, though that was, perhaps, not her intention.

'It's true,' Cressida said, 'I'm not putting on an act to hold off sympathy! I really do feel free. I can have as many people as I like to meals, and there's no fuss if everyone's hours late. I'd much rather cook than tell anyone else how to, and if the house is dirty I haven't got to run after some wretched wench and blast her into giving notice! And then start again with another one who'll scrub the carpets with the vacuum cleaner. Everyone who stays here will have to do their own cleaning' – out of the corner of her eye Cressida glanced at Felicity Brent who did not, however, appear to be listening – 'and if they do it badly it's their look-out. If they actually wreck the furniture one has to butt in and fuss, but it doesn't happen very often, anyhow, not as often as it did when I had maids.'

Miss Ambleside looked a little flustered, as if she felt the approach of defeat. She turned to her neighbour, who happened to be Jim Rimmington-Clarke.

'Now I'm sure you'll uphold me!' she said brightly. 'Surely you, as a man –'

What else could he uphold her as? Cressida wondered irritably.

' – would not like,' Miss Ambleside continued, 'to come home in the evening and find your wife always cooking and in a mess and not ready to talk to you?'

The Colonel looked as though he did not quite know how to answer this.

'Well, er –' he began doubtfully. 'I don't know, you know. I can't say I've ever seen Cressida in much of a mess,' he finished, with a little more assurance.

Everyone laughed. Miss Ambleside turned to Tori.

'Now you,' she said. 'You understand all about the comforts of life! I cannot believe that you would wish to spend all your evenings in the kitchen.'

Tori did not reply for a moment. Then he said, very seriously, but with his eyes suspiciously bright, 'Miss Ambleside. Since you ask me I must tell you that I think your niece has understood so much of the art of living that I could not permit myself to' – he searched for a word, wrinkling his monkey face into yet more lines – 'to enter a dispute about a subject which she is, so far more than I, able to support.'

Miss Ambleside, uncertain, as Tori had intended, whether or not he had agreed with her, rather hastily changed the subject. She realised how nearly she had said a most unfortunate thing when she had spoken of a man coming home to find his wife cooking. Poor Cressida, one should never have mentioned such a subject in her hearing, most careless of one, and it was to be hoped she had not noticed. Dear, dear, what a terrible business it had all been, and Simon so good-looking and well-off, and how difficult an affair like that made conversation. There were so many things that must not be said. Nearly five years ago, and seemed like no time. Well, fancy that, how time flew!

Jim Rimmington-Clarke, who was a slow thinker, came at last to the conclusion that if Madge was as good a cook as Cressida it wouldn't be half a bad idea not to bother about servants after the war. Leave a lot more cash for other things, he thought. Why, for a cook's wages he could get that extra reach on the river that was a damn sight better fishing than his own. And if a woman could cook and still look like

Cressida – By Gad, there was something to be said for the notion! The Colonel glanced at his wife, feeling a little guilty, as if she might have read his thoughts.

Madge, however, had done nothing of the sort. Oddly enough, even if she had she would not have been in the least disturbed. Cressida possessed the very unusual quality of being extremely attractive to men without provoking the slightest jealousy in women, even wives. There was something so detached and casual about her attractions that even women instinctively felt that whatever happened it wouldn't be her fault.

Madge was wondering, in fact, why it was that Cressida had not married again. One didn't know the details, of course, but one had heard the stories about her husband and some other man, and it had all sounded pretty grim. Still, Cressida didn't look the sort of woman who would take to cooking as an anodyne. She always seemed quite cheerful, and didn't look at all harassed, or miserable, or anything like that. Madge Rimmington-Clarke was very simple-minded and direct. She took people at surface value and was apt to suppose that anyone who was unhappy was bound to go about with a graveyard expression.

Mrs Yates was thinking, with quite a glow of pleasure, that it was rather wonderful, when you came to think of it, how completely Mrs Chance's views agreed with her own. Mrs Yates longed for the neat little kitchen she had owned in the days of the eight-forty to town. Life had been so cosy and simple then, and poor Willy so much more like himself. And, nice though Mrs Chance was, and lucky though they were to have found such a lovely place to stay, there was, after all, nothing like your own house. As for servants, Mrs Yates had never had any, and would have been at a loss to know what to do with them if she had. But it was certainly nice to have such a – well, startlingly beautiful person as Mrs Chance feeling the same as oneself.

Mrs Yates did not know that it was Cressida's gift for sympathy that made her a friend to almost anyone who needed understanding. Social distinctions did not affect this understanding, which was instinctive, and of which Cressida herself was quite unaware.

The thoughts of Mrs Yates's husband ran on much the same lines as hers. Had he been approached by Miss Ambleside with her question about coming home in the evening, his embarrassment would have been acute. He could never have brought himself to say in front of all these people that one of the things he longed for most after the war was just to come home and find his wife in the kitchen, so that he could sit by the stove in his slippers and watch her prepare his supper.

Mary Handley thought, almost unbearably, of the nine weeks that were all she had had of married life before her husband left the country. She thought of the hotels, in three different places, they had stayed in, and of the dreams they had dreamed about the house they would one day have. There had never been time to talk about houses, but it had been impossible not to imagine one, though imagination had not had time to dwell on details such as kitchens and servants. A house had been simply a place where she and Roger would be alone, instead of sitting in hotel lounges and talking in low voices.

John Greenacre, gazing in rapture at his lovely Felicity, hardly took in the subject of conversation. The only remark that registered with his brain was Miss Ambleside's question about coming home in the evening. The picture those words had conjured up made his mind reel. Coming home to Felicity. Perhaps not coming home to Felicity in the kitchen. The kitchen was not the room Felicity's glamour suggested as a background. John Greenacre's mind dwelt on breathtaking thoughts. The general aura of romance with which these were surrounded made him feel more than a little drunk.

Felicity Brent herself was the only person in the room who had not given the matter under discussion a single thought. She was wondering what line of approach would be effective with the extraordinary, but peculiarly attractive, little man with the remarkable name and rather odd, but very amusing, mannerisms.

Cressida was in the highly nervous state of one who has only just managed not to be carried away by temper. She had been so nearly angry with her aunt that she was still tired with the effort of trying to sound flippant. Oh, God, she thought, why can't I just be casual about it all? What the hell's it matter whether Aunt Jessie sees my point or not? It's idiotic to mind. And I suppose she's embarrassed now, because she mentioned husbands coming home in the evening. As if it mattered what she said, or what anyone says. It's all so boring and simply not real. I've got to have something real, and not just conversation for ever and ever. Tori knows . . . and I can't hurt him. Poor, darling Tori . . . oh, God, Charles, Charles. . . .

CHAPTER NINE

The *Alice Corrie* went down on the night of June 2nd, and at dawn on the 4th Charles Valery opened his eyes for the first time since the ship sank. Dawn that day was very beautiful. The sky was as delicately coloured as a thrush's egg. The sea was so calm that it looked as soft as milk, but its colour, subtly changing every second, took on a clearer radiance until, by the time the sun was fully up, it was shining with the hard brilliance of ice.

Charles Valery winced from pain of this intolerable light. He shut his eyes hastily. But after two days and nights of unconsciousness his senses were not to be lulled by shutting out light. Inch by inch, it seemed, he became aware of his body, and each area of returning consciousness was alive with pain that threatened at any moment to become unbearable. It became impossible to endure this creeping approach of torture, and Charles sat up with a violent wrench of all his muscles. A wave of agony leaped at him, so that for a few seconds he almost returned to the comfort of unconsciousness. But instead, his mind waked slowly to the necessity of discovering the cause of this apparently gratuitous anguish. He did not remember the shipwreck or the fire at first, but the memory of a face began to grow clearer until he recognised it as Harcourt's face.

Harcourt's face, twisted and distorted, his mouth stretched as if he was screaming, but no sound coming from it. Charles shut his eyes again, this time not against the light. Horrible, it was, that face, screaming without making a sound. But there was some other sound, that was why Harcourt's voice had been inaudible. Some other much more savage and overpowering sound. . . .

Charles tried to shake himself free of that sound. His eyes opened again, and again he saw Harcourt's face. This time he stared at it. Perhaps by staring it out he could dissolve memory. Harcourt was no longer screaming. His eyes were open and stared back at Charles. But Charles knew for certain that Harcourt was not looking at him. Suddenly it occurred to him that Harcourt's face was black. This seemed odd and unlikely. He studied the phenomenon carefully for some minutes. At last it dawned upon him that Harcourt might be dead. Surely no one could be alive and look like that. . . .

With difficulty Charles removed his gaze from Harcourt's face and let it wander over the immediate surroundings. After a little he discovered that he was looking at his own feet and legs, for some odd reason under water. He moved one foot a little and water lapped against his waist. He made a queer thin sound that seemed to have no connection with himself. His hands were in the water. The water felt like boiling oil. He caught sight of black hands flapping meaninglessly. With astonishment he realised that they were his own. He lifted one from the water and studied it carefully. Eventually he decided that it had been pretty severely burnt. Burnt. Yes, that was it, fire. Fire in a blinding sheet . . . fire roaring like some savage animal . . . and Harcourt's face, floating in a sea of flame. . . .

The whole thing came back to him then. He remembered all about the *Alice Corrie*, in which he had been voyaging from the States to England. He remembered the shock of the explosion, a torpedo, he supposed, because no aircraft had been heard before the shock. He remembered that he had been talking to Harcourt. Harcourt had been talking politics, he usually was. He always had some theory about the party to blame for the latest lack of success on the part of the English in some part or other of the world. Absurd, some of his ideas had been. On this occasion, Charles remembered, it had been the entire Government that had come in for one of Harcourt's attacks of recrimination. Harcourt was one of those people, and there were millions of them, who talked about the Government as if it was just some remote body, totally unconnected with the population of the country it governed. And yet Harcourt would be almost the first to assert that the English, including himself, were fighting to preserve the sanctity of democracy. Men like Harcourt, Charles thought, if asked to define the word democracy, would bring out all the right answers; government of, by and for the people, and all the rest of it. But what they really should say, if they could be somehow given a few moments of accuracy, was that democracy meant, to them, the right to blast the Government as often and as loudly as they wished, and to describe at length any scheme of their own which they considered would have been far more successful than the action by the Government that happened to be under discussion.

Charles put his hands over his eyes because the sunlight had begun again to hurt them. The act had several effects upon him. To begin with he became once more conscious of acute pain. His hands were unbelievably sore, and one side of his face felt as if the skin had recently been torn from it. Then it dawned upon him that, instead of sitting and thinking about Harcourt's face or his politics, he should have been trying to discover where he was and decide on action of some kind to remove himself somewhere else. He realised, with vague surprise, that he was sitting in quite deep water. In spite of the sunlight he opened his eyes and studied the situation. Harcourt's face appeared again. Oh, blast the man, why think about him so much? This must be stopped somehow. He reached out with one of his black and painful hands as if he would brush away the maddening vision of Harcourt's face. With a shock of astonishment he discovered that he was not only haunted by Harcourt's face, he was looking at it.

It was at that moment that complete coherence came to him. He realised that this was, in truth, Harcourt's face, and Harcourt himself lay there, in the water at the bottom of a fairly large boat, lay very still and stiff in the same water in which Charles was sitting. The only fact of which he remembered nothing was that his own courage had brought the body of Harcourt through those sheets of fire into that boat, that his blackened hands had cast off from the burning ship before he had fallen back beside Harcourt into the water at the bottom of the boat.

Charles decided that he had now to make a choice between two courses of action. Either he could lie quietly back in the water, which would be much easier than any other movement, or he must try to discover how much was the matter with him, and what was to be done about it. If he lay back, as every instinct urged, he would perhaps die in a fairly short time. Very restful. He looked round at the sea. There was nothing else to look at, and the sea, though beautiful, did not hold out much hope that any change he might make in his position would be worth the torture of making it.

The sun grew stronger, and its warmth was like the touch of life. The idea of dying began to seem absurd. Charles leaned gently against the side of the boat and let the sun continue its comforting work. He listened to the slight smack of water against the boat. The sound was soothing in the extreme, and it was quite easy to sit there and let thought drift. Very soon Charles began to lose his recently regained sense of reality. He did not think about action of any kind. He did not even wonder whether rescue was a possibility. A very light breeze crept over the sea, making the boat sway so gently that it could scarcely be said to rock. The motion, combined with the warmth of the sun, produced in Charles a state of half-waking dream, so that he ceased to consider time or anything else.

His thoughts wandered inconsequently from one irrelevant subject to another.

A ship, cutting through still water, spray at her bows making a crisp sound like flung grain . . . the reedy note of an oboe cutting through the rush of a great orchestra, like a warning . . . a sea-bird, with outstretched wings, apparently asleep on the wind . . . wind trying to smooth out a field of standing corn . . . the inrush of silence when, with engines cut, an aeroplane begins a long downward glide ... smoke drifting across a dark wood like a huge lazily waving feather ... earth a map one moment, and in the next turning into real fields and trees ... the flat outline of a house becoming suddenly three-dimensional and disappearing at almost the same instant ... sunlight through trees, turning the air green so that birds were like winged fish, flying under water ... water flowing under trees in a gleaming brown tunnel ... an open stretch of water and the light plop of a rising fish ... a wooden footbridge, one board missing, with moss on the hand-rail ... the river behind the woods at Brede....

Brede. Suddenly Charles could see his home so vividly that he had to open his eyes.

The sun continued to strengthen, the sky's colour became hot. The sea glittered like a jewel turned by magic into liquid form. The lifeboat made the centre of an immense circle in which nothing else moved except the light on the water. The circumference of the circle seemed to support the cloudless dome of the sky. Charles took in none of these things. He leaned against the side of the boat without moving and thought about Brede.

CHAPTER TEN

After three days of good cooking, hot baths and delightful weather for sitting in the garden, Miss Ambleside found herself genuinely regretting the fact that she was to return to London on the following day. Miss Ambleside, if set in her ways, was honest enough to admit that she had thoroughly enjoyed herself, meals in the kitchen and all. In fact, her honesty carried her to the point of realising that it would be quite an effort to go back to a way of life which required continual efforts to keep one's clothes up to the mark, incessant and difficult arrangements to fit one's engagements into insufficient time, and a clean pair of gloves at least three times a week, to say nothing of the terrible stocking problem. Life in the country was certainly simpler.

Miss Ambleside did not pause to consider that her experience of life in the country had consisted of delightful periods of sitting in the garden, punctuated without any effort on her part by excellent meals. She would have been surprised, and perhaps a little hurt, if anyone had told her that for three years Cressida had never managed to find time to sit in the garden.

The thought of another of those fearful train journeys loomed in a shockingly unpleasant manner. The nine o'clock news, on that Sunday morning, had cast quite a gloom over everything. Miss Ambleside found that, taking one thing with another, it wasn't easy to preserve the cheerful manner which was, one felt, one's duty, and showed that one, like the English as a whole, was 'taking it' nobly. Things didn't seem at all good in Egypt, she felt; it wasn't nice to hear of so many of our troops being taken prisoner, but, of course, as that nice Joseph McLeod kept saying, these battles went backwards and forwards so fast and so often that one never knew what map one would want next, and it didn't do to get depressed. After all, these new tremendous raids we were making would upset the Germans a good deal. But, on the other hand, it would be very trying if they stimulated the Germans into sending several thousand bombers over London, where one had lately begun to live quite a normal life again. Miss Ambleside's life in London had never been far from the normal. During the blitz she had done a great deal of visiting in the country. And now Miss Ambleside's gloom drove her to consider the possible advantages of leaving London again. One could open one's house in the country, but then there would be the trouble of servants. It was all very difficult and trying. Perhaps dear Cressida would keep one a little longer, until one could see which way things were going. But in that case one would lose one's hair appointment, and getting another was always problematical. There were difficulties, it seemed, whichever course one decided upon. Perhaps it would be best to return to town as intended. It wouldn't do to look as if one was panicky. And the Germans might take some time to make up their minds. And one could always go down to the Gethrins' at a

moment's notice, in spite of the bad cook. She had probably
left, anyhow. And of course it might take quite a time for the
Germans to make all those bombers.

Oh, dear, Miss Ambleside thought, if only one could see
a little ahead, how much simpler things would be. This
aspiration, which she unwittingly shared with the General
Staffs of all the belligerent countries, did not comfort her in
the least. She, and the General Staffs, merely became more
anxious and more irritable, because it was so annoying to feel
that at any moment something might happen which would
entirely ruin all one's plans and render all one's efforts a mere
waste of time.

'Well, Cressida dear,' Miss Ambleside remarked after her
Sunday lunch, 'I really quite hate the idea of leaving you all
tomorrow.'

Cressida, feeling weak-minded for saying what was
expected of her, said, 'Of course you mustn't go if you don't
have to, Aunt Jessie.'

'It's very sweet of you, dear –' Miss Ambleside began.

Oh, God, she's going to stay, Cressida thought.

' – but I really think I must get back. It's always so difficult
to upset all one's arrangements, you know.'

'I suppose so,' Cressida answered, without, she hoped, too
much enthusiasm.

Little did her aunt realise, she thought, how difficult
it could be to upset arrangements which nearly always
involved a drive of twelve miles. Twelve miles with a horse like
Beltane might take fifty minutes or two hours, according to
mood and the number of lorries encountered. A convoy, for

instance, would certainly entail missing a train, if nothing worse.

'It's been so delightful,' Miss Ambleside went on, 'you've almost made me feel I could enjoy running my own house again. That is, if I could cook as beautifully as you do, dear!'

Cressida smiled. She had an inward vision of her aunt, with all her rings flashing, poking nervously at a saucepan from a safe distance, as if she expected either to find a toad in it, or that the pan would leap off the stove and throw itself at her.

'But I'm afraid at my age I could hardly manage the work,' Miss Ambleside continued blandly.

Cressida found this remark extremely irritating. She was annoyed with herself for being irritated, which led to irritation doubled. She knew very well, and had suffered from, her aunt's boundless energy when it was social occasions that required its expenditure. Her aunt could rush from one function to another, sit on endless committees, attend innumerable exhibitions, provided that they were the thing at the moment. She could march round the Royal Academy, jotting down suitable remarks under well-known names in her catalogue, and do three hours shopping on the same afternoon and be ready for her dinner engagement, with the comments of *The Times'* art critic on the Academy at her tongue's end. It seemed absurd that she should imagine her strength unequal to the effort of cooking herself a meal.

'I shan't let that pass, Aunt Jessie,' Cressida said amiably. 'You've often worn me to the bone in London and looked brand new yourself at the end of the day!'

Her aunt smiled, obviously pleased. 'Well, it's just what one's accustomed to, I suppose,' she said. 'One gets too used to running about in town.'

'You can get just as used to cooking, you know,' Cressida remarked, only her eyebrows showing an indication of her real thoughts.

Miss Ambleside looked a little surprised. 'Well,' she said, 'I suppose that may be so.' She sounded extremely doubtful.

'And after all,' Mary Handley broke in suddenly, 'far more women have always done their own cooking and cleaned their houses *and* looked after their children than not. I don't see why it should be supposed to be so overpoweringly exhausting.' She blushed slightly. Mary sometimes came out with vigorous remarks, almost before she knew she was going to speak, and was always embarrassed by her own eloquence.

'Yes,' Cressida said, 'I'm glad that got said. I always feel those women must think us extraordinarily wet for making such a fuss about what they've done all their lives as a matter of course.'

'Yes, but, Cres, look what hags they are by the time they're thirty,' Madge Rimmington-Clarke put in.

'That's generally too many children and too little money,' Cressida said. 'I simply don't believe it's just normal work. Anyway, some people are hags by nature, and some get haggish by having to worry, or by having to do too much work to get enough to live on. Living in peace with a reasonable family and enough money wouldn't lead to haggishness even if one did all the cooking and scrubbing. And hags aren't confined to the so-called lower orders, either,' she added.

'Plenty of what "we" are pleased to call "us" look like sluts when they've been married a year.'

'And some look like the morning after when they've cooked one meal,' Madge said. 'I expect I do. Feel like it anyway!'

Cressida grinned. 'You take it too hard,' she said. 'If you worry about cooking it's always a failure.'

'Dare say you're right,' Madge said. 'I may manage it in time. There's another class of slut,' she added, 'exhibit A, I'd put it at. The little glamour piece who gets married and says, or looks as if she says, "Well, now I'm fixed I needn't bother any more."'

'Oh, Lord, yes,' Cressida agreed. 'More marriages are wrecked by that sort, powder all over the floor, and tooth-brushes all over the bathroom, than by any amount of philandering.'

'A solemn thought,' Madge said, 'and too true.'

'Too true indeed,' Tori began in his most airy manner. 'A philanderer may play and be recognised and do no great harm, perhaps. But a man who is naturally faithful, naturally what you would call nice, who becomes disgusted and then bored and then more disgusted! Ah! There you have the serious trouble.'

'Same with women, Tori. You can't have it all your own way,' Cressida said. 'Think of the poor young girl who marries love's dream and finds blobs of shaving soap drying on the bathroom basin.'

Tori performed one of his seated bows. 'And the same with women,' he agreed solemnly, his eyes very bright and mocking. After a little pause he went on. 'There is a thing that I have thought about this affair of going without servants. It seems to me a test, perhaps more severe because it does not appear to be one. Everyone speaks of the test of war, which takes many different forms. For women there is the test of courage, to go with men into danger, to bear hardship and discomfort, to work all day in factories, to be tired and perhaps afraid. But for me I think that to stay at home, to be unnoticed, to do every day the same things, to be bored, to be tired by work which no one sees, to live in the same way that you have always lived, with only the difference that it is upon you that all the work will now fall, there, I think, is the most severe test of all. There is no uniform, just old clothes becoming every day older, and no company such as a factory would give, no new interests, no sense of urgency, of being what you might call "in the war". Perhaps it may seem an impertinence for me, a European, to speak of English women in such a way?' Tori's eyebrows rose inquiringly.

'Go on,' Cressida said, 'you're forgiven before you start.'

Tori grinned. 'Thank you,' he said. Then, turning to Miss Ambleside, he continued. 'I have very many English friends, and they are most kind so that I have travelled a great deal about your country. I have seen much of what your women have to do. I have, perhaps, been able to – to judge of their activities in a way better because I am not English. I can see from a distance, as you might say, and so see more. No one could admire more than I the women who work as men and with courage as great, but it is not for them I would speak. For me I prefer to forget women while they are in uniform and to think of those who are still in their homes, those who undergo the test of which I spoke. And for some it was at once too severe. They have failed at the beginning and have gone to live in hotels and the houses of other people. Some have made a start, complaining all the time. It has become a struggle, and some have failed and become, as Cressida has said, sluts. Many have continued the struggle, but it has remained always a hardship. They sigh and speak of after the war when the servants will come back. But the others, the few for whom the test was no more than a bridge to be crossed, they have already their reward. And it is a simple thing, this reward. It is just that they have discovered the freedom of a true family life.' Tori spoke with such sincerity that his words did not sound pompous, in spite of his rather stilted English.

Of all his audience, Mrs Yates was, perhaps, the most moved. Her heart warmed to Tori as it had never done towards anyone in this, to her, rather alarming household. How funny, she thought, that a foreigner should be the one to say what she had always felt. The freedom of family life. Of course it was that. People were always saying exactly the opposite, that a family was such a tie, that one was never free to do anything else, and so on and so on. But what, Mrs Yates asked herself, being far too shy to ask anyone else, what could possibly be more attractive than the bliss of making a home for one's husband and children? So-called amusements, games, parties, paled into futile ghosts beside the living warmth of a human home life. Perhaps, Mrs Yates thought honestly, perhaps I'm too dull to want anything else. That may be why I'm so satisfied.

It did not occur to her that her own instinctive unselfishness had anything to do with the case.

Mary Handley thought, with longing that brought tears to her eyes, that she would give all she had to have been tested in the way Tori had mentioned. She felt, without conceit, that she would have passed successfully.

Madge Rimmington-Clarke was uncertain whether she was more irritated or uncomfortably aware of her own inadequacy. The wretched little man was right, she admitted, but it was all very well for him to talk. What about the people who violently loathed cooking and grubbing about in the house?

Miss Ambleside, through no fault of her own, was out of her depth, and thought comfortably that as the little man's remarks did not apply to her in any way it wasn't necessary to take much notice of them.

Felicity Brent was bored and wished that the man would be amusing instead of reeling off sermons and gazing at Cressida Chance. She had had about enough of the endless conversations that seemed to go on in this house and was looking forward to returning to London the next day.

Cressida, who had guessed more or less what Tori would say, remained comparatively unmoved.

'Well,' she said cheerfully, 'I've always thought a lot of marriages were held together by the servants, and the sooner that sort cracks up the better. I'm sure you're right, Tori, but you must admit it's hard on women who hate cooking!'

Better turn the thing into a joke, she thought, before everyone gets either angry or too solemn.

Tori caught her tone instantly.

'Hard? No!' he exclaimed brightly. 'It is a question of fashion only! When cooking shall become the fashion, of more effect than a new hat or a new shade of lipstick, then there will not be so many who hate it!'

At that moment John Greenacre joined the party, having achieved a free afternoon by various complicated arrangements with his brother officers. His eyes, as usual, went first to Felicity's face, and happened to observe Cressida at the same instant. Cressida was standing behind Felicity, preparing to clear the table, and doing so in a manner that would make it pretty well impossible for Felicity not to help. John Greenacre was struck by the loveliness of Mrs Chance when she smiled.

Cressida gave him a slightly prolonged edition of her smile. 'Have some lunch?' she said, 'There's still something somewhere.'

'Oh, I've had my whack, thanks awfully,' John said. 'I didn't think I'd get here so early, but I got a lift down in a truck.'

'Coffee?' Cressida offered him, and he took it gratefully.

'Gosh, this is wizard,' he said after a mouthful, 'I wish you'd teach Felicity how to do it.'

Felicity looked, if possible, more bored than before, and said nothing.

'When – when we come back next week, I mean,' John went on, a little shyly.

Cressida, in one glance, took in his pleasant face and Felicity's unpleasant but lovely one. Oh, Lord, she thought, they can't get married!

'Come on, let's go out. It's a marvellous day,' John said to Felicity.

She showed no enthusiasm. 'Damned hot,' she said, getting up as she spoke and wandering out of the kitchen, as if she had no idea that anyone ever washed up.

John's eyes followed her to the door but he did not go after her. He brought his coffee cup to Cressida, who was standing by the sink.

'It's been most frightfully good of you,' he began hesitantly, 'having Felicity here like this, I mean, and letting me run in and out, and all that. I –' He picked up a wet spoon and at once dropped it on the floor with a clatter. 'Oh, damn. I'm awfully sorry, I'm so ham-fisted. I do hope it's been all right – I mean that you – haven't minded us, or anything?'

Poor lamb, Cressida thought, apologising for her already.

'Of course I haven't,' she said. 'You know I hardly notice who's here most of the time.' This was far from true, but it sounded comforting, she thought. 'You must never begin to feel a nuisance,' she went on, 'because I should feel obliged to gush over you, which would be such a bore.'

'Well, it's marvellous of you,' John said sincerely, 'I – couldn't begin to thank you.'

'Please don't try,' Cressida said, 'we should both get madly embarrassed. I'd much rather just guess!'

'Well – well, thank you!' John said and laughed.

Cressida gave him another of her sudden flashing smiles, with the result that he forgot he was supposed to be following his Felicity and began to dry the things Cressida was washing. She let him do this without comment.

If there was a little more time, she thought, it might be an idea to take the boy in hand. It must be obvious to almost anyone that in marrying Felicity Brent he was heading for disaster. Cressida, though the last person in the world to interfere with anyone, felt that she would, in this case, be almost justified in putting a spanner in the works. She thought about the four days that Felicity had spent in the house. It was difficult to remember a single agreeable moment.

On her first morning Felicity had announced that she must go shopping and get her hair done. Cressida had looked up buses for her. Tori had conveyed her to the bus stop, telling her on the way what a remarkable and charming woman Mrs Chance was. Felicity had not been amused by this or by the long, slow bus drive in a very old and spring-less bus which stopped, it seemed, at almost every other cottage on the way, either to drop a parcel, pick one up, or merely exchange the time of day with a friend of the driver. She had returned, thoroughly exhausted, in time for supper that evening, having spent the afternoon in a cinema watching a film, which, after an hour and a half of it, she remembered having seen in London three months previously. On her second morning she was an hour late for breakfast and refused to eat anything except toast and marmalade. Not having brought any rations did not prevent her enjoying quantities of Cressida's marmalade. The rest of that morning she had spent at the telephone, making several trunk-calls which entailed her being called back, so that someone else was continually answering the telephone and having to find her to take the call. As a result of the telephoning three young men had arrived in an R.A.F. car and had spent the afternoon with Felicity by the river, taking on their way home a handsome tea off Cressida.

Then there had been the visit of Daff. Daff had arrived on the back of a motor-cycle ridden by a young man in sandals and a dirty sweater, who had given Cressida what is known as a big rush, while Daff amused herself with Felicity. Cressida had disliked the young man intensely, and the rush had been a failure. The young man had remembered suddenly that he had an urgent engagement elsewhere, and had departed in clouds of exhaust and without his girl-friend. Towards supper-time another session with the telephone had begun, with the object, apparently, of getting Daff removed. This end had not been achieved and Daff had remained, first for supper and then, after more argument and telephoning, for the night, on the second bed in Felicity's room.

But long before she reached the bed Daff had made herself felt in the house. To begin with she sang. She knew two complete dance tunes, with words, one with half the words, and one with all the words but half the tune. Her voice was piercingly high, but she did her best to lower it to the hoarse cooing of a noted torch singer. The result was odd and very trying. The singing had begun in the bath, which she had on arrival, having announced as she leapt off the motor-bicycle that she stank. To this opening remark Cressida had silently agreed, with the reservation that she would have preferred the good smell of oil, natural to motor-bicycles, to the indefinable mixture of not-very-expensive powders, scents and hair lotions not intended to be used together, of which the aura surrounded Daff. Daff's bath had lasted an hour and the passage had been full of steam for another half-hour, while the whole house smelt like a cheap hairdresser's for most of the day. After her bath Daff had been prostrated with thirst and had finished three bottles of Cressida's beer, and had then strolled down the drive to the village in search of a pub. Cressida knew the local was never open at midday, but let her go without a qualm. Daff had been comparatively quiet during lunch. Except for a habit of using American slang with a pseudo and unconvincing accent, she had done nothing actively irritating. Later in the day she and Felicity had again walked to the pub, this time escorted by John Greenacre. Daff had been more than a little drunk when she returned, three-quarters of an hour late for supper. Her lateness was actually a mitigation of her behaviour, because it meant everyone else had finished and did not suffer from her desire to sing, this time during the meal. Cressida had taken a good deal of care to ensure that John Greenacre should have no opportunity of apologising for her. But his whole face had been an open, if silent, apology.

At breakfast, which she ate at eleven the next morning, Daff announced that she was due for her interview for the call-up that morning, and supposed something would have to be done about getting to it. Something, it was evident, done by someone else, because Daff herself seemed delightfully carefree in spite of her hangover. She did not, however, show any anxiety about her chance of attending her interview punctually.

'Julian's sweetie,' she had announced, 'was ten days late because she wasn't going to muck up his leave. They couldn't kill her, even then, and she's grubbing in some filthy factory quite nicely, and has her nights to herself.' This remark had caused Daff to go into hysterical laughter, and Felicity broke her rule of impassivity so far as to snigger.

'You're so bloody lucky,' Daff had continued, 'getting hooked up just in time. I guess you did it on purpose.'

To Cressida's surprise Felicity had looked more than a little uncomfortable and could apparently produce no answer to this remark.

Daff had then given a harrowing account of the life in store for her if, as she put it, the press gang copped her.

'You even have to wear army pants and bra in the A.T.S., my sweet, though I don't see how they get to know unless they have a strip-tease act from time to time.'

Cressida, with the double incentive of getting rid of Daff and ensuring that she would reach her interview, eventually drove her in the dog-cart to the station. She had encouraged Beltane to his most alarming speed, but Daff, hardened, no doubt, by pillion-riding, had been unmoved, and it was Felicity who once more clung unhappily to the back of the seat and decided to stay in the town with Daff and return in the evening by bus. This she had done, arriving at ten-thirty, having had no dinner. Unfortunately Cressida had been in the kitchen shutting up the boiler and had been unable to avoid offering Felicity some food. She had left her to eat it in the kitchen, and had the next morning found the remains and the dirty dishes scattered on the table.

And now it was Sunday. Tomorrow Felicity was to go back to London. In four day's time John Greenacre was to join her there and, unless providentially prevented, would marry her.

Cressida finished the washing-up and sighed. Oh, well, everyone had to make their own hash of life, she supposed. But it was difficult, sometimes, not to tell them what they were in for.

There were times, Cressida thought, when life seemed most depressingly pointless. There were millions of charming people in the world, but for some obscure reason they did not seem able to get together. People everywhere were wasting their lives. They were worried, bored, or actively unhappy. They were overworked or underpaid, or both; they were dissatisfied with their circumstances, envious of other people's, who, in their turn, were unsatisfied for some different reason. People had jobs which did not interest them, while the jobs they might have done well were done by others who were bored by them. Even the successful people of the world were seldom noticeably happy; in one way or another success let them down when it seemed that happiness must have been achieved.

Was it, Cressida wondered, simply that human nature was not yet basically capable of happiness? Or was it that happiness itself was an invention, a sort of spur, created by man's instinctive desire to have something to encourage him through a life of drudgery? Could it be that this – this mass frustration – what a hideous expression, she thought – was a fundamental cause of the appalling mess humanity had made of human life?

War was supposed to be merely an accumulation of individual selfishness, restlessness and jealousy, grown until it broke the bounds of civilisation. With the progress of civilisation wars had progressed, if one could use such a word in connection with what looked more like retrogression, to the savagery of animals. It could not be denied that civilisation had improved the well-being of the human race, but on the other hand war had grown in horror until it had reached a peak of insensate fury that could lead nowhere but to ultimate chaos. Could this hideous monster, this universal expression of unbridled hate, really have grown out of such insignificant trifles as personal acquisitiveness and the dislike of man for the man next door?

Cressida gave it up. The question was so huge that it needed thought and discussion, for which there was, at the moment, no time. There never was any time. Life in these days seemed to require all the available time for its maintenance, so that there was none left for actual living.

For five years, Cressida thought, I've wasted life. Five years without Charles, and in two more years I'll be forty and a hag. She shrugged her shoulders slightly. Selfishness, she thought, selfishness at the bottom of everything. I've tried to think about the causes of war, and it's boiled down to worrying about myself and the approach of middle age.

CHAPTER ELEVEN

That Sunday night six bombs were dropped on Brede
Somervel. It was the first air raid the village had had. On
at least two hundred occasions there had been sirens without bombs, and once three bombs, without sirens, had fallen
on a field of clover at midnight. This time the sirens went
first and so the six bombs became an air raid and not an
accident.

It was Cressida's fire-watching night. She heard the sirens
with a distinct, if slightly guilty, sense of relief. Once every
three weeks, for two years, she had sat up all night, trying in
various ways to endure the struggle with sleep and boredom.
On perhaps a dozen occasions the sound of the alert from the
camp about three miles out of the village had given a sense
of reality to her vigil. Sirens at least meant that she had to go
out and walk as far as the first house in the village and back,
repeating the exercise, theoretically, until the All Clear
was sounded. Cressida had enjoyed these occasions, except
on the nights it had been raining. Half ashamed of herself,
and knowing that she would rather die than admit it, she had
never been able to prevent herself feeling that, for an hour
or two, she was at last taking part in the war. This rather

childish thought had nevertheless given her a pleasing sense of responsibility.

Quite alone, in an utterly silent night, in some of the quietest country in England, she could never help feeling a sort of pride because she was awake and waiting for danger, while everyone else slept. A man or a child looked defence-less, and sometimes unbearably touching, in sleep, and so did a village, Cressida discovered. Even the cattle, snuffling in the fields, roused in her a new and absurd protectiveness.

Between Brede Manor and the village there was a stretch of rising ground from which there was a view of several hundred acres of cultivated downland. Sometimes, on a night of moon-light, the sight of the standing corn, a misty silver blanket on the earth, would give her an almost passionate sense of guardianship. It was so easy to imagine fire, leaping crazily across those quiet acres, devouring in a few moments the food that would keep hundreds of people alive for weeks. And perhaps, perhaps one night she would be there in time to smother the beginning of fire before it could get a hold on those endless fields. These slightly dramatic fancies were apt to be interrupted by cold and sleepiness, so that she usually ended by yawning and wondering how long it would be before she could get into bed.

Sunday, as Felicity had so bluntly remarked at lunch, had been very hot. The evening seemed even hotter. The moon rose early and became at once obscured by cloud which was not, however, heavy enough to darken the night completely. At about eleven o' clock, when the house was drained of active inhabitants, Cressida went to the kitchen to make herself coffee, her one hope on a fire-watching night. She was, as usual, shamed by the rush of black beetles to shelter as the light went on. As usual she assured herself that in old houses black beetles occurred, and were not the result of dirt. She remembered with a grin the remarks she had made to the servants about black beetles, and the enormous efforts with powders and even fumigation that had annoyed so many cooks. Well, now she knew, she thought, and gave no more than a shudder as the beetles scuttled.

Tonight the kitchen was unendurably hot. With the black-out in place it was impossible to remain there for long. In fact, it was difficult to endure any room with the air shut out. Cressida realised that it was going to be a thoroughly trying night. If she tried to read she would be stupefied with heat. If she sat in the dark she would go to sleep. She could not walk about indefinitely, and so the prospects for the night were not good. The sirens, in fact, were her one hope. If one walked about before they went one might be too exhausted to do anything if bombs did arrive. And it was fatal to stay outside unless one was walking. Cressida could never forget one night of delicious warmth when she had sat in the dry remains of an old straw stack. She had eventually sprung to her feet with the sound of the All Clear ringing in her guilty ears, which even now burned at the memory.

And so, when the sirens went at five minutes to twelve, Cressida was distinctly relieved. She took a torch and a whistle, most inadequate armament, she considered, to counter acres of fire. She walked on the grass bordering the drive, because the sound of her feet on the gravel so disturbed the silence, which always seemed to have a quality of magnificence in the country at night. Also there was the possibility of hearing a nightingale. And, she admitted honestly, the sound of her own footsteps was apt to be more than a little frightening, as if it might all the time be covering some other less human sound. Fear of the darkness, Cressida had discovered, was a queer, unpredictable thing. She had often walked miles at night and enjoyed it. But there had been occasions when something, some quite ordinary sound or perfectly reasonable shadow, had startled her and put an end to all enjoyment. Nerves, she thought, when left to themselves, were quiescent, but once jarred by some shock, however slight, might easily become over-alert and so make every step a conscious effort of control that was, eventually, exhausting and quite prevented appreciation of the night's beauty or the soothing charm of silent country.

So she walked on the grass until she reached the tarred road, upon which her rubber-soled shoes trod with commendable soundlessness. She walked up the rise in the road past the cornfields, but tonight she could not see more than a few yards of them. She stopped for a moment, listening to the delicate sighing of a slight breeze that gave an impression of coming from very far away, and seemed full of the scent of the thousands of unseen acres it had travelled over. Cressida became aware of the sound of an aeroplane engine, throbbing gently somewhere in the enormous grey-dark sky. Not alarming in the least, that tiny, delicately powerful and even beat, sounding far more like the pulse of the night than the possible approach of violent death.

The sound passed over, very high, and died away as gently as it had begun. A great white owl drifted across the road, just above the trees, in a total and ghostly silence far more menacing than the sound of the distant aeroplane. Another aeroplane, far lower, swept across the sky in a burst of the waspish fury of a fast single-engined machine. Cressida continued her walk. She reached the first cottage in the village and turned back. This time she could see from the high ground a faint glow growing on the horizon. Stairmouth, she thought, getting it again. She stood and watched the glow deepen. She thought, as she had before, how absurd it was that she should be standing there in the most utter peace imaginable, in country of which the safety seemed inviolable, while that seaside town less than thirty miles away was being ravaged and shaken by fire and sudden death.

Stairmouth, with its permanent association with luxurious shops, neat lawns, neat flower-beds, shiningly neat bathing-huts, disreputable children sucking ice-cream cones, and cold wind, was a place impossible to connect with bombs, fire-engines and hurrying ambulances. The untidy horror of casualties, burnt-out buildings, and holes in the tram-lines, seemed quite fantastically out of place in such a well-conducted neighbourhood. An air raid in London, Birmingham, or any other large, grim town, was instantly a horrifying thought, but for some reason an air raid in Stairmouth was, however reprehensibly, slightly funny. It required an effort of mind to admit the equality of horror in either case.

Cressida walked on. The quiet night had become grimmer for that faraway glow in the sky. The silence itself seemed to have taken on a different quality, intense, doubly precious because it might not last. Cressida felt extraordinarily aware of it, and, in consequence, it began to frighten her. She dug her hands into her trouser pockets and told herself she was being absurd. Tonight was like any other night, as peaceful, as remote from anything warlike, as uneventful as any of the eight or nine hundred nights that had passed so serenely for Brede Somervel since the beginning of the war.

The clouds over the moon thinned. Cressida reached the gates of Brede Manor, which were now visible as dim but elegant outlines. She stood looking at them for a few seconds. The lovely lines of the high wrought-iron wings caught and held her eyes always, though she must have seen them many hundred times. The gates were famous in the county as an outstanding example of the work of local craftsmen of an earlier century. Cressida remembered now the first time she had seen them.

It had been a month after her marriage. Simon had driven her into the country to see a friend of his, to see Charles Valery. Cressida remembered that drive, in Simon's black Bentley. She remembered sweeping through village after village at the terrifying speed Simon always maintained, which had seemed so thrilling and was so dangerous. Brede Somervel had just been another village, and then those high iron gates had come suddenly into view, standing open, their intricately worked, delicate lightness giving the impression that a puff of wind might at any moment swing them shut again, thus closing for ever the way to the bewitched country beyond. The designer of those gates had done more than carry out a perfect piece of craftsmanship. In some way he had managed to create an atmosphere with his patterns, so that the grounds of the manor were not just a piece of country shut in by a gate, they became a place apart, a little strange perhaps, but magically lovely, enclosed by gates that were the barriers of fairyland.

Cressida had cried out in sudden excitement, that first time. She remembered catching Simon's hand on the wheel.

'Well, we're here,' Simon had said, laughing at her excitement, 'this is old Charles's place.'

Old Charles's place. This beckoning road, winding between silvery poplars, running away from reality, running away from those gates that might so easily close against human intrusion, that seemed to hover on the verge of movement, like cobwebs magically still, that could not, surely, be just the gates of old Charles's place.

But Simon had swung his car round and driven it through the gates without so much as a side glance at them. Cressida's excitement had risen until her heart hurt her, and at the same time she had been shaken by a sense of familiarity so strong that she felt recognition rather than mere admiration when the house came in sight for the first time. Ridiculous, impossible and only half-coherent words had sung in her head. Mine . . . mine . . . it's mine . . . it's always been mine. . . .

And then Charles had been there. He had been standing on the front-door steps. Just a tall, fair-haired man in a grey suit, walking down the steps with a stick which he managed so nonchalantly that it was not immediately obvious that he needed it because he was lame. Cressida had been introduced to the old Valerys. She had, with an enormous effort, talked to them and made suitable remarks about their lovely house, trying all the time not to listen to the singing in her heart that was making a mockery of her attempt to behave in the rational manner of a week-end guest.

For more than a year after that Cressida had not seen Brede again. The old Valerys had died during that year, and then Charles had made his offer to let Simon his house, so much too big for him to live in alone. At the time that had seemed to be the answer to Cressida's queer premonition of ownership. But it had not been, not, at least, the whole answer.

At this point in Cressida's reminiscences reality asserted itself, and six bombs fell upon Brede Somervel in as many seconds. Six bright flashes snatched the pattern of the gates from darkness and plunged it back again into deeper darkness. Cressida found herself in the ditch with her face pressed into long, cool grass. Three thoughts, John . . . nearest stirrup-pump . . . I'm not hurt . . . chased themselves in that order through her mind.

She got out of the ditch and started to run towards the village. She could not have explained then or afterwards how it was she knew her own house was untouched. But she did know and ran towards the village.

A choking smell that was a mixture of high-explosive, brick-dust and torn earth, and would have meant death to those who knew, grew stronger with every step she took. The darkness became deeper than it had been at any time that night. It was like a wall that had to be pushed away before any progress could be made. Cressida knew she was coughing from time to time, and only then did she realise that she was still almost deaf from the blast of the explosions, which had been at the time so loud that her ears had scarcely registered them as mere sound.

Far away in the sky a panic-stricken German boy on his first flight over England, his aeroplane lightened by the weight of the six bombs he had wildly let go, forced his machine to the limit of its speed in a frantic effort to escape the night fighter his nerves had conjured up from a chance patch of cloud. With his heart choking him, he swept on through endless darkness, his aeroplane fleeing like a mad thing from nothing.

Cressida, wondering desperately whether John was awake and frightened, and telling herself firmly that she mustn't go and see yet, reached the village. She ran into a human figure, a torch flickered for a second, someone murmured something.

'. . . up t'Northeast's place. . . .'

Oh, not Northeast, not old Northeast. . . . But it had to be someone.

The smell became altogether overpowering. Other carefully screened torches appeared, and men in white tin hats. The darkness grew less thick. A woman carrying a white haversack that Cressida recognised as belonging to the First Aid Post passed at a run. A figure on a bicycle followed swiftly, ringing his bell as if he had been an ambulance. The ceaseless bell was as urgent as a message tapped in Morse. Figures became more and more clearly visible. For some seconds Cressida did not appreciate the reason for this fact. But, as if her feet automatically carried her in the right direction, she hurried on and into sudden blinding glare.

The village trailer-pump passed her at that moment, six men pulling it at a trot and puffing with urgency. Cressida was irresistibly reminded of the last A.R.P. exercise held in the village, when every service had been ready, waiting for the whistle. She could not help remembering the sight of every member of the First Aid Post, attached to a bicycle, like competitors at the start of a race, each complete with equipment, and the stirrup-pump parties in little clusters with buckets already full. She remembered the wardens, very smart in their clean uniforms, standing about the road, trying to look as though they were there by pure chance. This time, she reminded herself, the First Aiders had been shaken out of their beds in utter darkness. The wardens had had to fumble for what clothes they could find in desperate haste. The members of the fire party had had to assemble from the ends of the village, and one of them had nothing over his pyjamas, she noticed. This was the real thing.

And it was 'up t'Northeast's place. . . .'

The thatch had already gone. The white walls on the roadside still stood, like barriers against the fire that sprang from within them. Old Northeast.

And then Cressida saw him. In the light of the fire his bent figure was plainly visible. He was on his knees, dangerously close to the fire, scraping with his hands at a huge heap of rubble that seemed to have sprung up, like a molehill of nightmare size, upon the piece of ground that had been old Northeast's neat back garden. Cressida knew that tears of thankfulness were in her eyes. Old Northeast was all right. He even looked most touchingly like himself, bent, with his hands in the earth. But he seemed to want something, under all that mess. Cressida ran to his side and spoke to him. He took no notice whatever, but went on scrabbling with his hands, like a dog, frenziedly digging for a bone. Cressida caught the words he was muttering.

'. . . just you bide, I'll get t'ye . . . get y'out . . . out o't' muck . . . just you bide, mother. . . .'

Old Northeast's gardener's attitude was no longer merely touching. For a few seconds the shock of implication in his broken words stunned Cressida. The roar and splutter of flames rose and fell in waves behind her. Another sound accompanied them. A clear, steady note coming on the wind. The All Clear.

All Clear. All over. Go back to bed and put away the tin hat for another time. Go back to bed while old Northeast scraped and scrabbled for his wife, buried under what had been one side of his cottage; old Northeast's cottage, that stood like a shell behind him, roofed and curtained with a mixture of dying fire and spurting water, which competed for its final ruin.

All Clear. Turn over in bed and sigh comfortably. Oh, well, that wasn't much of a show.

The rest of that night was never perfectly clear in Cressida's memory. She did remember kneeling beside Northeast, digging and scraping until her hands bled. She remembered cutting herself on what turned out to be the corrugated-iron roof of old Northeast's pathetic home-made air-raid shelter. She remembered men with picks and shovels, and other men with a stretcher. She remembered sitting, it seemed for hours, with her arm round the bent shoulders of old Northeast. She remembered him trying to tell her what had happened, fumbling with his words, like a child who was only learning to speak.

'. . . wanted it, she did, that old shelter, look . . . no good, I telled her . . . won't get me out o' bed, look . . . but she wanted it. . . .'

She remembered having her bleeding hands washed in the First Aid Post, and someone making a joke about her being the only casualty, forgetting in the relief and excitement of reaction that there had been one real casualty, who had not needed First Aid. She remembered standing outside the cottage belonging to old Northeast's brother, Joe, watching the two old men go in together in silence.

And she remembered walking through the gates of Brede Manor with Tori, who had been there somehow, as dawn was breaking. The cloudy night had cleared, and the dawn was delicate and lovely. Brede looked as serene, as finely outlined as an old coloured engraving.

And so Brede Somervel had its first air raid. Two bombs had fallen in fields, one in the churchyard, one on an already roofless barn, one in the woods above the local pub, and one upon Northeast's home-made air-raid shelter, where it had killed old Mrs Northeast, who would have been seventy-six at Michaelmas, and who had always insisted, in spite of her husband's ridicule, upon getting out of bed and sitting in the shelter he had made to please her, not altogether because she was nervous, but partly because she felt in some obscure way that she was doing her duty by putting up with such extreme discomfort without a grumble.

CHAPTER TWELVE

Towards the evening of his first waking day in the lifeboat, Charles Valery became conscious of the sound of an aeroplane engine. For some minutes it meant nothing to him and he did not move. He had remained almost abnormally still all day, because no reason for moving had occurred to him, and because he was subconsciously afraid of discovering how much movement would hurt.

It had been a pleasantly warm day, without much breeze, and with enough cloud to prevent the heat of the sun becoming too great. Charles had spent a long time studying the level of the water in the boat, and had discovered that, by evening, it had lowered very slightly. This, it would seem, must mean that the boat was not leaking, which was fortunate, because any attempt to bale out suggested an unthinkable amount of exertion. One other immediate problem had held his wandering thoughts for a few moments at long intervals. This was the problem of Harcourt. The thing to do, Charles realised, was to put poor Harcourt in the sea. It should be a simple matter and take no more than a few seconds. Charles arranged in his mind exactly how it could most easily be done, but his body did not react to the suggestions of his mind. Charles told himself that it was his hands that were the trouble. It was better, really, not to find out how badly they were burned. There was nothing to be done about them except not use them.

It was the sound of the aeroplane that roused him more completely than anything else had done. For four years Charles had been testing aircraft for Western-Masterson's Airplanes, Inc., and the sound of their engines had become as normal to him as the sound of his own breathing, and very often just as important. After four years Charles could never hear an aeroplane without listening intently for the slightest roughness, the most minute irregularity in what would sound to another man like a perfectly running engine. And so he listened automatically to the thin drone which meant a four-engined machine flying too high to be visible. He stared up into the lightly clouded sky, trying to work out the direction of the sound. In spite of the assertions of ladies in the London suburbs Charles could not tell whether or not the aircraft was German. He did not even consider the question. In any case it did not matter. If he could not see the aeroplane, its pilot could certainly not see him, and the nationality of the thing was, therefore, of no importance. Nevertheless, though he did not realise it, the sound of that anonymous aeroplane was of most vital importance to Charles, because it roused him from inertia that might easily have slipped into death.

The thin drone died away and left nothing but the light smack of water against the boat to break the silence of the empty sea. But it had brought Charles Valery to life.

Almost without knowing how he did it, Charles moved,

stood up, bent over the body of poor Harcourt, lifted it and let it slip as gently as possible into the alleviation of the sea. Afterwards he stood in the stern of the boat for a long time, watching the colour of the sea deepen and the sky become increasingly remote with the coming of night. In a curious detached way he was happy. The problem of his rescue had not yet begun to trouble him. He knew nothing of the procession of days and nights whose uneventfulness would turn hope to anxiety and anxiety to fear and ultimate nightmare. And so he was happy because he was spared something that men long for often, and try uselessly to obtain by all kinds of methods, something which the most intrepid of them would do well to dread, the knowledge of the future.

After a time Charles's returning vitality manifested itself in the simple form of hunger. With some difficulty, owing to the water in the boat, he explored the vessel's fittings and found food and water in sealed canisters. He also found a neat package wrapped in green oilsilk. He unwrapped it and found charts. Neat, beautifully designed and printed, spotlessly new, they lay across his knees and he was no longer alone in a world of water. At that moment these meticulously correct, clean Admiralty charts were as comforting as the sound of a human voice, as cheering as a candle in darkness.

But it was now too dark to read them. Charles finished eating instead. Every movement was slow and painful, so that a great deal of time passed while he was doing so. Charles did not realise how fortunate this was. He did not think with much concentration about anything except the immediate needs of his body. When it came to a question of sleep he realised that

he was cold. The prospect of spending the night in a foot of
water was not attractive. During his search for food he had
come across a zinc dipper, and with this he began the process
of baling. Very slowly the water level sank lower. It became so
dark that the dipper's weight was the only sign of its empti-
ness or fullness. The sea and sky had become one darkness.
Charles worked mechanically and did not notice that there
were stars, not only overhead, but in all directions. After
unmeasured time the dipper began to scrape upon wood, and
there was less and less weight in it as it returned to the side
of the boat. Charles's slow swinging arms slackened, and the
tiny splash of water rejoining the sea became infinitesimal,
like the rise of a minnow. At last the dipper fell from his
fingers and clattered on the bottom of the boat. The noise it
made seemed outrageous, and the returning quiet more
intense for the disturbance.

Charles looked up for the first time since he had begun his
long task. The stars seemed to be whirling round his head in
a dizzy and reasonless dance.

'. . . the old star-eaten blanket of the sky. . . .' Some lines
of poetry came into his head from another, perhaps only
imaginary life.

'That I may wrap it round me and in comfort lie,' he
finished, pleased because he had been able to complete the
quotation.

In another moment he was asleep. He lay as chance had
placed him, with his head wedged between a coil of rope and
the edge of one of the water canisters, and slept as soundly as
an exhausted child.

CHAPTER THIRTEEN

The bombs that fell on Brede Somervel had several results besides the tragic one of destroying the peace of the last few years of an old man's life. To begin with, they provided everyone in the village with the opportunity of telling everyone else exactly how deeply asleep, or how wide awake, they had been at the time of the first explosion. But besides being an excuse for chatter they were valuable as a test for the passive defences of the village. Four stirrup-pump owners discovered that their pumps did not work. Two members of the First Aid Party found that the batteries had rotted in their torches and could not be removed without permanently ruining the torches. One of the wardens had had great difficulty in finding his tin hat because, owing to summer time, the downstair windows of his house had not been blacked out and he could, therefore, not turn on a light to look for it. Bill Piney's wife, who, it had always been supposed, was thoroughly flighty and bound to be hysterical in an emergency, had been the first person on the scene to help old Northeast to his feet when the bomb had, in the unlikely manner of such things, blown him out of his cottage unharmed. Mrs Brandon, on the other hand, who sat on every possible committee and told everyone what her brother-in-law in London did and said under a variety of circumstances connected with air raids, had spent the important moments of the night under her dining-room table. This, however, no one knew. For the first time in her life Mrs Brandon was thankful that no servants slept in her house. She could thus return to her committee meetings with her shame undiscovered; but her remarks about her omniscient relative became less frequent, which was to the advantage of all. The crater of one of the bombs that had landed in a field had made a good beginning to a drainage scheme that had been in the mind of the field's owner for some time, and was likely to have remained there but for the incentive provided by the sight of so large a part of the work already done. The bomb in the churchyard had destroyed the stained-glass windows, and it was found that the interior of the little building was enormously improved by the additional light thus obtained. The glass, it was now openly admitted, had not been good. It had been the gift of a Victorian of pious intentions but no artistic taste, and without it the little church returned to its original and touching simplicity.

But above all, the bombs taught the people of Brede Somervel something that none of them were aware of, the simple value of life as opposed to death. Though few could have expressed it, everyone was for a time intensely conscious of being alive, less ready to grumble about trivialities, but readier to enjoy the simple pleasures of routine that usually passed unremarked. There was, until the return of peace dulled it, a sense of active friendliness, of affection, between the little collection of people who had all escaped death together. Normally so familiar with, and often so bored by, each other, they had never before realised how much affection existed between them. People who hardly spoke to one another stopped in the street and indulged in quite long conversations. Everyone, though unaware of it, was alive with the simple joy of living, a sensation surely worth the price paid for it in fear.

Only old Northeast, sitting for the rest of the night in his brother's cottage with a cup of strong tea growing cold beside him, was not aware of any joy.

But, if he had known it, he might have been able to find comfort in the fact that other men, remembering Mrs Northeast, perhaps looked at their own wives with newly opened eyes. Perhaps the loss to old Northeast was cancelled out by the gain in conscious affection between men and their wives who, in long years of custom, had become to each other only slightly more important than the rest of the furniture of their homes.

Perhaps the rise of enthusiasm in the village, the new interest in First Aid classes, the extra shillings saved, the extra kindness expended for a neighbour, the added energy which made all forms of civil defence an interest rather than a boring addition to an already full day's work were, taken together, worth the price of one life.

At Brede Manor the next morning Cressida accepted three separate offers of cooking the breakfast, and stayed in bed until eleven o'clock. But she did not sleep. She lay with her eyes shut and thought about old Northeast, and about the thousands of other harmless men and women who had had their lives ruined by one of the apparently gratuitous accidents of which this war seemed to be made up. Somehow death seemed more bitter when its victim had not been given the opportunity of offering his life to his country. Accidental death, in the middle of a war, seemed a hideous waste. It was impossible to imagine a more harmless couple than old Northeast and his wife, who had probably never in their lives done a consciously unkind action. It was pretty certain that neither of them had in the least understood the causes and purpose of the war.

But who does? Cressida's mind asked in despair, and could find no answer.

Beyond a kind of mass-produced anger with the enemy, the average person in England was probably almost without a vindictive thought. The famous British character was, in fact, strangely lacking in the capacity for hatred. Perhaps that was where its strength lay. Hatred was a violent, ungovernable thing, and no match for cold reasoned anger, the kind of anger that had at last been roused in the tolerant, mentally lazy English. If a census of emotion could be taken in the two countries it would certainly be found that the Germans hated the British far more fiercely than the other way about. Neither country had the personal and terrible reasons for hatred that the occupied countries of Europe knew too much about. But hatred of the British had, in Germany, been artificially whipped to maniacal fury, which would, perhaps, in the end weaken those it possessed to the point of exhaustion, whereas the anger of the British would grow, unaffected by passions of any kind, and so be too strong for the crazy hatred that opposed it.

Cressida got out of bed eventually with an aching pity for Northeast in her heart. None of these abstract ideas, she thought, would be any sort of comfort to him. Nothing she could say or do would help him to find happiness in the rest of his life.

The rows of cabbages outside the kitchen window were, that morning, heart-rending. Each of them had been planted with individual care which years of repetition had never lessened. For perhaps fifty years old Northeast had planted cabbages, and still these small operations were lovingly carried out. His gnarled, rough old hands were still gentle with the most tender plant. And now, in one second, crazy violence had ruined his life beyond repair.

Cressida stared at the vegetable garden, scarcely aware of the tears in her eyes. And then she saw him. He was bent, in the extraordinary attitude he achieved in spite of his age, so that his hands reached the ground though his knees were stiff. He was barely visible behind a row of peas. As she watched he straightened himself very slowly, as slowly moved one step to his right, and then resumed his hairpin attitude in order to plant another lettuce. Cressida wanted to go out to him, to talk, to do anything that would show her sympathy. But she did not move. There was nothing to be done except to leave him with his plants.

She felt an arm slipped across her shoulders. It was Tori, and for some moments he said nothing, looking as she was, at what could be seen of old Northeast behind the peas. Then he said, very quietly, 'There is a man who has already won.'

Cressida drew a deep breath and turned away from the window.

'Yes, Tori,' she said, and then went on suddenly, 'But what good has it done him to win? He – wasn't fighting anything, he – How can there be any point in – I mean, how can last night have anything to do with a war between us and the Germans, Tori? It – it simply doesn't make sense.'

Tori remained at the window and did not move or look at Cressida.

'It is not the Germans,' he began at last, 'who are in this war the worst enemy. This is not simply a war between two nations or between many nations. It is not a matter that will decide itself because one country or another will win.' He paused for a moment and then went on. 'It is not one war but a million, many millions, for it is war within every man and woman, war that has not just begun, but war that has always been. Cressida, there is war now in all the world, not only internationally and with guns and bombs, but in men's hearts and minds with weapons more dangerous still. In each human being is their own war taking place, a war of thought, of feeling. Always, if they have, perhaps, not known it, men have fought in their hearts. Selfishness has fought with generosity, cruelty with kindness, each attribute of human nature with its enemy. And perhaps –' He paused again, as if at a loss for words.

Cressida knew it was not for lack of ideas, this hesitation of his. In his own language Tori would not have had to pause. There was about him an extraordinary sense of mental strength, the more noticeable for his fragile appearance. He gave the impression, more strongly than anyone she knew, of being a man who knew his own mind. This did not mean, as it often did, that he was set in his ideas. It meant that he knew his mind because he had discovered it for himself by a process of reasoning and examination.

Cressida said nothing, because she knew that if Tori could not decide what to say, no one could do it for him.

'Perhaps,' he went on at last, 'perhaps it is that there has been in so many of these small terrible wars defeat, defeat for those qualities which we must call by a name to avoid a great string of words, so we will call them simply kindness, which is of all perhaps the most important. Perhaps for so long the kindness in human hearts has been defeated by greed, selfishness, personal desires, for comfort, power, money, what you like, that can make a man forget so simple a thing as love towards his neighbour. There have been, perhaps, so very many of these small, but so crushing, defeats that the enemy has grown strong. The greed, the selfishness, the cruelty have taken in their victorious hand so much power that they have been able to make the whole world a madness of war. And it is now not a question of which country will kill the most of another country's people, or destroy of another's creations the greatest part, or bring to ruin most completely the work of his enemy's brains and hands. It is not a question only of whether England will win or Germany, or whether Fascism, Communism or Democracy will become victorious. Victory of a party, a nation or a creed can never be a final victory, for in such a victory there is always one who loses. In true, in perfect victory there must be no losers!'

Tori's words seemed to wait, suspended, unfinished. Cressida forgot everything except what he would say next. Tori was still looking out of the window. He went on as if he thought aloud.

'But for war to be won without a winner, to be lost without a loser, how is this to be understood? How, except it be clearly seen who is the enemy? Who is the worst enemy all men must fight till the victory without a vanquished be won? To ask that little question is to see the answer. The worst enemy every man must fight is himself!' Tori took a quick breath, and his next words were spoken more practically, less as if he was lost to his surroundings. 'It comes to a question,' he went on, 'of whether there is still enough of what we are calling kindness left in the hearts of men to triumph at last and for always over brutality, greed, cruelty. Is, we could say, Christianity strong enough? Ah – !' Tori's exclamation was extremely Central European in its vigour. 'Ah! I do not mean churches or preaching, but the qualities of Christ that God gave to men, are they still strong enough? Is the goodness of Christ still within the power of men to reach? Impossible, you will say, Christ was a god. But I say He was a man, and what a man has done once a man can do again. There have been men whose goodness was to be seen and who have been called without untruth Christlike. But of such, how few! And yet in every man is there this seed of goodness, in every man the free will to choose what he will be, what he will do. Not once, but a thousand times he may choose, a thousand times win or lose the war against himself. And by the mercy of God it is never too late. Never. Always there is another beginning. Always.'

The intense sincerity of Tori's words had produced an atmosphere in the room in which it was suddenly easy to express thought.

'Another beginning,' Cressida said, 'another new world beginning from chaos.'

Tori whipped round, so that he faced her.

'Yes!' he said, so eagerly that he almost took the words out of her mouth. 'Yes, another new world, beginning as the old one, from chaos. But this time there is a difference, so great a difference. In the first beginning the chaos was of the universe, man an embryo without power to control the forces at war in that chaos. But of all those warring forces it is the little embryo which has evolved and grown so strong that it, that man, can control Nature herself. It is man who has become the great power in the world, and it is man who has brought about this second chaos from which another beginning must come.' Tori paused, then added, 'If it is not to be for nothing that God created the world.'

'This time,' Cressida said slowly, 'this time I suppose the new world won't have to start so far back. I mean – it'll begin where it left off.'

'Indeed yes,' Tori answered at once. 'And there is the great difference between the first and second beginnings. This time man will have to help him all the knowledge of the centuries that have passed, he will have control over Nature, he will have the power of science, he will have all that is called the advantage of civilisation. And if the spirit of man has been strong enough to grow itself, to evolve from elemental chaos, what will it not be strong enough to do, what may it not build upon the foundations it has laid?' Tori's enthusiasm was so infectious that Cressida began to speak before he had finished. But she got nowhere, because Tori's eagerness carried him on regardless of interruptions. 'If,' he hurried on, 'if, if, if! If the – the motive power behind all this new beginning is the good, the great one which in the first beginning moved God to create the world so that He could see that it was good. If it is the great motive of love, kindness –'

'Kindness.' Cressida echoed his words. 'But it's so easy, Tori. Kindness is the simplest thing in the world.'

'For you, yes!' Tori said with so much vigour that he might have been hurling an insult at her. But there was no insult in his bright dark eyes which were fixed upon her face. 'For you it is easy to love, to be kind, because always you have the will towards kindness. But for everyone it is not so. I would say that there are a thousand, a million persons in the world for each one who is truly kind. For kindness means more than just – just the absence of unkindness! There are, perhaps, not as many as one unkind person in every million. But it is not enough to be not unkind!'

'I know what you mean,' Cressida said, 'the really kind people are the ones who would rather do a dirty job them-selves than think of someone else having to do it.'

'But exactly, exactly,' Tori replied quickly, 'you – you understand too much! You have it, this kindness and – you have beauty as well. But there is much beauty in the world, too much perhaps because beauty alone, for what is it but to make men mad? And so foolish!' he added, with a sudden return to his normally flippant manner.

Cressida, who realised that his change of mood was purely protective, because his feelings were running away with him, picked up his cue.

'Well, Tori,' she said lightly, 'from you that's a good one!'

'Ah, you laugh!' Tori replied instantly. 'You think I would set myself above the power of beauty and you laugh. Well, you are right! If I should do so it would be for you to laugh. But alas! It is I who shall laugh, to cover my foolishness, which is so great as the foolishness of other men. For beauty I have passion' – his hands became as eloquent as his words – 'but too much! So that I am as dust in a great wind! But – Ah, no, you shall permit me to finish!' He silenced Cressida with another vigorous gesture. 'For beauty I have passion enough,' he continued, 'but for the kindness of a beautiful mind I have love.' He ended very simply and without a flourish. He took one of Cressida's hands and kissed it.

'So!' he said lightly, 'I shall leave you and you shall prepare beautiful food with no more talking to distract!'

Cressida smiled at him.

'You're a comfort, Tori,' she said, and meant it. 'But you're right. There's always cooking!'

Tori shrugged himself as far as the door. There he turned and said, 'Indeed there is always cooking. In this brave new world that we shall build upon science and learning, how dull will it be if we have not good food to nourish our good intentions!'

With that he vanished, whistling with perfect accuracy a theme of Bach, complete with every trill and flourish.

After the exhilaration of listening to Tori, Cressida's mind relaxed while she cooked. She let it dwell easily upon variations on the theme of kindness, or rather the various meanings that had become associated with the word. If one described anyone as kind, she thought, was it quite that high virtue which should save the world that one meant?

She's so kind, but – but a crashing bore, and I don't want her patronage. Or, of course she's very kind. . . . Words which often meant one could think of no other asset for an unattractive character. It's very kind of you, generally preceded a firm refusal of an undesired invitation. And one could not overlook the implication in the Elizabethan sense of the word.

Words, Cressida thought, words, words, words. Powerful, vitally important, beautiful, and so often merely the clothing of insincerity. Words should be taxed, they should be rationed, so that scarcity might fix their value. Scarcity could procure appreciation for almost anything. One had for years averted the eyes from dried prunes, and now the purchase of a pound of the revolting objects was a highlight of the morning's shopping. Words, in this terrible freedom of too much speech, were become as dried prunes, wrinkled and arid, shrunken out of all resemblance to their original luscious beauty. If words were as scarce as prunes, their preciousness might become appreciated. Tori used words well. Tori, who spoke English in a stilted and sometimes difficult manner, gave words the gusto of their true meaning. The English, she thought, were shy of their own language, and still more shy of any other! But they borrowed from other

140

languages, they invented slang, they used absurd hyperbole, rather than say quite simply what they meant. Perhaps that was why it was effective to hear a foreigner using simple words in their true sense. Great speakers of all nations could, of course, use their own languages superbly, even great English speakers. Was it simply that only the great orators had courage enough to give words their real meaning? But why should courage be necessary anyway? Oh, well, she thought, why speculate about it. Think about cooking instead, which is at least constructive.

CHAPTER FOURTEEN

Miss Ambleside decided that after such a very disturbing night she could not be expected to face that journey to town, which had been hanging over her with an increasing menace as the time for it approached. Tomorrow would do just as well, really, if one caught a rather earlier train. Also it would be much pleasanter to travel without that Brent girl, who was, one hoped, to leave today. Miss Ambleside sought Cressida and informed her of her decision, not, of course, realising all that it meant for Cressida to have to make another arrangement to get her to the station.

During lunch the recurrent topic of transport was exhaustively discussed.

Felicity Brent showed no inclination to alter her plans, and as a taxi was already ordered for her Cressida had to admit that there was no reason why she should. When the discussion was apparently closed, Tori suddenly took a hand in it. He turned to Felicity and said, with all the appearance of marked interest, 'So you must leave us already? That is too bad. But for me, how fortunate!'

Felicity Brent showed for once a little interest in what was said to her. She looked genuinely surprised. Was this queer man at last going to take notice? she wondered. It was about time, certainly.

Tori continued without a pause. 'I too must be in London today, and so, perhaps, I may give myself the pleasure of accompanying you?'

'Oh, yes,' Felicity said, 'do.' Her flat voice was as flat as ever, but there was slightly more expression on her lovely face and she even smiled faintly.

'You are most agreeable,' Tori said untruthfully, making her one of his implied bows. 'I shall look forward most pleasantly to our journey.'

What's he up to now? Cressida wondered.

Fallen after all, Madge Rimmington-Clarke thought. Always imagined he had more sense.

I wish he'd cut out that nice Greenacre boy, Mary Handley thought, he'd be far more likely to be able to handle her.

Mrs Yates did not think at all. She was permanently out of her depth in the society of people she could never hope to understand, and had very sensibly given up trying to rise to the surface for more than a few occasional moments.

Miss Ambleside was annoyed. She had found Tori increasingly charming. Not the least part of his charm had been the fact that he ignored Miss Brent in a manner that Miss Ambleside found very soothing. Most unfortunate, she thought, most. It would have been quite delightful to have had his escort on the journey. The journey might have been quite pleasant. But one could hardly change one's plans again in so very short a time. Altogether very trying and unnecessary.

Tori, unmoved by the interest he was perfectly aware of having created, continued to make himself agreeable to Miss Brent for the rest of the meal. The assembled company even had the doubtful pleasure of hearing the lovely creature laugh for perhaps the first time since she had arrived at Brede.

Tori certainly did things well, Cressida thought with amusement. He was nothing if not thorough. Was it, she wondered, all a rescue act on behalf of John Greenacre?

After lunch Tori manœuvred Cressida into the garden, leaving Miss Brent with a look that was enough to flutter the most hardened heart.

'Tori, what are you up to?' Cressida asked as soon as they were out on the lawn.

Tori laughed. 'Ah!' he said, 'I hoped to surprise you also. It was – necessary,' he added less flippantly, 'that you should not have to simulate your astonishment.'

There was a moment's pause. All suggestion of casualness had fled, quite suddenly. Cressida could hear her own footsteps in spite of the long grass.

'Tori! It's –' She dropped her voice to a whisper, although there was no one in sight for at least fifty yards on all sides. 'Is it – the job?'

'Yes,' Tori answered, 'it is the job.'

Although he spoke lightly, his little monkey face was completely serious.

'Tonight,' he went on, 'or tomorrow, perhaps, I go back.'

Involuntarily Cressida drew a sharp breath. 'But –' she began. But Tori interrupted her.

'Ah, no,' he said softly, 'no, you shall not be alarmed. Everything is arranged. I tell you nothing because it will be more easy for you to know nothing!'

'Tori, you – you haven't had a long enough – rest and – and it's crazily dangerous,' Cressida said before she could stop herself.

She knew, as she spoke, that her words would have less than no effect on Tori. She was not, however, entirely right. For a few moments Tori's expressive face was ravaged by an emotion he did not try to conceal. He looked suddenly vulnerable, like a man stripped of his armour in the face of appalling danger.

'That may be,' he said quietly, 'but – I shall not be too much afraid since you are afraid for me, Cressida.'

'Tori, I –' Cressida began, but he stopped her again.

'You shall say no more,' he said. 'It is well that I go while I am strong, as you have made me. Because if you –' He did not finish, but said instead, with a sudden return of his old liveliness, 'Ah, how fortunate it is that I have so good an excuse for running away! The lovely Felicity, she does not know that she is suddenly of so much use!'

'How – how long will it be?' Cressida asked quickly.

'That,' Tori answered, 'will arrange itself.'

He turned as he spoke and began to walk back towards the house. Cressida said nothing.

'You will say,' Tori went on, 'that I do not tell you where I go or when I return, that I am what you call casual, is it not? That you do not trouble yourself with me because of this unmannerly behaviour, which you may find, perhaps, a little – *an*noying?'

Tori's eyebrows rose to sharp peaks and his shoulders seemed inclined to follow them.

'It'll be difficult to look annoyed, Tori,' Cressida said, trying to speak as lightly as he had.

'But you will be successful, Cressida. It will be better so. And if it should be thought that I – amuse myself with the little Felicity, that also will be well.'

As they approached, the lovely house seemed to glow with a warmth of its own. The unmown lawns softened the formality of its outline and made it homelike and very gracious. The beauty of Brede Manor lived; it was more than just a successful arrangement of brick and stone.

Tori stopped suddenly, his eyes fixed upon the house and its background.

'This,' he said softly, 'this is beauty to remember. I shall go where there will be no beauty, no truth, nothing but lies and fear and – cruelty.' For a moment Tori's voice shook. Then he straightened his shoulders. 'But I shall know that all the time there is this truth, this beauty, which shall live though the house be destroyed. To know that is to have the strength that will make of lies and fear no more than a dream, an unreality, powerless.' He paused, no longer looking at the house but at Cressida. 'And to this,' he went on, 'you belong, Cressida. You belong to truth, and if I am not afraid of fear it is because of what you have given me.'

'Oh, Tori, what have I ever given you?' Cressida asked before she could stop herself.

In another moment, she thought, I shall have to cry.

'Faith,' Tori replied simply, 'so that I can no longer be afraid. Because of you I believe in the good in men's hearts.

And now you shall go in,' he went on, so quickly that she had no time to answer. 'You shall go in to your beautiful house and make for me one more picture that I shall see always when I do not have it to look at.'

Cressida walked on without a word. Tori's quiet, unemotional voice had a power which made it impossible to hesitate, even for a second, in carrying out his simple request. She dug her hands into her trouser pockets and stared at the house, a little blurred now because of the tears in her eyes.

Tori stood watching her, utterly still. For him the picture of the house had faded. All the light of the sun seemed to be concentrated on Cressida's pale, shining hair. Like most Europeans, Tori had always cherished a vision of woman as a creature of elegant curves in clinging skirts. But as he watched Cressida in her trousers his whole soul looked out of his eyes. There she went, walking with smooth, easy strides, independent, demanding nothing, asking for no protection from him or any other man, behaving, in fact, in exactly the opposite way to the woman of a man's dream. And yet he knew he loved her as he could never imagine loving a woman again.

At the door of the house she turned back towards him and made him a little gesture with one hand. There was something curiously young about her momentary attitude, half awkward but wholly graceful all the same. She still looked very modern, very independent, very self-possessed, but also, quite suddenly, very lonely.

After she had gone into the house Tori still watched the dark, empty doorway. For him she still stood there, in that sudden moment of loneliness.

CHAPTER FIFTEEN

By the time she reached her room Cressida realised that she was not, after all, going to cry. For some reason her last sight of Tori's small figure, standing so quietly on the calm, green lawn, made tears seem absurd. Tori had looked so slight, so fragile, so unlike a hero who was about to face danger as terrifying as any nightmare. Seeing him stand there, surrounded by peace and safety that had the assurance of permanency, made it almost impossible to realise that in twenty-four hours he would be in a country where he could never stand quietly in the open, looking at beauty; a country in which he would have to be suspicious, in which he would have to watch every human being with eyes narrowed by mistrust, with mind continually alert and without rest for a moment. Tori, who stood in the sun and watched her leave him as if she merely went into the house first, would soon have to hide from the daylight and walk cautiously in darkness, in a country of shadows and whispers, where only fear swaggered in the sun and decency crouched behind closed doors. And he was not going out with the reckless bravery of a man who flung himself into unknown dangers. His journey required the far more terrible courage that could carry him back into the horror of a nightmare of which the memory had never ceased to haunt him.

Cressida had always known that Tori was in touch with an organisation in his own country. He had told her nothing more, no details, no hints even, of what he might one day have to do in connection with it. Cressida had asked him nothing. It was easier to look as if you knew nothing if you actually knew nothing. But, as time went on and Tori remained quietly at Brede, Cressida had almost begun to forget that he was not really living there, quietly writing a book in order to make up for the income he had left in the hands of the Germans. And so the shock of his sudden announcement was so much the greater. It left Cressida with the feeling she might have had on waking from a dream to find the dream was reality.

In an hour Tori was gone. He had simply stepped into a car in which Felicity Brent was already sitting and driven off, after a farewell of the most casual kind which suggested nothing more than a weekend's absence. His manner had been at its most flowery, but his eyes, Cressida could see, were shallow and unrevealing, as if he had already begun to hide his thoughts from even the most searching eye.

That night, the moment she lay down in her bed, Cressida found herself crying with so much abandon that she could not even try to stop. She cried until she was exhausted, like a child who has forgotten the reason for his tears but still cannot control them. But, unlike a child, she did not fall asleep when her tears had ceased of themselves. Instead she found herself so wide awake that she could not stay in bed. Her mind was completely refreshed, as if tears had cleared her thoughts so that she realised them for the first time.

She stood at the window and thought of the various occasions in her life when she had cried as she had that night. The little incidents passed through her mind, each one of them looking more foolish than the last. Small, ridiculous tragedies; having a cold on the night of her first hunt ball . . . spilling ink over a suit that had just been taken from its tissue-papered box . . . watching one of her old retrievers die . . . seeing Dolphin off to school. . . . And other occasions, when tears had been impersonal, merely the result of emotion aroused by a book or a film, or a parade of soldiers. . . .

On and on it went, this procession of ordinary, simple emotional incidents, none of which had had any lasting effect on her life. Over real tragedy, over the blow which had finally and completely changed her life, she had not been able to cry. She thought of that tragedy now, calmly and in detail, in an entirely detached manner, as if her recent tears had drained her of emotion.

She remembered the beginning of that appalling, utterly unreasonable quarrel between Charles and her husband, Simon Chance. Looking back, it seemed to her that she must have known it would come. She must have seen Simon's jealousy growing daily more vicious; she must have realised that his irritability was becoming more easily roused. He had been so spoilt all his life, so good-looking, so successful, so certain there was nothing his charm could not do for him. His friendship with Charles Valery had appeared to be another of his successes. To go into partnership with a racing-stable, to be offered a home as lovely as Brede, had all seemed to Simon quite natural, quite an obvious result of his own worth. But, very gradually, Charles's superiority had begun to show, in small, unobtrusive ways. After an argument, in which Simon had got his way, it had become suddenly clear that Charles's opinion was, in the end, the right one. Simon lost his temper with a horse and Charles mastered it by hours of patience. Charles was always just a little more successful than Simon, though he appeared to mind much less whether he was or not. Simon –

Cressida checked her thoughts. There was no point, now, in going over all the tiny absurd incidents which had culminated in that final quarrel. Even the reason for that quarrel had been tiny and absurd, not worth remembering.

But it was too easy to remember Simon, as she had last seen him, standing outside the stable-yard, arguing passionately with Charles, who was sitting in his car for some reason or other. She remembered Simon's sudden crazy fury, which had made him shout outrageous insults at Charles, insults which all the stablemen must have heard. She remembered how Charles had pulled Simon into the car so that they could get out of earshot until his temper subsided. She remembered the grey Lagonda streaking away from the stables, the tyres spitting gravel, Simon snatching off his hat to avoid having it blown away by the speed at which Charles was driving.

There memory stopped for a time. For two hours or so life had gone on as usual, and then Charles had come back to Brede alone.

For a second Cressida shut her eyes. It hurt, after all, to remember Charles's face as he got out of the police-car, helped by a sergeant. It was unbearable to remember how he had looked, leaning heavily on the stocky little man in uniform, wincing every time his weight fell on his lame leg, dishevelled, utterly unlike himself. But with her eyes shut the vision of Charles's thin, haggard face was more vivid than ever.

Cressida moved away from the window. The room was only half dark and she found a cigarette and lighted it. It was silly, she thought, to torture herself like this over old tragedy, just because she imagined she was strong enough not to mind. Just because she had cried so thoroughly about another man, it was absurd to suppose that emotion would not be able to upset her again for the moment.

Suddenly she found that she knew why she had been crying.

It was not simply because Tori had gone away, and because she would miss him, and because the circumstances of his departure had been full of emotion, and because his careful casualness had been so touching. All these reasons might have produced tears, but she knew she had cried for none of them.

She had cried because Tori loved her so much, and because she would never be able to love him in the way in which he needed and deserved to be loved.

She went back to the window and flung out her cigarette-end. Oh, why, she thought almost angrily, why is everything like it is? Charles went away five years ago. I don't even know what he's doing. I may never see him again. He may have changed so much I wouldn't know him. He may have changed so much I wouldn't love him. And I want Tori. I want him as a lover. I want the fun we could have together, the loveliness we could make of life. I want to make him happy, to make him forget the hideous things that have happened to him. And I want him, I want him. . . .

Her own sudden honesty frightened her, but she forced herself to go on facing the spate of truth. It wasn't often, she knew, that one's best-hidden thoughts became so alarmingly clear.

I don't want to go on wasting my life like this. I don't want to be middle-aged and have nothing to remember. Tori would give me a memory that would last for ever. . . .

There she stopped again. A memory. That was just it. Only a memory. Tori would give her a lovely memory and she would go on loving Charles until she was dead, and perhaps even then.

Oh, God, how can I know, she thought in despair, how can anyone know what to do?

Tori would know the answer and I can't ask him for it. Even if he was here to ask. I can't go and ask him for a little fun. He's too good, so much too good, for someone else's remains.

And how on earth, she thought, returning to a lower and less emotional plane, can I stand here like this and think the things I'm thinking? Is everyone really so detached from life that they can take their own feelings apart as if they were inventing a plot for a book? Go on, finish the story, find something genuine in it, something that will really prove how I feel.

There wasn't much more of the story. But every detail was as clear as if it had happened a week ago instead of five years.

There was Charles, limping into the house on the arm of that little police-sergeant, obviously on the verge of collapse but determined to tell her himself about the crash. She remembered how he stood in the hall, turning to watch her follow him into the house. She remembered his exact words.

'I smashed the car, Cressida, and –' For a moment he had seemed unable to go on, but somehow he had pulled himself together. 'And I've killed Simon.'

He had said just that, in front of the police-sergeant who was obviously taking down every word to be used in evidence, although he had no actual notebook in his hands. Charles did not seem to realise that there was anyone there except Cressida. She had instinctively tried to stop him talking, not knowing she was doing the very thing that would make things so much worse in the end, not knowing, really, what she was doing at all.

Then, in the short, jerky sentences of a man still half stunned from shock, Charles had told her more.

'We – we were arguing. He – tried to make me stop the car. He wanted to get away. I didn't want – to finish it until – he'd calmed down a bit. And then –'

'And then you hit Mr Chance, did you not, Mr Valery?' A very concise, official voice asking that frightening question.

Oh, no, that was later. That wasn't what the little sergeant in the hall had said. That was another official voice, afterwards, at the trial, when Charles was in the dock on a charge of manslaughter. A charge, as the prosecution had most carefully shown, that was only just not murder, because of the risk to himself Charles had incurred by being in the car with his victim.

'. . . and you have heard the evidence of witnesses to the quarrel between Mr Valery and Mr Chance, to the frequent quarrels, I feel I may say . . .'

The clear, slightly pompous tones of the prosecuting counsel were so easy to remember.

'Mr Valery was, I am given to understand, an extremely, I might say an unusually, competent driver . . . no traffic on the road in front of him at the time of the – er – accident . . . the one place in the neighbourhood where a car would be certain to overturn if it should leave the road . . . long grass, which would break the fall of anyone who should succeed in jumping clear as the car crashed. . . .'

'And you hit Mr Chance, did you not, Mr Valery?'

That was where that question had come in; just there, after the remarks about the long grass.

You hit Mr Chance so that you should jump clear and he would not be able to.

Those words had not actually been said, but the implication was clear enough.

'Yes, I did.' Charles's quiet, weary voice had been in startling contrast to the smug legal tones.

'Why, Mr Valery, did you do a thing which you must have realised to be very dangerous, driving at a speed which witnesses have stated to be most alarming?'

'I – lost my temper. He was – trying to take over the wheel.'

'Does it not occur to you that Mr Chance was, perhaps, right in so attempting to control the car? Do you not feel he was justified?'

And more and more of those long pompous questions, so worded as to make it more and more evident that Charles had been driving at a criminal speed and without due care, and all the rest of it. Dozens of total strangers in the witness-box, men and women who had just happened to be in a bus which had turned out of a side road just as Charles's car flashed past, just a few seconds before it had been hurled off the road by a sudden, uncontrolled swerve. A whole bus load of witnesses gratuitously provided, people who didn't know Charles, or anything about him, but had happened to see an exciting accident; people who had seen the driver of the Lagonda hit his passenger, just under the ear, and then jump clear as the big car crashed over the steeply banked roadside to overturn, and then subside upon the man who had not been able to jump.

It had made such a good story, all the details had hung together with such damning effect. The witnesses had all been so anxious to assist the law. They had been, from the safety of their reliably driven bus, so shocked by the speed of the great grey car, in which they would, most of them, have so much preferred to be driving. The presence, by pure chance, of all these people had seemed to make the tragedy more appalling somehow. It had turned it into a sensation, a dramatic story for the newspapers, a story which was all the better because Charles and Simon were well-known already, at least to everyone who followed racing. Simon's flamboyant personality had always surrounded him with glamour anyhow, and Charles had that year won the National, riding his own horse. Circumstances seemed to have combined to make the whole affair as sensational as possible.

And yet, in the end, it had been the presence of that very bus-load that turned the verdict in Charles's favour. Surely, his defending counsel had pointed out, surely a man with evil intentions would not have deliberately staged an accident without making some effort to see that he was not observed? Surely no motorist could ignore the presence of anything so large as a bus, so very close behind his car? If he had intended to knock his passenger unconscious and then crash the car, surely no man with an atom of intelligence would fail to notice such a concentration of witnesses?

And so the trial had ended and Charles had been acquitted. But that had been the end of nothing. There had never been an end to the business, unless the total disruption of two people's lives could be called an end.

Cressida had not stayed to hear the judge's summing-up of the case. Afterwards she had read the careful, well-chosen words, that had made it quite clear that Charles's acquittal was due, not to insufficient evidence, but to the fact that the evidence was based on surmise and could not be supported by proof. The speech had left no doubt in anyone's mind that Charles was culpable to a criminal degree, but no mere opinion, even that of a judge, could alter the course of the law. Cressida knew that hearing those words must have been intolerable to anyone who knew Charles. She knew that his urgent little note, begging her to leave the court after her own evidence, had been justified. Nothing but that note could have made her go, but it had been impossible not to obey the pathetically few words he had scribbled. '. . . please, Cressida, if it's the last thing I ever ask you . . .'

Cressida, remembering all this, put her hands over her eyes. But she could not shut out the picture of that hotel bedroom with the white enamel telephone, where she had sat, waiting to hear the result of the trial. She had sat for perhaps an hour watching that shining and silent telephone, with the words of her own evidence hammering themselves into her brain, as if it was necessary that she should be reminded of them.

The cultured, pleasant, utterly impervious prosecuting voice . . . '. . . my painful duty . . . realise how painful . . .' Considerate, merciless padding . . . '. . . understand that you did not appear to be completely – astonished, shall I say . . .? Perhaps some reason that you knew of . . . anxious, perhaps, that Mr Valery should be careful what he said to you . . . the sergeant of police . . . a witness . . .'

Very careful questions. Nothing said that could be called libellous, but enough implication to hang a man. One careless word in answer, one unsteady movement, one breath of anxiety, it seemed, would be enough to prove that Charles had wanted a rival out of the way so that she would be free. . . . The proof of motive, which was all that was lacking. . . .

Cressida did not know that her face had been as blank as a china mask. She had felt that her sick anxiety must be brilliantly clear to all. As she walked out of the court she had felt that even her back might be taken as a sign that she could not face the accusation that had not been made in so many words, the suggestion that had not needed any words.

And then she had waited, in that quiet, luxurious bedroom with the white telephone. The telephone bell had rung. She had picked up the receiver, which had been cold and slippery in her shaking hand. And Charles had said, 'Cressida, it's over. I'm going away.' And she had found it almost impossible to say anything at all except, foolishly, to ask him where he was going. He hadn't answered that. He had just said he would be at Brede that evening to fetch some things. He had refused to let her drive him down. He had said, 'I'm going by train,' and rung off, and she hadn't known where he had been speaking from.

She remembered every moment of that drive down to Brede in Simon's Bentley. Until she found herself alone in the car, racing through familiar country, she had not clearly realised that Simon was dead. There had been no time before. No time to think of anything except that Charles might go to prison.

She remembered Charles arriving at Brede in a taxi from Wichlesbury, later in the evening, when she had been there for some time, waiting again. He had looked, somehow, like a stranger, like someone arriving at a strange house, rather nervous because he did not know who would be there. He had been in such a hurry all the time. He had scarcely spoken to Cressida, beyond a few business-like words about the house and the solicitors who would arrange to look after it and see about repairs and so on. Those east windows, where the rain had begun to come in . . .

It had been horrible, that conversation, like a nightmare. Even after five years Cressida could remember the sense of panic that had almost choked her, while the minutes rushed by, and Charles was going away, perhaps for ever, and talking jerkily about lawyers and repairs to the house. Exactly like a nightmare, in which something terrible was always just about to happen, in which one was held down, powerless to alter the course of events. But, unlike a nightmare, this time the terrible thing had happened. Charles had gone away and she had stood at the doors of Brede and watched him go.

If it had not been for John, she would have gone with him . . .

If it had not been for that iron barrier of restraint Charles had surrounded himself with, she could have said . . .

If there had been more time. . . . If, if, if . . .

But it was no use. One couldn't change the course of life with a series of ifs. Life went on, and one went on with it. There was no time to look back.

Downstairs in the hall the clock struck one. No, there certainly wasn't time to look back, and she had spent half the night doing it. Tomorrow there was a lot to do. Must remember about getting Aunt Jessie to the station. Must certainly go to bed now.

CHAPTER SIXTEEN

After four days in the lifeboat Charles Valery began to feel restless. He no longer found it possible to lie in a state of semi-collapse between one meal and the next. He was beginning to recover from shock and from his various burns. Also his knee was beginning to hurt him intolerably.

For ten years Charles's knee had been in the foreground of his life. For a long time after the original injury it had seemed that a physically active career was at an end for him. But Charles had refused to accept such an idea. His tenacious endurance had made it possible for him to ride again. No one knew that he had often been forced to wonder whether activity was worth the pain that so frequently followed. Once or twice this pain had exasperated him to the point of wishing that he had lost his leg altogether. Often it seemed that the life of an acknowledged cripple would be preferable to the endless effort to look as if nothing was the matter, to walk about using a stick as if it was an elegant affectation rather than a damnable necessity. Charles had always known that one day the effort would be too much for him and he would have to give in. But he had put off the thought, from day to day almost. Next year, next month, next week, he would give up riding and his knee would benefit from the rest and not worry him so much. But, somehow, there had always been just that one more day, or race, or occasion of whatever kind, that must be got through before he could admit defeat. It had become a childish sort of game, this putting off of the time when he would have to grow up and face facts. He had told himself that next time his knee kept him awake all night he would give up riding. Then it was next time he lost a race, next time he won a race, and so on and so on. Then he had set himself the apparently distant goal of the National. But, like all other goals, this one had not been impossibly distant after all. And decision had become no easier. To win the National and then give up riding had seemed unsporting, as if he was afraid to give anyone the chance of beating him. Also, with sensitiveness he knew to be absurd, he had felt that it would be showing off, advertising the courage that had carried him to success, a kind of exhibitionism of which the idea horrified him. He could not, in the very moment of success, ask for pity. He had told himself a thousand times that this subservience to public opinion was childish, a weakness any man would be ashamed to admit. No one with any sense, he told himself, minded what anyone thought. But he had gone on minding, just the same.

Now, when enforced inactivity and a cramped existence in the boat had caused his knee to stiffen and hurt him as much as it had ever done after the most violent exercise, he was reminded once again of other occasions in his life on which he had been driven to feeling that the effort of living was not worth making. Why, after all, did one go on against all reason, with the apparently pointless determination to live? Why now, especially, when half the world had bent its energy upon killing the other half, was it so essential to preserve one's own tiny and useless spark of life? Why not follow poor old Harcourt to peace at the bottom of the sea?

The wording of his thoughts struck him. Poor old Harcourt, he had said. Why poor? If Harcourt was to be envied his calm resting place, why think of him as poor? Was that unconsidered little word, automatically applied to the dead, really the answer to everything? Was life so wonderful that the dead were poor because they no longer lived? If life was really the effort it seemed to be, why were those who had escaped from it poor?

Charles could think of no answer to any of these questions. Or rather, he could think of none except the terrifying one that death was so much more horrible than anyone could imagine, and so life must be clung to at any cost to avoid it. And yet that wasn't an answer either. No one had so far succeeded in avoiding death, and so why make so much effort to escape the inescapable? If death was horrible, it would be just as horrible in twenty years' time, and why bother with the twenty years?

Well, Charles thought, why am I bothering?

He decided that it was time he made some slight attempt to answer at least one of the string of questions that had so freely asked themselves. So he applied his mind to the last, which was personal, and therefore could surely be tackled? Having so much time and nothing to do gave him an excuse to review his life with a thoroughness that would, in other circumstances, have been too much like the introspection of a confirmed egoist. The result of this exercise showed him that his life so far had fallen into three parts.

There was the life before the accident which crippled him. There was no need to ask himself why he had wished to live that life. He had enjoyed every moment of it. And happiness, when it was instinctive, precluded introspection.

After the accident another life had begun. This had been a life of trying to return to the previous one, of struggling against a disability that threatened the happiness he had been scarcely aware of until he saw it in retrospect. After several months of looking enviously at the past he had gained the moral strength to look forward instead. He had discovered the futility of retrospection. That discovery, instead of leading to despair as it might have done in a weak man, had given him a new encouragement to live. He had found out that there was pleasure to be got out of rising above disheartening circumstances. The excitement of winning a race, after imagining he would never ride one again, was infinitely more satisfying than he could have guessed. This, he realised, was because something gained from life at a price became naturally more valuable as the price increased. It was, of course, a truism to say that easily gained pleasure inevitably became boring. But, as with most truisms, it was not until he had found out the truth of it by experience that it meant anything more to him than a rather irritatingly obvious statement.

The third part of his life was not quite so easy to review. Although it had now lasted for nearly five years the beginning

of it was still very close, still very vivid. And it still had the
power to hurt.

Perhaps because he was afraid of looking too closely at
those last five years, Charles found that his attention was
inclined to dwell on his immediate surroundings. He became
acutely conscious of the sea, spread around him like a sheet of
winking sapphires. He watched the delicate drift of the few
tiny clouds in the intensely blue sky. All this space, in varying
tones of blue, accentuated his isolation and gave him a sense
of self-consciousness, almost of shame, as if he was just a
tiny ugly blot, left by carelessness on an otherwise superb
arrangement of colour.

So that the glittering sea should not mesmerise him,
Charles shut his eyes and began once more to face the past.
The last five years. It was a little easier to look back at them
now, after he had seen himself dwarfed by the immensity of
a colour scheme on which he was merely the blot.

He could look back at himself, a little blot, and therefore
of no consequence, on the day he had killed the man who
had been his best friend. He could remember Simon's crazy
burst of temper, out of all proportion to the immediate
cause of it, some small argument, not worth remembering.
He remembered dragging Simon into the car, so that his
ridiculous anger should not be watched by the grooms and by
Cressida.

Cressida.

How absurd, Charles thought, to have ever imagined
it would be possible to stop loving Cressida. Quite as easy
to forget one liked sitting in the sun. Loving Cressida was

something one took for granted, like the joy of sunlight, and did not need to remember. Well, there were people who lived without sunlight, and he had lived without Cressida, and would continue to do so. That was, he thought, if he lived at all, which seemed at the moment fairly doubtful.

All this, he thought, was not getting him any nearer an answer to the question about the reason for making so much effort to live. Cressida would have been a reason. But as he had known for five years that Cressida would never concern him again there must have been something else that had made him constantly alert to snatch at life when death was close and easy.

For four of the five years he had been away from England, Charles had lived, so to speak, in constant touch with death. Life had been a sort of competition with death. That, thought Charles, sounded extremely macabre, and suggested a tense and prolonged struggle with nerves always keyed to snapping-point. In reality life had been nothing of the sort. It had been sometimes exciting, always interesting, always vivid. But it had also been light-hearted and extraordinarily carefree; carefree because he had a job he knew he was good at, a job in which he was entirely dependent on himself and in which the risks he took concerned his own life only, and were, in fact, a safeguard for the lives of other people. Besides all this, it was a job he loved.

Charles's sensitive, beautiful hands, strong and gentle with horses, were peculiarly apt with intricate machinery. Unlike most men who had lived a great deal with horses, he had always been attracted by machinery. It had meant more to him than a mere fascination of noise and oil, irresistible to boys of any age. The intricacy and smooth precision of a well-running engine had been to him a shining wonder, the nearest approach man's brain had made to the creative genius of God. And of all forms of machinery, surely the most brilliant, the most inspired and the loveliest must be the aeroplane? Here, it seemed to Charles, was at last a dream come true, the dream of Leonardo, and of other men who had dreamed ahead of their time and been thought mad. Here at last was release for the spirit of man, always straining at the leash which held his feet to the earth. Here was a power that could rise above the laws of Nature herself and resist gravity.

And so Charles had been happy during this third part of his life. His happiness had been perhaps deeper because it had nothing to do with human relationship. It would sound odd, he thought, and rather foolish to use the word security in describing the life of a test pilot, and yet his happiness had been secure. It had depended upon something that was under his own control, upon a machine that would obey his hands and answer his lightest touch, and not upon the unpredictable reactions of another human mind, over which no one could have perfect mastery.

Well then, he asked himself at this point, why had he left that satisfactory and exciting life? Why had he decided upon a course of action which had, as it turned out, landed him in a peculiarly uncomfortable and profitless situation? Why, in fact, had he suddenly found that he could no longer stay out of the war?

He was quite aware that his motive would be misread by anyone who might pause to consider it. It looked, he thought, as though he had stayed in America as long as that country was technically at peace. That, however, was not the truth. His job of testing aircraft was now more important than ever, and he could have kept it indefinitely. If he had remained in the States his life would have gone on almost exactly as it had done for four years. He need not have felt that he was not doing enough, that, to use a revolting expression recently forced on the language, his war effort was insufficiently great. Such unnecessary ideas would not have troubled him. So what, his mind reiterated, what was it that had made him restless, unsatisfied with an entirely engrossing job? Why had he suddenly felt that irresistible urge to get into some actual fighting? And why bother to go back to England first? He could as well, and with much less trouble, have gone with men from the States and killed some Japanese, if it was merely violence his restless spirit required.

Charles thought over all the well-sounding, and probably more or less accurate, definitions of what were known as war aims that had been made by able and thoughtful men, whose job it was to tell the various peoples of the world what they were fighting for, what they were thinking about, or what they would be thinking about if they thought at all. In passing it struck Charles that one of the differences between totalitarianism and democracy was that the dictators told their people what they must think, while democratic leaders set out to show theirs what they were thinking. Whether or not these two methods of influencing mass thought came to the same thing in the end remained to be seen.

The more Charles thought about the advertised purposes of the war, the more remote and impersonal they appeared. No one would deny them goodness and truth, but they were still too big for the average mind of humanity. The average mind, he thought, could not be anything but small. The great minds of humanity could have a very light influence on an average necessarily arrived at from the immense number of minds which could scarcely be said to exist at all. A great aim, a magnificent purpose, however noble, would ultimately fail of its object if it remained outside the grasp of the persons it was designed to influence.

The words of the Atlantic Charter achieved admirable simplicity. There could scarcely be anyone who would disagree with the aims it set forth. But those aims were large and impersonal, essentially so because they formed a comprehensive definition of an enormous, world-embracing purpose. What Charles was trying to get at was not the general aim of the war, but the tiny, intimate reasons individual men must have if there was to be found a basically true answer to the question, Why am I fighting?

If put to every individual in the world, that little question would probably be instantly answered. There were dozens of answers which would ostensibly serve. Fighting for my country, fighting because it's my job, because I obey orders, because I hate the Germans, because I'm frightened, because everyone else is fighting.

How many men would give that last answer, Charles wondered, and yet of how many was it not probably true?

Men would fight for all kinds of reasons, good and bad. They would fight with magnificent courage and selfless heroism. But it would be interesting to know how many men, in any given battle, were there because the others were there, because it was easier to move with a mass than to think for oneself, because it was better to do what everyone else did, rather than make oneself noticeable.

Fear of individuality was supposed to be an English characteristic. Englishmen were trained from boyhood to behave in a uniform manner, which was an admirable doctrine unless carried, as it often was, to the point of absurdity, to the point where individual sense was subordinated to uniform behaviour. Charles could distinctly remember sweating miserably in a thick jersey on a July day at school because no one had told him to take it off. Individual inclination, even in so personal a matter, must be checked in the resounding name of discipline. Either all the boys must take their jerseys off or no one must. And so it had gone on, and Englishmen had become the doers of the right thing throughout the world, the doers, that meant, of the things other Englishmen did. Carried to a logical extreme, this doctrine of uniform behaviour could conceivably arrive at a point at which every individual in the world acted against his own inclination and fought because all the others were fighting. Imagine the converse, Charles thought. Imagine every individual suddenly fired with the truth of his own desires. Imagine every individual crying aloud his hatred of killing his fellows. What would that be but an end to war?

But, Charles's mind uncomfortably demanded, does every individual hate killing his fellows? Well, does he?

Is it because he does that the weapons of war have always

been attractive in themselves, fascinating to use, irresistible to play with? Swords, daggers, bows and arrows, all the weapons men had invented had been things of beauty, things that were bound to attract men's desires, things so exciting that their purpose could be overlooked in the thrill of handling them. What was more magnificently beautiful than a battleship firing a broadside? What boy could fail to enjoy roaring over all obstacles in a tank? Could anyone be unmoved by the sheer beauty of wave upon wave of fine aeroplanes overshadowing even the birds in their power and grace? Even a tired foot-soldier with a Bren gun must get a thrill from the vibrating mechanism of his fascinating weapon.

Would men be so anxious to fight if they had nothing to fight with but ugly bits of blunt lead?

Charles checked the trend of his thoughts. How easy it was, he thought, to be led away from the original purpose of all this thinking. Was he any nearer to an answer to his first question, Why am I bothering to go on living?

He knew that he was not. But to another question, the question of why he had suddenly wanted to get to close grips with the enemy of his country, he felt he now had an answer. From the bottom of his mind, dug up, perhaps, by so much thought, a very simple vision emerged. It was a picture of Germans in uniform clattering up and down the staircase at Brede, of German armoured vehicles roaring through the gates of Brede, those gates whose gossamer loveliness should open upon nothing but sacred peace.

That answer had the ring of truth. So what? Charles asked again.

That answer came easily also. So there'll always be war. There'll always be men who own grass and trees and lovely homes, and men who do not. There'll be men who own grass and trees and want more of the same. International Communism would seem to solve those problems, but there were, apparently, so many cogent and irrefutable reasons why International Communism could not be made to work. The very mention of such a thing led to such impassioned argument that one's mind became exhausted at even the thought of it. Charles shied away from pursuit of the subject. Laziness, he thought, laziness was the trouble, with him and with most of his fellow men; men who talked of and fought for freedom, and who really wanted nothing less.

Absolute freedom would saddle a man with fearful responsibility. It was safer and far less trouble to do what one was told than to have the freedom to think for oneself.

Charles remembered a phrase he had once heard or read. 'The fearful loneliness of freedom.' He could not remember the context of the words, but they did not really need one. Was it, he wondered, a fact that the human soul, having once been part of some pre-natal whole, went through its earthly incarnation trying to become once more part of some protective, all-embracing entity? Trying, in fact, to achieve the very opposite of freedom? Could that fear of 'the loneliness of freedom' account for man's eagerness to form societies, clubs, teams, and even nations? And might it not finally lead to the formation of a world?

Logically it certainly might. History had shown how greatly the size of communities had already grown. There had been a time when war meant a squabble between one village and the next, or even one castle and its rival. Then it had become a matter between the Scots and the English, between the North and South in America. And now a man from a lonely ranch in Texas would go and fight in the jungle of Guadalcanal, a boy from western Australia would fly over a German city, an Indian would march through Africa. If boundaries could thus grow, surely a time might come when the world would be its only boundary?

From boyhood onwards men were taught what was known as the team spirit. A great many people, whose thoughts leapt small fences but were unaware of the great ring enclosing those little obstacles, sneered at the team spirit; some went so far as to condemn it as the nucleus of war. If you were taught, they said, to play for your side, to play for the school, or the college or what not, it was not a long step to fighting for your country. And so the cricket matches at your prep school were the first steps to the ultimate competition in murder in which you would take part as soon as your country became involved in war. But, if you managed to see further than the small fences, was it not possible that the team spirit might carry men beyond war?

Wasn't it possible that the team spirit could bring men to a point at which they would live and work, not for the school or the nation, or even the State, but for the world? The size of a society depended upon locality and distance. With distance diminishing before the advance of science, world membership, from being merely fine words used by politicians, became suddenly a possibility, more than a possibility. Arrived at by those simple steps in reasoning, it became a certainty.

The steps in reasoning, Charles reminded himself, were easy enough. The actual steps were a good deal more complicated and difficult.

But it doesn't matter, he thought, how difficult and complicated it all is if there is something visible at the end of the journey. Even the possibility of an answer made the effort of argument worthwhile.

His head subsided against a coil of rope. He had forgotten about his knee. He shut his eyes and was instantly asleep.

CHAPTER SEVENTEEN

Three days after Felicity Brent had left for London, John Greenacre walked yet again up the now familiar drive of Brede Manor.

It was curious, he thought, how much emotion that drive had been the scene of in the last week or so. He remembered his first walk there, when he had been so nervous, so horrified at himself for approaching such a house to ask for lodging, when every turn in the drive had increased his diffidence. And the following times when, sick with excitement because he was going to see Felicity, he had scarcely noticed the scenery at all. And now. Now he was going to tell Cressida Chance that he would not, after all, be using that grey and yellow room whose luxury had always looked a little too dream-like to be true.

And this time he did not know what he was feeling. A week ago, if he had been told of the errand upon which he walked today, he would have been stunned by shock and misery and intolerable disappointment. Now he felt nothing at all. At least he felt no emotion, merely a mild surprise at himself because he was calm enough to go and see Cressida Chance instead of writing her a letter. He did not even realise that he hadn't written because he wanted to see Cressida Chance.

All the way up the drive he thought about Felicity's letter, not because he wanted to think about it, but because he felt it was up to him to try and discover his own feelings, or the lack of them.

'. . . after all I can't marry you . . . sorry . . . joining the W.A.A.F.s . . . Yours, FELICITY.'

A stiff, unimaginative note, written without any apparent feeling, just a duty letter, it sounded like, just an excuse for not keeping some casual date.

Reading that boring little note, John could not be expected to guess that it had been written by a girl in the grip, for the first time in her life, of a genuine emotion. He would have found it impossible to visualise Felicity, sitting at the end of a telephone which did not ring, Felicity restless and nervous, unable to go out in case she missed the telephone call which did not come, Felicity waiting for two days and then, in an angry fury of disappointment, writing that dull little note to the man she should have married the next day, Felicity deciding for a variety of hardly coherent reasons to go and join the wearers of those boring uniforms after all, to risk the loss of glamour entailed by service pants and cotton stockings.

John Greenacre would have been astounded if he had known that this transformation, as remarkable as any conjuring trick, had been brought about by the funny little monkey of a man with the unpronounceable name who had, somehow, always managed to make his presence felt, even in a room containing Felicity. He would have been even more astounded if he could have watched Felicity on that railway journey, with the same odd little man in attendance. Any woman could have told him, of course, all about Tori's power of attraction, but he could not be expected to see it for himself. Any woman could have told him that four hours of Tori's unflagging attention might easily cause a flutter in any woman's heart, especially if Tori's intentions were directed to that end. To finish that journey with a pressing invitation to dine, accompanied by a look which meant so much more than an invitation to dine, might easily excite even the most sophisticated female mind. And if, as in Felicity's case, the sophistication was only veneer, the excitement was likely to be the more genuine. If anything was wanted to make that invitation still more attractive, it was a parting from the giver of it with the details of the date unsettled; a parting with a tinge of uncertainty, with a promise to ring up and make arrangements. And then no telephone call. No telephone call, no word of any kind to explain the apparent loss of interest, or complete forgetfulness of that pressing invitation. No woman could have survived such treatment at the hands of a man of Tori's personality. In a girl as spoilt and conceited as Felicity, disappointment would be coloured by rage and exasperation and any number of other vigorous sensations, the exact nature of which was not important. Importance lay in producing in the bosom of Felicity Brent a genuine emotion. In this Tori had most thoroughly succeeded.

Tori himself might have been mildly surprised at the impressive success of his perfectly deliberate experiment. But he had no time even to remember it. If he had shaken the girl out of an intolerable attitude to humanity and given her the chance to make something of her life, he was quite unaware of it. He needed all his attention for other purposes.

And John Greenacre walked up the drive of Brede Manor not knowing what he felt.

Cressida met him, as she had the first time, at the front door. She was wearing yellow trousers this time, of coarse French linen, and a dark brown shirt. For a moment John Greenacre found it easier to look than speak.

When Cressida saw him, she remembered with a pang of pity that it was actually tomorrow that he was to marry the glamour baby. She tried to greet him in a suitably cheerful manner, but felt that her efforts were unconvincing.

'I –' John began uncertainly, 'could I – talk to you?' What a damnfool question, he thought, when he was doing it already.

Cressida said yes as if his remark was the most natural in the world.

'I'm going down to the stables,' she went on, 'so come and talk on the way.'

Much easier, she knew, to say awkward things to someone walking beside one. One didn't have to face their eyes. The poor boy had awkward things written all over his face, she thought, and would evidently need a lot of help in putting them into words.

She started for the stables. John, striding beside her, walked faster and faster until it looked as though both of them were intent on nothing but violent exercise.

'Well, you talk,' Cressida said, 'I'm out of breath.'

John laughed and slowed down, and the atmosphere became easier.

'Thank you,' he said gratefully, 'it's – it's marvellous of you. I mean you make things easier somehow. The fact is – I've had a letter from Felicity –' It is easy, he realised with surprise, I don't mind saying it a bit. 'And – she says – well, the whole thing's off. She says she can't marry me.'

Thank God for that, Cressida thought, and said, 'John, I'm sorry.' Well, it's true, she told herself, I am sorry for him because he's had to have it this way. 'Did she,' she went on, realising that she must help him a little more, 'did she say why, or would you rather not tell me?'

'Oh, no,' John said instantly, 'I'd rather. But – well, she didn't exactly say anything much, except that she was going to join the W.A.A.F.s.'

Cressida stopped and put her hand on his arm.

'Look,' she said, 'tell me just one thing, and please don't think I'm being tough and unsympathetic. But – are you unhappy about it?'

Better make him see straight off, she thought, before he's had time to decide how he ought to be feeling.

John turned and looked at her.

'No,' he said simply, 'and that's what's so – well, I simply don't understand.'

'I'm terribly glad you came and told me,' Cressida said. 'And if you don't mind I'd like to tell you why. I expect it sounds rather heartless to talk like this, but I think it's better to say everything at once and then you don't have it hanging around.' She smiled at him in a way that would have taken the sting out of any words. 'You see I – was quite worried about you! I know it was interfering and inexcusable of me, but I always knew you and Felicity were – not the right answer to anything. That sounds rather revolting and flippant, but it gets it over quickly!'

John took a deep breath. He looked younger suddenly, and Cressida realised thankfully that she hadn't said the wrong thing.

'But,' he began, 'but I still don't understand. I mean, how can you – love a person – frightfully and then – well, suddenly not mind? It – it seems crazy.'

'It's very easy,' Cressida answered, and this time her voice was completely serious.

Too easy, she thought, remembering herself and Simon. She had loved him, as John had said, frightfully, and then suddenly – Well, this was nothing to do with herself and Simon, she reminded herself, and don't drag your own troubles into someone else's, she added severely. She did not pause to consider that without her own troubles she would not be much good at handling other people's.

'But, doesn't that mean – that – that the whole thing's just – bunk? I mean I – can't imagine feeling more than – than I did.' Or can I? he thought suddenly.

'I know,' Cressida said, 'no one ever can! At least not till it's over, and then it's even more difficult to imagine how you actually did feel!'

For a time John said nothing, and they walked on in silence and gradually less and less rapidly. Then John began again.

'You know that's extraordinarily true. What you said just now, I mean. And yet if you'd said it to me last week I'd have laughed.'

'Or been madly angry,' Cressida replied. 'That's why it's never any use telling anyone anything! You can hammer heavy truth into people till you're sick, but they don't believe you till they've found out by experience how right you were.'

'All the same you might tell me one thing,' John went on, and grinned. 'If – if feeling like I did doesn't mean a thing, how the hell are you ever safe?' He spoke almost jauntily, and Cressida realised that his shyness had vanished, probably for ever.

'You're asking a lot,' she said. 'And – I don't know if I can produce an answer. But –' She hesitated, knowing what she wanted to say but not knowing how to say it.

How ridiculous it was, she thought, to have all this difficulty with words. One imagined that one thought in words, and it wasn't until trying to write or speak one's thoughts that one discovered how untrue this was.

'Well,' she went on at last, ' I think the real answer is that you never know whether you're safe or not because that's the last thing you think of at the time!'

John's face grew gloomy.

Cressida laughed. 'Don't look so miserable,' she said, 'I won't quite leave it at that. But what I'm going to say probably won't do you much good because you won't believe me.'

'I will,' John interrupted vigorously. 'Or anyhow I'll start by meaning to.'

'That's something,' Cressida said. 'Well, I think part of the trouble is that what's called "being in love" can happen so damned often to the same person. And so few people admit that. It's considered rather shocking and sinful not to think that love is final and all that. It's that mixture of romance and priggishness that will talk about Love in capital letters as if there was only one of it! And yet almost everyone, if they really thought about it honestly, must find it hard not to admit that they've been in love more than once. And what's more, that every time it happened it seemed that "this time was different". But it usually isn't.'

'Well, is it ever?' John asked gloomily.

'Yes,' Cressida answered at once. 'It's different when you know someone and find that you love them. You can be in love with a mere acquaintance. You can fall in love with a total stranger, at first sight and all that! And the trouble then begins because the moment you're even a little in love you start idealising the stranger, pretty well making up a character for them which may turn out to be entirely imaginary! You can't really love anyone until you know them. That sounds extremely simple and not worth saying, but it's not a bit simple. Some of the trouble comes from not getting to know a person till you've married them!'

'So the marriage-is-a-gamble line of talk is pretty accurate,' John remarked.

'Often, yes,' Cressida answered. 'But it needn't be, if only – well, if people would only realise that it's absurd to marry anyone without knowing whether you could talk to them for hours on end without getting bored. And I mean talk, as opposed to just throwing a few remarks into a necking session!'

John laughed, but he said nothing. After a pause Cressida went on.

'The difficulty is that when you're in love the physical side of the business wins so heavily, anyhow at first. The very idea of just talking seems absurd. But – but if you can get so interested in a conversation with someone you're in love with that you forget about wanting to kiss them, then – well then it looks as if you're safe to go ahead. Does that seem to make sense?'

John took a deep breath. He was vividly reminded of several occasions when, alone with Felicity, he had felt the fire in his blood threaten to devour him, and then, when they had been out together, in public places where he couldn't kiss her, he had been carried along by the thought of how wonderful it would be when they were alone again. Apart from that thought, he could now honestly admit, those intervals of conversation only had been boring. He could even remember wondering, in great agitation, what on earth to say to her next.

'I simply don't know what to say,' he began. 'It's – I mean it all sounds so simple, but I'd never have found it out myself!'

Cressida laughed. 'I expect you would,' she said lightly. But she thought: I don't believe he would. He's just the type that gets married in a rush and is bored for the rest of his life, if not actively miserable.

She thought of the dozens of married couples she knew, who were apparently quite happy, not openly faithless, and did not actively quarrel, but who never seemed to want to be alone together. Society was made up of people like that, she thought; people who had to run around and go to parties and be constantly surrounded by other people; couples who, if they were alone, would even turn on the wireless rather than face the prospect of just talking. And yet all life was not long enough, no time could be too long, to talk to someone whose mind answered your mind, so that conversation was like a double set of thoughts, carrying each other along indefinitely.

'Well,' John began uncertainly, 'if – if you were so interested in your wife that you didn't want anything else, how is it that – that you could ever bear to be with other people? I mean, would a party be simply a crashing bore?'

Cressida laughed. 'Well, not quite,' she said. 'I don't mean that a perfect marriage consists of endless conversation! I only meant that the thought of endless conversation wouldn't be a sort of bugbear. And, of course, one would want to run around and do things with other people sometimes. But the best part of the party would be the drive home!'

How can I talk like this? she asked herself suddenly. How can I know about perfect marriages? But she did know. She knew that a perfect marriage meant all the fun in life was twice as amusing while it lasted, and when it was over the drive home was the best part of all.

All at once she had a vision of herself, with a man walking beside her. It was not John Greenacre, in spite of his physical and very large presence. It was not the man who had been her husband. And it was not Charles Valery who had appeared out of some cranny of her subconsciousness. The face of the man beside her was Tori's face.

'Yes,' John Greenacre said quietly, 'I see what you mean.'

See? Who? Oh, yes, yes, of course.

'Oh, well, I'm glad. Oh, Lord, we seem to have walked miles. I'll have to rush back I'm afraid.'

Cressida heard her own voice, speaking in the most natural manner possible. It sounded strange to her at that moment.

'I say, I am sorry!' John exclaimed. 'Have I wasted hours of your time?'

'Of course not,' Cressida answered, 'I've – loved it. But all the same I've got to go and see Springett.'

'And I'll have to make a pretty heavy dash for the camp,' John said. 'I'm late already. But – I must tell you how – how terrifically grateful I am –'

'That's all right,' Cressida interrupted. 'Please don't go on. But – if it's any good to you, come round whenever you like.'

'I'd love to,' John said, and evidently meant it. 'Well,' he stopped and faced her, 'well, thank you,' he said simply.

Cressida realised that this was one of those pauses from which almost anything might emerge. It required swift action on her part, because, at that moment, her own mind was in no state to cope with 'almost anything'.

'Well, good-bye for the present,' she said smiling, and turned away as she spoke.

She knew that John watched her until she reached a corner in the path. She could not help realising that the young man was more than half-way to being in love with her already. She knew that there were two courses open to her. Either she could treat him with heavy patronage, as from the distance of the twelve or fourteen years between them, and probably calm him into plain friendship pretty easily, or she could be human and kind and let him go the whole way.

Well, it wouldn't hurt him, she decided. It's probably just what he needs.

She walked on, but she was no longer thinking about John Greenacre.

CHAPTER EIGHTEEN

It was Sunday, a fortnight after the bombs had fallen on Brede Somervel. In that fortnight the village had returned gently to its normal, uneventful life, a life so rooted in traditional calm that even the raw scars left by the bombs were becoming merely part of the scenery, scarcely more noticeable than the new ditch a farmer was digging at the bottom of his orchard or the new bit of spile fencing that had recently replaced the iron railing round the churchyard. Only the ruin of old Northeast's cottage stood, as if withdrawn and self-conscious in its untidy charred state, as a reminder of the swift tragedy of war.

On this Sunday, on the coast of Africa, thousands of miles away, the little battered, sun-scorched town of Tobruk had surrendered to the Germans, and even in Brede Somervel the summer air was full of a deep, poignant sadness, as if something lovely, some hitherto unshakable truth, had been violated.

Tobruk. Just a name. Until recently a name unknown to more than a handful of the human race: an unremarkable, sharp little name that had been suddenly transformed into a symbol of gallantry, known all over the world, loved with an almost personal love by men and women who could not even find it on the map. The little name had become a challenge, a rallying call that could lift the heads of the weary and put a spring into exhausted feet. And now it was just another collection of half-ruined houses the Germans had taken, to be mentioned as casually as possible in the news bulletins, to be explained away as being not so very vital to the new line of defence which our armies had taken up. But all the explaining in the world would never reduce that little word to unimportance. It would remain for ever glorious, with other words that had been brought to birth and baptised by heroism that would never die though a million heroes died. Words. Names. Tobruk. Bataan. Corregidor. Dunkirk. And another name, that was only now stirring before its birth to glory, Stalingrad. Names that would be spoken for generations with pride and tears.

Today Tobruk had fallen and the tears of half the world brought no relief to Mary Handley, who dared not cry.

Cressida, suffering as a born comforter who is powerless to comfort, stood outside the doors of Brede with the dogs, waiting for John Greenacre, who had just telephoned to ask if he might come up. The dogs watched her, tense with love and anxiety about their walk. Their fixed gaze drew her eyes.

When John arrives there'll be three of them, she thought, and suddenly hated herself. Poor John. And poor Mary. And I'm no use to either of them, no use to Mary. How can I stand here and – just think about going for a walk?

But the answer was in the eyes of the dogs. Live in the present. Deal with every moment as it comes. Life would disintegrate if tragedy was given the power to control the little ordinary happenings of the day. For the dogs nothing mattered except the immediate question of whether or not they were to get their walk. Well, it wasn't safe to forget such little questions. It wasn't safe to let life become one enormous, unanswerable question.

Cressida's attention was distracted from the dogs by the crackle of gravel under the tyres of a bicycle. The freckled face of Tommy Pinhorn bobbed towards her, like a hot red moon. Cressida's heart thudded once, so that it nearly choked her. She could not take her eyes from the telegram in Tommy Pinhorn's grimy hand.

The boy dismounted and grinned vaguely at her. He held out the telegram and Cressida watched her own hand take it as if it was the most unimportant action in the world. Her other hand extracted sixpence from her trouser pocket and gave it to Tommy Pinhorn, who grinned again, less vaguely, and remounted his bicycle.

'Thur'll orlways be ur' Ningland,' he sang cheerfully as he vanished down the drive.

I've got to look at it, Cressida informed herself, I've got to take it to Mary.

For several seconds the sight of her own name on the envelope meant nothing to her. Telegrams, today, must be for Mary, whose husband was in Tobruk. But the name on the envelope was written in large round letters and could not in any way be thought to look like Handley.

Cressida opened the envelope and read the message.

'Thursday and Friday nights please am bringing Rilla if no answer.'

No address, so no answer was possible. Poor old Dolphin. Just an ordinary telegram after all. One of the thousand ordinary ones that arrived with the heart-stopping image of death in their wake. Dolphin coming for two nights. Forty-eight hours' leave. Bringing Rilla.

Cressida crumpled the telegram in her hand and noticed John Greenacre, standing with the dogs in the drive. She had been right, she saw, about the look in his eyes. She said, 'Hullo,' in a normal manner, and John started trying to look less like the dogs.

'Is it,' he began, 'I hope – you haven't had bad news – or anything, that telegram –'

Cressida smiled. 'It was my brother,' she said, 'he wants to come down for two nights on Thursday. I'm glad you'll meet.'

Funny, she thought, how one takes it for granted that they will. John, in a fortnight, seemed to have become as much an inmate of the house as if he actually lived there.

'Well, I'm afraid we won't,' John said, 'I'm off tomorrow. I came to tell you.'

'Oh, John, how sudden,' Cressida said, thinking, what a futile remark. I wonder if I'll ever grow out of saying things to fill up pauses. 'Is it just another move, or what?'

'What,' John said. 'I'm crashing in on the war at last.'

By this time they were walking across the daisies on the lawn.

'You're lucky,' Cressida said. 'But I shall miss you.'

John did not seem to be going to answer this remark. He walked on, looking firmly in front of him.

'I suppose I don't ask where,' Cressida said after a little, knowing that he was in the condition of needing to be made to talk.

'Actually I don't know,' John said, obviously relieved to have something handed to him to say. 'It seems – pretty odd, to be teed up and not know what for. I mean, it'll be a bit of a drop if I land up in Poona and play tennis of an evening. But I suppose we're piling up in front of Rommel, if we get there in time. Looks a bit grim, doesn't it?'

'Yes,' Cressida said, 'it does. Are you getting any leave?' she added, so that the grimness of the situation should not take charge.

'I'm going home tonight. It's – going to be a bit grim' – John's adjectives were apt to run in packs – 'for my mother, you know. I thought – if I didn't tell her it might be simpler. D'you think so, or –?'

'I think I should tell her,' Cressida said. 'I think it'll be better afterwards, even if it's worse at the time. That's what I'd feel anyway.'

Oh, John, she thought, John. A little boy of six in a tank, with shells bursting . . . a child running about on the deck of a ship while an aeroplane screamed out of the clouds and was gone before the bombs had time to burst. . . .

Cressida shook herself. He's six, she told herself firmly. This isn't anything to do with me. But this other John had a mother too, although he was six foot tall and had fallen in love twice within as many months.

'I wish we were like cats,' she said as lightly as possible, 'and didn't recognise our young when they grew up.'

John laughed, as intended, and the atmosphere was lightened.

'It'd simplify things a lot,' he said, and went on to give Cressida a lively description of the way his C.O. had fussed round that morning, looking at every bootlace and toothbrush. 'Bit hen-like, but he's a good old sausage,' he ended.

The old sausage, Cressida knew, was a Major of about thirty. She was once more reminded of the fact that she had put her hair 'up' before this boy could walk. It was odd that age should cease to mean anything as soon as one was old enough to meet grown-up people who hadn't been born when one had been already a grown-up. I wonder, she thought, if it's the same when you've seen them grow? She tried to imagine herself feeling younger than her own son. It wasn't easy, but even the idea was full of a pleasure too enchanting to grasp. It would be like being in love without any of the fuss, she thought, and suddenly could hardly wait for the years to pass.

They had reached the woods by this time. The mossy ground was wet and cool, and the trees cast black shadows across the clean bright green of new bracken.

John said suddenly, 'I'm glad I came today. It'll be something to remember.'

This is beauty to remember . . . Tori, standing out there in the sun and saying that . . . to remember . . . .

Everyone was catching at things to remember. The war made beauty painfully precious. It gave tremendous importance to simple things like bracken and a view of an old house. This extra appreciation was, in a way, another of the cruelties of war, as if beauty was recognised only when it was almost too late.

'Someone else – said something like that a little time ago,' Cressida said. 'I sometimes wonder if – going away and all that is the price we're made to pay for being allowed to – to see, instead of merely looking.'

John did not answer for a little while. Then he said slowly, 'I see what you mean. You could walk here every day and never really see the trees. Or at least, I could, I suppose! You – you must have seen them before,' he ended in a rush.

Cressida smiled. 'Yes,' she said, 'I have, but – but I had to learn to, you know! That sounds fearfully heavy. Learning to see. Learning to listen. The maddening things people say when they want to rub in how much more they get out of life than you do! I remember being mad with rage when I'd been thrilled at a concert and was trying to tell my music teacher about it. She said, "Ah, yes, child, but you must wait till you've learned to listen!" I could have wrung her neck, but she was dead right, of course.'

John laughed. 'I know,' he said, 'I've always wanted to be left to enjoy myself my own way without any bother with understanding! But I think I've begun to see there's something in it.'

'You have to find it out for yourself,' Cressida said. 'I'm certain that's the only way. A lot of so-called teachers don't appear to realise this at all. They just drive impersonal facts into you and give you bad marks if you're bored! Of course one doesn't think of it at the time, but if you look back at school you'll probably see which of the teachers taught you anything. I don't remember who said it, but I always remember the words "some teach, some teach you to teach yourself, and some just keep order".'

John laughed again. 'By Gad, yes!' he said. 'I'll never forget our maths master. Lots of chaps thought he was a bit crazy, but he had what it takes. He used to be so excited over the sums he was explaining that it felt as if he'd just discovered how to do them himself for the first time. God knows how he kept it up year after year. Amazing chap. I can't remember being half as interested in any other class. I used to get the feeling I was racing him to the answer and had quite a chance of winning. I didn't realise all that at the time, of course, but it made me keen on maths all right!'

'You were lucky,' Cressida said, 'to have enthusiasm handed out like that. I can't remember loving anything at school. The whole episode was just a series of black dots on the holidays!'

They turned out of the woods and took the road back through the village. They passed the little church with its glassless windows and the bomb crater among the tombstones. John wondered what it would be like to have bombs smacking all round continually, instead of just dropping at night in the distance, what it would feel like to be the bombs' objective instead of just being missed by chance shots. Cressida was thinking much the same thing. In a few weeks, her thoughts ran, he may be living among bombs and shells, and we shall just walk past the craters in the fields without looking at them. We shall stop talking about our bombs, and he may be blown to pieces by one.

For some reason neither could find any real drama in their thoughts. Both were surprised, and even a little shocked, because their thoughts produced no emotion.

John's switched easily to another subject, and this time there was no lack of emotion.

Cressida Chance is the most beautiful person I've ever seen, he thought, and if I'm knocked off it will have been worth being alive just to have this walk.

I'm safe because John's only six, Cressida thought. I'm selfish and safe, and it's someone else's mother who's got to get through embarkation leave.

They arrived at the lovely gates of Brede Manor. John stood still.

'I won't come in,' he said.

Cressida turned to him. 'All right,' she said.

Thank God, John thought, she isn't saying, oh, do!

'I'd like to tell you,' he went on aloud, 'that – that you're the most lovely person I know and I – well, I love you. Good-bye, Cressida.'

Suddenly looking taller and very much older, he bent and kissed her, as naturally as a child, and almost with a child's emotionless ease.

'Good-bye, John,' Cressida said, 'bless you.'

He marched away without looking back. Cressida thought how odd it was that she had never noticed before how enormously broad his shoulders were. She turned in at the gates. She did not think about her feelings but she knew she was happy, in a tired, impersonal sort of way, as if she had finished a job successfully and was now free of responsibility for it.

John dug his hands into his scratchy pockets and marched on. He looked as if he was quite prepared to march into battle like that, with no protection except the joy of living which was making his heart light.

Halfway up the drive of Brede, Cressida increased her speed. But she did not escape the vision of Tori, very slight and delicate-looking, so thin and agile he might have been made of wire. 'This is beauty to remember . . .'

And then, on the doorstep of Brede, as always, the ghost of Charles Valery met her. Limping down the steps, talking about repairs to the house. . . .

CHAPTER NINETEEN

On his fourteenth day in the lifeboat Charles Valery saw smoke on the horizon. He had opened his eyes after one of the short snatches of unconsciousness which had begun to take the place of real sleep. It was an hour after sunrise and the sky was clear and pale, so that the little smear of smoke stood out like a thumb-mark above the horizon. For several minutes Charles did not take in what it meant. He no longer expected his eyes to encounter anything but washes of sea and sky, and so his mind did not immediately register the sight of anything else. His first thought, as always for the last week, was water. The water was not finished, but Charles had to make an increasingly strong effort to drink less every time he was thirsty. He no longer took the smallest interest in food. And the charts had begun to frighten him. It was better not to know how many sea miles lay on every side before land could appear.

On this fourteenth morning his eyes dropped from the smoke smear to the water-canister before he was sufficiently awake to know what he had seen.

He told himself that he must wait till it was hotter, and removed his eyes from the water-tin. Then it occurred to him that he had seen something different from the simple colour effects of every other morning. Without moving his head he raised his eyes to the horizon once more.

Very like smoke, that little smear, he thought. Well, there wouldn't be any smoke on a picture of sea and sky. Far from being a traffic lane, the Atlantic was just a colour scheme, and there was no place for smoke on it. Charles began to exercise his fingers, noticing that the burns were almost healed, though his hands looked like wrinkled cardboard still, and felt like it too, he decided. The next thing, he knew, was to wait for the pain in his knee to start. When that happened he would stand up at once, before it became too difficult to move. There was no need to hurry. He had the whole day to sit and stand alternately, before he would be tired enough to get another blank in sleep.

A little breeze sprang up and rapidly strengthened into a fairly brisk wind. Charles's eyes returned to the water-canister, but today something drew them to another tin object, close to the water-container. He had noticed it before, of course. It was a smoke-float. No use because it did not hold water. Just some patent kind of smoke generator, several of them stacked in a neat row.

Suddenly the message of his eyes reacted on Charles's brain. Smoke. Smoke!

He scrambled to his feet. With shaking hands he began to unfasten the tin generator. Oh, God, what a fool, what a damned idiot! Wasting time when there was smoke – *smoke* on the horizon!

Charles could scarcely read the few printed words on the lid of the generator, beneath a protective covering of sticky varnish. Something about a striker . . . quite simple . . . lid was stiff, but it came off and there was the striker, neatly stuck down with surgical plaster. . . .

The fuse was dry. The generator was going to function. It worked perfectly. A column of astonishingly thick, black smoke curled before Charles's unbelieving eyes. God, what a cloud. Must be visible for miles.

He tried to peer through or round it to the other smoke wisp. Now and again he caught a glimpse of it, like a feather stuck into the sea. It looked smaller now, or perhaps that was just nerves. It would look small compared with the enormous cloud over his own boat.

Charles did not know that the smoke on the horizon was a hundred times thicker and covered a much larger area than the cloud he had released. The ship whose funnels belched that smoke was hull down by now. But the cloud Charles had unloosed like a genie from a bottle grew every second more dense and climbed indefatigably into the sky.

The wind began to play with it, scattering it so that it covered an even larger expanse of the empty sky.

But as it grew larger, so it became thinner. The wind, with mischievous energy, dissolved the head of the column into a mist so thin that it faded into the sky's pale colour. At its foot a gap appeared, between the smoke and the container. The genie was free of his bottle. An area of sea grew clear above what was now just an empty tin. The escaped genie became just a wisp of dirty air. The wind swept it away as if it had been an offending cobweb on a clean, blue wall. Charles's eyes strained towards the horizon. The horizon was a clear, hard line, clean and sharp, entirely free from even a suggestion of smoke.

Charles put his thin, dry hands over his aching eyes. He sat down, suddenly too exhausted to stand. For the first time since he had awakened in the boat he felt thoroughly ill.

When at last he raised his head, his eyes fell upon the three remaining smoke generators in their neat holders. To his own ears the sound he made was like the attempt of an animal to laugh like a man. Without another glance at those tormenting, useless signals, he seized the water-tin and took a long, satisfying drink. The tin was very light when he put it down.

The day's routine proceeded. The undeviating revolution of the earth presented in due course each appropriate part of its surface to the beams of the indifferent sun. The expanse of the Atlantic was carried through warmth back to shadow, unaffected by the antics of the million atoms scattered by humanity upon its shifting waters. Night came in the area of Charles's consciousness as fourteen other nights had come, with a magnificently decorative display lavishly provided by the stars.

Half a dozen times Charles started out of sleep, shaking with nightmare. The nightmare was the same every time. A little feather that appeared one moment on an empty sky and was gone the next.

CHAPTER TWENTY

Cressida drove Beltane once more in the direction of Chilbury. For three miles she tried to school herself into the state of detached hospitality which she hoped would help her to deal with the presence of Rilla Hamar. She had met Rilla several times in London, and each time the presence of the singer had had the same effect upon her. It had made her feel about twice lifesize.

Rilla Hamar had that effect upon most people. It was not because of her own smallness, nor could it be ascribed to any physical fact. Rilla Hamar's measurements were probably what would be classified as standard size. But somehow she appeared so complete, so compact, that she made other women look either too big or else all unfinished ends. Perhaps this was partly due to a trick she had of never keeping her eyes still, so that they darted over the figure of anyone she looked at in little quick jerks, as if the other person was too large to be seen in one piece.

Cressida tried to imagine Rilla at Brede and failed. Rilla Hamar's background was vivid and alive, but it was not a background of the country. She always looked, Cressida thought, as if she was a portrait of herself, painted against a sort of

Surrealist vision of London. There were always lights in the picture. She created for herself an aura of continual light, but the light of the sun did not form any part of this nimbus. Theatre lights of all kinds naturally came into it, but not only these. There were visions of lighted cars, of silver fox furs glittering under streetlamps, of silvered shafts of rain shining outside the windows of a limousine, of glowing lighted door-ways, of the flash of plate glass as it was snatched aside to allow her to pass, and of the light from a shaded lamp falling softly on her shining head.

Cressida scratched Beltane's broad back with the end of her whip and the old horse's skin quivered with appreciation. He stamped along at a great rate, the ring of his hoofs suggesting the vigour of a young animal.

Chilbury looked a little drab that morning. There was no sun and the road was dusty. Most of the cottages needed paint, and the inn sign was very chipped and faded. It seemed to Cressida, who knew she was thoroughly over-sensitive this morning, that the whole village had retreated nervously before the arrival of the woman for whose presence it was so inadequate a setting.

Oh Lord, Cressida thought, if I'm like this already, I'll break up when she gets here.

She got down from her high seat in the dog-cart and gave Beltane an unnecessarily hearty slap of affection, of which the vigour seemed to be directed more at herself than at the horse. Rilla Hamar in a dog-cart, she thought.

A cold little breeze rustled through the village. Cressida turned up the collar of her old tweed coat and walked up the road a little, feeling very healthy, and very conscious of her thick, square-toed shoes. Beltane, hitched to a post, fidgeted placidly.

The Wichlesbury taxi scuttled into the village and stopped. Rudolph Standing emerged, looking, as he got out, as if he could never have been inside it. He bent and opened the other door of the car. Rilla Hamar descended on his arm.

I wonder if she's ever got out of a car by herself? Cressida thought, and then, Oh, my God, how beautiful she is.

Rilla Hamar said some perfectly ordinary words and immediately the spell of her lovely voice fell upon Cressida like a caress. For a moment Cressida felt that her own voice would be an intrusion.

Fortunately she managed to overcome her feelings and so conversation was not brought to a standstill. It proceeded, in fact, with some animation, because Rilla Hamar somehow managed to give quite ordinary remarks the glamour and point of good stage dialogue. She was anything but affected or stagey, yet she managed to convey an impression of artistry carried to such a pitch that it became the extreme of simplicity. On the stage, apart from her voice, Rilla was a good actress. In real life she was a brilliant artist who had achieved the supreme art of being natural.

'I'm sorry it's so cold,' Cressida heard herself saying, as if the cold was her own fault entirely.

'It's almost nice after the train,' Rilla said. 'It was so hot, and there were seventeen people in the carriage, which makes one feel so guilty.'

Cressida laughed. 'It's nice to meet someone who doesn't

take crowds as a personal grievance,' she said, realising as she spoke that she was falling rapidly under Rilla's fascination, and feeling already, as Rilla always made her feel, as if she was at least ten years younger than the other woman. The truth being just the opposite, Cressida found it necessary to remind herself frequently that she was not a little girl, gaping at a sophisticated and rather frightening woman of the world.

It was easy enough to think critically about Rilla Hamar when she was not there in the flesh. One could study her, pick her character and appearance to pieces, even hate her for tormenting Dolphin. But once in her presence there was nothing to do but admire her.

Dolphin, in the meantime, had fitted suitcases into the dog-cart and helped Rilla into the front seat. He did the same for Cressida, made the usual remarks and appeared outwardly normal, but Cressida knew that every sentence was a conscious effort, and that he was suffering as much as if Rilla Hamar held his heart in her hands and was wringing the life out of it.

Dolphin climbed into the back seat. His arm lay along the side of the cart, protecting Rilla. The jaunty little feather in her hat blew backwards and touched his cheek, but he did not move so much as an eyelash. Cressida looked at Beltane's ears, but out of the corner of her eye she was very much aware of Rilla's hat, a light-hearted affair of felt so delicate that it looked brittle, a Bond Street sketch of a country hat. Cressida shook back her own hair, blowing freely in the breeze, and felt it must look thoroughly wild.

The drive back to Brede seemed infinitely shorter than the one out. In no time, it seemed, Cressida was turning Beltane through the gates, or rather she was holding the reins with all her strength while the horse hurled himself round the corner. Rilla, with a swift glance from side to side that made the feather in her hat dance like a mad thing, cried out in admiration of the gates.

'Oh, surely,' she said, ' these are most lovely. "The gates of heaven, blown apart by lovers' sighs . . ." I hate people who quote and I apologise, but I'd have had the words on the brain for a week if I hadn't let them go. And, Cressida, I've never seen such gates.'

She knows, Cressida thought. She's got everything. Oh, poor Dolphin.

'They're very famous,' she said, feeling that she could hardly have produced a more banal remark if she had tried.

'Oh, but it's beautiful, so perfectly beautiful,' Rilla went on, as every turn in the drive justified her admiration.

When Beltane stopped at the doors of the house she was silent, but still as eloquent as ever.

Cressida explained the necessity of leaving her to Dolphin while she took the horse to the stables. She did this very firmly and rapidly, so that Dolphin should have no chance of offering to do it for her. Suddenly she could not endure the strain of being a third party any longer.

She drove off thankfully, leaving Dolphin to his fate.

Dolphin followed Rilla into the house. He watched her in the frame of the open doorway. He watched her pause and then walk across the great cool hall to the lovely curve of the staircase that was at once just another background for her delicate, almost unreal elegance. Rilla Hamar wore a suit that could be technically described as being made of tweed, but she gave the impression that she and her clothes were as fragile as china.

'Oh, lovely, lovely,' she murmured to herself, and then, 'I shall be grateful to you always,' she said to Dolphin, 'just for bringing me here.'

As she spoke she turned her head, with the little, quick movement so characteristic of her, and so graceful in spite of its bird-like swiftness. Rudolph Standing looked enormous beside her, and more like a Viking than ever.

'Let's go up,' he said, speaking for the first time since their arrival in the house. His voice had an edge on it that made his words very like an order.

Rilla walked up the curving stairs, touching the wrought-iron rail with her fingers as if she loved the feel of it. Dolphin followed her so closely that he could easily have touched her, but it seemed to him that she moved, as always, in quite another world, quite alone, as if she walked within a glass case whose walls kept her permanently out of the reach of human hands.

He opened the door of the grey room for her and shut it quickly after himself. With a sudden, almost rough movement, he took her in his arms, as violently as if he had really broken through thick glass to reach her.

Cressida, when she returned from the stables, picked up some letters that had come by the second post. There were three for Rilla Hamar and a bill for herself. Three letters, when she had scarcely set foot in the house. Even those letters helped to create the atmosphere Rilla carried about with her.

Their instant arrival seemed to exaggerate Rilla's importance. Other lives, it seemed, hung upon her actions, even an hour could not go by without contact with her.

She must, Cressida thought, live what is known as a full life.

Cressida shuddered mentally at the expression. It called up visions of diaries full of scribbled dates and times, a long succession of engagements and appointments, taxis continually being called, the telephone constantly ringing. . . .

Well, she can have it, Cressida decided, as long as I needn't. In spite of her decision she had to admit that there was something about those visions. It was easy to imagine Rilla's life, easy to visualise her, lovely, fragile, always cool, always a little late, but never flustered, just delicately breathless, always forgiven instantly, no matter who had waited and no matter for how long. She would always find that the best table had been kept for her, that a car was always at every door, that flowers were always about her head and under her feet, at any rate metaphorically, and often actually.

Rilla supplemented these visions by appearing on the staircase, a perfect portrait of herself staying in a country house. She had taken off her hat, which gave her tweed suit a totally different appearance. It had now just the right touch of informality, the *dégagé* elegance of an artistically unfinished sketch. She walked downstairs in the most un-selfconscious manner possible, but there could be no doubt that she had made an entrance beautifully in a beautiful setting.

'Cressida, I'm so enchanted with your house,' she began, 'and I couldn't have imagined a more lovely room. I couldn't bear to leave the flowers –'

Nice of her, Cressida thought sincerely, to notice the flowers when her life is lapped in them.

She picked up Rilla's letters and gave them to her. Rilla glanced at the envelopes and put them down unopened on the nearest table. Her eyes swept the room and she had quite clearly lost interest in her letters, and, in fact, would probably forget them altogether.

As if merely looking could not satisfy her, Rilla moved about the room, occasionally touching things, very carefully, as if she felt they might not be real. She seemed to study even the pattern on the Persian carpet by the fireplace, like someone who wanted to make sure of remembering it for ever.

'I do love staying here,' she said, as if she had been in the house at least a month. 'I love it, Cressida.'

As she spoke she wove another kind of spell about her. Her close examination of the room seemed to have given her possession of it. And yet she preserved a charming appearance of gratitude. She never took anything for granted, although she must, Cressida knew, be almost satiated by the loveliness that was always provided so eagerly for her approval. It was this gift of spontaneous appreciation that was one of the reasons for her instant success in all kinds of company.

Having, as it were, taken possession of the room, Rilla's eyes began on an inventory of Cressida herself. Cressida, quite aware of this, and feeling quite a foot taller and two broader in consequence, could not help being amused by such frank scrutiny, as completely without offence as the gaze of a child.

'You are so like Rudolph,' Rilla said at last. 'So much more than I had remembered.' Her eyes did not leave Cressida's face, but they did not rest upon the whole face, they took in, it seemed, one feature at a time. 'I think if I was your mother,' she went on, 'I should die of conceit! That both should be so beautiful does not seem to be fair!'

Cressida had to laugh. She had also to admit to herself that it was nice to be told one was beautiful by anyone as beautiful as Rilla.

'What isn't fair?' Rudolph Standing had come downstairs and broke into the conversation.

'That your sister should be as beautiful as you are, my sweet,' Rilla said, laughing at him.

Rudolph picked up Rilla's letters, as if they were the only things in the room he could see when he wasn't looking at her.

'You'll forget these,' he said, 'if you don't read them now.'

To Cressida's eyes he looked as though he hated the letters, because they were something of Rilla's that had nothing to do with himself. Actually he was wondering whether Rilla would forget letters from him, when letters were all the contact he could have with her.

'They are unimportant,' Rilla said, but she took the envelopes and opened one of them. She did not read the letter, however, but rustled it back into the envelope and once more let the little pile drop, this time on the sofa.

'Ah, no,' she said, 'I must go out. It is all so lovely I can't wait. Rudolph, you must let me see the garden.'

She darted out of the door as if she was afraid someone would stop her, but not too quickly to leave an impression of herself, framed in the doorway against the background of the lawn outside, poised and lovely, her dark hair shining and her small, pointed face alight, half turned over her shoulder.

Cressida went upstairs without saying anything. She saw her brother pick up Rilla's letters. This time he put them in his pocket and followed her out of the door. Cressida found this simple action very touching. It was a pathetic attempt at possessiveness and seemed to show that there was nothing he would not do, in spite of his jealousy, to save her from the effects of her own vagueness.

Upstairs the Yates baby was crying with great energy and maddening persistence in a room at the end of the corridor. Cressida caught a glimpse of Madge Rimmington-Clarke leading her small boy, aged three, in the direction of the lavatory. This domestic interlude, demonstrating the less romantic side of married life, seemed suddenly sordid after the atmosphere of enchantment Rilla Hamar had carried with her into the garden. Cressida sighed with exasperation.

Love! she thought.

CHAPTER TWENTY-ONE

About six o'clock that evening Dolphin came into the kitchen by himself and found Cressida, as usual, cooking.

'Well, I'm off at last, Musty,' he said lightly.

The use of the old nickname, dug up out of a childish past, made him suddenly a little boy again. Mustard and Cressida. Musty. Years since anyone had even remembered the silly little joke that had seemed a stroke of brilliant wit to the children who had thought of it.

'I guessed it must be that,' Cressida said, not giving way to the sentimental appeal of the nickname. 'One does not ask where,' she added.

'One does not know,' Dolphin said. 'Report at somewhere in England with a suitcase full of short pants and then –' He shrugged his tremendous shoulders.

'Does,' Cressida began uncertainly, 'does Rilla know?'

'No.' It appeared that he would add nothing to the clipped negative. But he went on suddenly, 'I'm not going to pull any soft stuff to –'

'Dolphin, don't be brutal,' Cressida said, not entirely sure whether she meant the brutality was directed at Rilla or at himself.

Dolphin, in the same dilemma, asked sharply, 'How d'you mean, brutal?'

Cressida wrestled with the old problem of thoughts, clear in her mind, which would not allow themselves to be caught by mere words. The brutality of too much self-control . . . leaving unsaid the things that might make memory bearable . . . the damned little words 'if only –' . . . talking about repairs to the house when there was no time. . . .

'Well, it – it'll hurt, terribly, Dolphin. She – you can't leave her without – giving her a chance.' I couldn't have put it less well, she thought.

Dolphin made a bitter little sound. Perhaps it was a laugh that didn't come off.

'A chance!' he said. 'I – there's damn well nothing I haven't already said.'

'But if you just go, there'll always be something you haven't said,' Cressida answered, 'and that's what I mean by being brutal. Or part of it, anyhow.'

I'd better get on a bit, she thought, and said, 'Look here, Dolphin. Now that we are on the subject, tell me one thing. Do you know Rilla loves you, or are you – just hoping?'

'I know,' Dolphin said at once, 'but – Oh Lord, it's no good trying to explain. I suppose I – understand but – I couldn't make anyone else.'

I suppose I understand. Poor, darling Dolphin, he doesn't understand at all. Cressida made another effort and went on.

'Try, Dolphin. It – may help.' He's got to be made to talk, she told herself, partly as an excuse for her own persistence.

Dolphin grunted. 'Well,' he said flatly, 'she says she'd marry me if she loved me less!' He made an unconvincing attempt to laugh at himself and then finished, 'So if that makes sense, there it is.'

'Well, go on,' Cressida said, feeling like a teacher with a hesitating child. She knew that this attitude was the only possible one. As soon as emotion got into a discussion of this kind all hope of clarity would vanish.

Dolphin looked at his sister, and this time his smile was genuine.

'You old robot,' he said, with cheerful affection in his voice for the first time, 'and maybe you're right at that. Well, all right, we'll have it in straight lines with a neat margin. It's like this. Rilla says that she can't marry me because that would be a whole-time job. She's already got one of those. I – even if she did marry me I – naturally I wouldn't expect her to give up singing. I mean, she –'

Dolphin's straight lines were not going too well. Cressida felt he needed help.

'I know,' she said, 'the well-worn theme of career $v.$ home and all that. But Rilla isn't – she hasn't got a career, Dolphin. She's got – well, it's a duty, although that sounds wrong somehow, but it does mean something, especially now. And if she gave it up she wouldn't be the same person.'

'That's it exactly,' Dolphin said gratefully. 'That's what she says. If she didn't sing she'd be only half alive. And if she sings at all it's got to be a full-time affair. She says she won't – land me with half a wife!' He laughed again. He sounded relieved because he had made a sort of joke of it.

Cressida, thankful to have got him started, knew that now there was nothing he might not say. Conversations which were difficult to begin, were even more difficult to stop, once under way.

'She's perfectly right,' she said. 'I hope I'd have the guts to do the same if I had to!'

Dolphin looked slightly astonished.

'That's one way of looking at it,' he remarked gloomily.

'It's the only way I can see,' Cressida went on quickly. 'Dolphin, don't you see what you're doing? Can't you see how brutal you're being?'

'Well I – well, damn it –'

'Yes, you, you poor fish!' Cressida interrupted with energy. 'You're making a tragedy of the whole thing and letting yourself wallow in gloom because she won't give you what you want, when it's you that won't give her what she wants! Oh, my dear, I'm not being unsympathetic, but I've got to make you see.'

'For God's sake go on then,' Dolphin said. 'I couldn't see less than I do now.'

'Rilla loves you, Dolphin. She loves you so much that she won't marry you because she can't give up her whole life to you. She can't give you something that isn't hers. She matters too much to too many people to be able to do what she likes with her life. She's clear-minded enough to know that and to know that it isn't just a question of personal satisfaction for her. It involves far more than that. To do her job properly she's got to be herself and know herself utterly. She's got to be one complete person. So she won't make a hash of your life and hers by trying to be two people at once. But that doesn't mean you aren't part of her life. You probably are, Dolphin. I think she probably needs you as much as she's ever likely to need anything. She – she's human, my dear, as well as that bit extra that makes her different, that puts her on a different plane. She's a woman as well as an artist, and it's the woman that keeps the artist alive. As a woman she's in love with you, and as an artist she's in love with all life. That's why she won't marry you. She won't make a promise she knows she can't keep, that it would be wrong for her to keep! Oh, I know all the stuff about artists not being tied by rules and so on, it's just used as an excuse most of the time, but there is truth in it, all the same. Just because a lot of scrubby people who paint, or write, or something, have to call themselves untrammelled artists who mustn't have their impulses frustrated, it doesn't mean that there aren't real people, real artists, who really can't be held down by rules that were made because ordinary society is feeble enough to need them. Rilla's not just a woman with a lovely voice. She might have as good a voice and be just a good singer. It's her personality, her under-standing, her love of life that make her an artist. And to love life you've got to understand it. That includes understanding love, and you can't understand love by yourself!'

Cressida paused, slightly exhausted by her own eloquence. Dolphin said nothing at all, but his silence was not unappre-ciative. After a little Cressida went on.

'Rilla wants you, Dolphin. If you hold out on her because she won't give you what isn't hers, her life will never be complete. Now do you see?'

Dolphin straightened his shoulders. He looked as if he had just awakened from sleep, and was bewildered by the daylight. Like a man who clings to the known when faced with the unknown, he said, 'But I – Cres. I can't be – just one of the many. I – couldn't stick it, I – She's never alone, never! And if I –'

'Dolphin, don't be a fool!' Cressida snapped at him. 'If Rilla loves you, it's you that'll always matter. If there are all those others, they won't. I said Rilla was in love with all life. Well, she is. She's almost in love with the chairs in this house! She can't help it if some of the things she loves are human. But that won't mean she can't love one person more than anything else, and permanently. And if that person is you, you'll have everything, even if she has a dozen lovers. If it isn't –' Cressida waved her hands, as if words failed. 'Well, it's up to you, Dolphin,' she added, 'and – if it's any comfort to you, I can't imagine you being a failure!'

For a few seconds her affection for her brother was startlingly obvious. It retired, however, beneath the comfortable mantle of sisterliness, before the display became embarrassing.

'I won't say any more till my immoral advice has sunk in,' she said lightly. 'Where is Rilla, by the way?'

'She went up to have a bath,' Dolphin said.

His commonplace words seemed to refer to a time so long past that he could scarcely remember it. He left the kitchen, looking a little dazed.

Later that evening, when the whole party was collected at dinner, he still looked dazed. His condition had spread to include Rilla so that, although they both spoke when spoken to, they seemed to be alone together. Cressida, whose perception, though clothed in the blandest unconcern, missed nothing, noticed the difference in her brother's whole appearance. She decided that no one else was likely to observe this, because his efforts to behave naturally were quite successful. But Cressida realised that, though he and Rilla did not exchange a single remark, for neither of them was there anyone else in sight.

Well, she thought, I seem to have done something. Suddenly her own loneliness rose up so vividly that it almost choked her, with the result that she became extremely lively and chattered as brightly as if she had not a single care in the world.

CHAPTER TWENTY-TWO

There was no one in the house upon whom the presence of Rilla Hamar did not work some kind of a spell during the two days of her visit. Miss Ambleside, who had stayed twice as long, and talked more than twice as much, came and went leaving nothing behind her except a vague relief because it was no longer necessary to try and live up to the social atmosphere she had encased herself in so thoroughly that even meals in the kitchen had begun to be occasions when one had to make conversation, instead of merely talking at will.

The Yates never got over the fact that they had stayed in the same house as the famous Rilla Hamar, that she had not only dined at the same table twice, but had passed the marmalade at breakfast, which constituted a far more intimate contact.

The Rimmington-Clarkes were less overawed and for that reason less comfortable in Rilla's presence. Miss Hamar, they felt, was, after all, only an ordinary young woman who happened to be able to sing. It was quite easy to talk to her but, for some unaccountable reason, anything one said sounded instantly pointless. Most of the people who made one feel foolish were by all means to be avoided, but Rilla

Hamar's attraction seemed, perversely, to increase with the increasing sense of one's own inadequacy. One felt a fool, and liked it, Jim Rimmington-Clarke said privately to his wife, making, for him, an unusually apt remark. But in spite of this odd liking, he and his wife would have been more comfortable if they had merely sat and gaped as the Yates did, from an unbridgeable distance.

Mary Handley, whose fate it was to be either bored or shy with other women, fell instantly under Rilla's spell, with almost the abandon of a schoolgirl in the throes of a crush.

On the second evening of her visit, Rilla, on the way to her room, was summoned by the voice of Cressida's son, who was in bed with his door open, listening intently for her passing.

'Miss Hamar,' she heard in the little boy's clear, precise voice, 'will you come and see me for a minute, please?'

During the three or four seconds it took her to cross the room to his bed she was treated to his lovely smile.

' My mother says,' he said at last, 'that you are one of the best singers in the world.'

The statement did not seem to require an answer, and Rilla wisely made none.

'So I should love it if you would sing to me,' John ended, and produced a second edition of the smile.

Rilla, who had received with perfect calm similar requests from more people than she could ever remember, became suddenly a little girl, flattered and a little shy because another child admired her. She said nothing but began at once to sing a little gentle song in German, as if she knew instinctively that strange words would enhance the effect of the music on the little boy. At the end of the song John made no sound. He lay absolutely still, the expression on his little pointed face as intent as if he was still listening. Rilla began another song, in English this time.

'There is a lady, sweet and kind . . .'

By the time the song was over Rilla could see John's lips moving as if he repeated the words to himself.

'I love that,' he said, 'and I can sing it too. My mother does, you know.'

'Does she?' Rilla said. 'Well, I sang it because it reminds me of your mother.'

'Oh, yes,' John said, 'that's what I think. Will you sing it again, please?'

Rilla went over to the window and sang it again. This time her whole heart was in the song and there were tears in her eyes at the end. The little boy did not ask for any more. Rilla could see that his tranquillity would become sleep in another moment. She went back to his bedside.

'Would you mind if I kissed you goodnight?' she asked, as politely as if she had been a child asking a favour of a grown-up.

John thought for a moment without stirring.

Then he said, 'I'd like you to.'

As she bent over him he put out one hand and very gently touched her hair. His gesture, limp and a little vague with sleep, was infinitely touching. Rilla found it was all she could do to kiss him with circumspection and without the emotion she knew he would resent.

'Most people,' John murmured sleepily, 'don't ask, you know. And then I hate them kissing me.'

Rilla's laugh was irresistible. John smiled again and was in the next moment asleep.

Outside in the passage Cressida was waiting.

'I was listening,' she said. 'I'm glad one of us has managed to make you sing! John'll never forget it.'

Rilla suddenly took hold of Cressida's arm, as if she needed to lean on something.

'He's so adorable,' she said. A slight break in her voice made her, for once, young and vulnerable. She went with Cressida into her room.

'Sometimes,' she began again, in the queerly young voice Cressida had never heard before, 'sometimes I almost wish I – I hadn't got a voice!'

Cressida, suddenly aware of the fact that she felt older and more sure of herself than ever before in Rilla's presence, put her arm round the other's shoulders.

In an instant Rilla was clinging to her, like a child to its mother.

'Oh, I love him so,' she said brokenly. 'Oh, Cressida, I love him so. I don't want – anything else. I want to marry him and – and have children and – and –'

She was crying now so that Cressida could not hear any words. Cressida's shyness, her sense of inadequacy and clumsiness left her at once. The poised, charming woman Rilla Hamar's voice had created had become a heartbroken girl, in love for the first time in her life. That lovely woman would return. She would once more enclose Rilla in a glass case, she would once more walk aloof, completely in control of herself. But for the moment human emotion made Rilla Hamar as helpless as a child.

Cressida heard herself saying the foolish, sentimental words which in cold blood would have made her blush, but which seemed, at the moment, to be the only possible things to say.

Finally, sincerity having rescued her words from the abyss of banality, Cressida said, 'This – this had to happen, Rilla. You – you'd never have been able to sing as you will now if – it hadn't happened like this.'

Rilla's tears became a relief instead of an anguish. Cressida realised thankfully that, banal or not, she had managed to say more or less the right things. Emotion, she thought, certainly helps one to get away with anything. I never thought I could be so patronising, and to Rilla of all people.

Rilla became coherent and said, still a little unsteadily, but with an attempt at a smile, 'How do you know all this, Cressida?'

Cressida said nothing. She could think of no reasonable answer to that question. She could not even answer it to herself. It was easy to give advice and comfort, she thought. It had been quite easy to tell Dolphin what to do, and quite easy to comfort Rilla, much easier than trying to decide what to do oneself. Perhaps that was why everyone was so ready to interfere with other people's worries. Much less trouble than dealing with one's own. Perhaps interference was just a play for retaliation, a cry for help. Well do I, Cressida thought, really want someone to tell me what to do with my life?

All the time she was gently stroking Rilla's head. It still seemed to her incredible that that head should be buried on her own shoulder, that Rilla Hamar, whose arrival had been unnerving, to say the least of it, should have abandoned herself to the comfort of Cressida's hands.

'Darling,' Rilla said at last, lifting her head, 'I'm sorry I've been such a mess, but –' she made a little gesture which somehow managed to convey everything she had not said. 'You could never know,' she went on, 'I could never begin to tell you how – how wonderful you've been. Oh, Cressida, if we – ever make anything of our lives it'll be – because of you!'

'That,' Cressida said, 'is just one of those remarks one laughs off but' – she paused, and added in a less flippant tone – 'but is very pleased to have made to one.'

Rilla smiled. 'I know now,' she said, 'what Rudolph means when he says you always know the answer.'

After Rilla had gone, Cressida still stood in her room without moving.

So I always know the answer, she thought. Well, they don't even know the question this time.

CHAPTER TWENTY-THREE

Two days after the appearance of smoke on the horizon, Charles Valery's boat was spotted by a patrolling aircraft which signalled his whereabouts to the nearest convoy. Within an hour Charles was picked up by a corvette. It was all as simple as that, but it had been a long time coming. And the last hour had been the longest, the hour that had elapsed between the time of the aircraft's disappearance and the first sign of the ship. During that hour Charles had lived mentally through days and weeks of thirst. The vanishing of the aeroplane had seemed to him more terrible than the vanishing of the smoke. Smoke might be an hallucination, but an aeroplane must have a man in it. And if a man could come and go without seeing him –

In that last hour Charles decided that of all the activities of human beings, thought was the most futile. If he was now to die slowly, of a madness of thirst, what good had it done him or anyone to sit in a small boat in the middle of the Atlantic for uncounted days and nights trying to evolve theories for the reorganisation of the world? If the greatest idea of all time were to dawn in his brain now it would not fill the water beakers. An idea for the salvation of humanity would not save him from a tormenting death.

Charles eyed the sea over the boat's side. It would have been better to go over with Harcourt after all. Well, it wasn't too late for that. Death was the one thing it was never too late for. The greatest thinkers of the world had succumbed to death in the end, in spite of their tremendous ideas.

Ideas. Everyone was full of ideas, and what good did any of them do? For centuries the world had been cluttered with men with ideas, and with the books of men who had committed their ideas to paper and were now uselessly dead. It was true that the books of these dead men were read by the living, and the living continued to evolve theories and to fill the world with more books, which would, in their turn, be studied, perhaps admired, perhaps agreed with, and then –

Well, and then what? What had all these centuries of thought and ideas led to but the most atrocious, the most insane and appalling war that any man's mind could conceive of? After centuries of civilisation war had merely grown more uncivilised, more abominable, larger and more horrible, until it had reached the proportions of a world nightmare with potentialities for evil beyond the bounds of imagination. War was no longer a struggle between nations, it was a disease of humanity, an irruption of accumulated evil that had increased in power with every outbreak.

For the disease of war there seemed to be no analogy. It was not to be understood by comparing it with physical disease. The science of medicine, starting from less than scratch, had proceeded with unwearying perseverence until it had acquired a measure of control over the evil of physical disease. But the growth of knowledge, the advance of civilisation, had gained no such control over the evil of war. With every outbreak of physical illness, medical science gained in knowledge and power. But with every outbreak of war, evil and horror were the gainers. Doctors of medicine became richer, mentally at least, in relation to the measure of their success in the healing art. But success in war did not mean an increase in the riches of a nation. Victory demanded a price which retarded the development of a nation's wellbeing only slightly less than defeat. With every success the Germans were weakening themselves, acquiring new enemies, not only outside their boundaries but within them. If they were to gain the world they would gain nothing but an enormous mass of hatred, which would strain their physical force to breaking-point. For any nation to conquer the world would be the end of all hope of peace. And since complete conquest was not the end of war, it must follow that there was no end.

Except annihilation. If that was the answer it was certainly not worth continuing with the struggle against death. The dream of world-membership seemed to have faded into no more than the memory of an idea that had sounded good once.

And it was not even a new idea. Citizenship had been preached and lectured about for years. World-citizenship had begun to take the place of the lesser idea, but it was still just a subject for lectures, still something people would read about and hear spoken of, and perhaps discuss. And then forget about in a new enthusiasm for the point of view of one side or another in the latest quarrel between men or nations.

At this point Charles closed his eyes and allowed inertia to creep over his senses.

In this state of physical and mental exhaustion he allowed himself to be assisted into the corvette's lifeboat, and from it on board the ship. He was put in a bunk and given hot drinks. Habit made him utter intelligible thanks, but to his mind even comfort meant very little.

The rest of the voyage proceeded uneventfully. The friendliness of the ship's officers made no impression on Charles's mind. Their casual cheerfulness seemed to shut him away from them more thoroughly than if they had spoken a foreign language. To them Charles was just another poor devil hooked out of the sea, more silent than most perhaps, and much less anxious to retail his adventures than some.

After five days the convoy put into port at dawn of a day that was already quiet and heavy with the promise of coming heat. Charles stood on the deck of the little ship, wearing a selection of borrowed clothes that did not fit him, and looked at England. His only emotion was a mild surprise at his lack of the feelings proper to such a moment.

England changed from a grey outline to a grey collection of unattractive sheds and houses divided from the ship by a strip of oily water with cabbage stalks floating in it. Only the gulls were beautiful, and even they betrayed the swift beauty of their flight by indulging in raucous, greedy screeching, altogether out of keeping with their majestic loveliness in the air.

Charles parted from the ship's company in an apparently normal manner, with all the hand-shaking and gratitude suitable to the occasion. He spent three days in a hospital, bought himself some clothes and necessities, and listened to the wireless. He left the hospital, outwardly a thin, tired-looking man with badly scarred hands, but otherwise in no way remarkable. But as he waited on the dusty platform of a railway-station for a train to take him home, surrounded by dozens of other men and women of his own country, he knew that he was as much alone as if he had landed naked from the sea on a desert island.

CHAPTER TWENTY-FOUR

Cressida left Beltane noisily munching in his stable and began the walk back to the house. She had returned from Wichlesbury in the late summer dusk, after leaving Rilla and Dolphin there to catch the night train to London, chosen because it would be cooler than travelling by day. Cressida had driven them into the town and dined with them at an hotel. All three had managed for an hour or so to act the parts of people dining at an hotel for no particular reason. Cressida was tired. It was very tiring to talk in public to someone too intimate to make small talk anything but a futile waste of time. It was tiring to talk against a silence that might admit the shadow of fate. It was also tiring to be the third party when love was already being tortured by the hours that hurried towards parting.

Cressida could still hear Rilla's lovely voice, still see her exquisite head, and her face as composed as if she was merely under the discipline of perfect stage acting. Dolphin was less of an actor, and he had not achieved Rilla's poise. And beside his love another preoccupation had begun to show in his eyes. He already had the look Cressida had sometimes seen before on the faces of men on the verge of departure to war, the look of a man ceaselessly aware that he was going into battle with the responsibility for other men's lives in his hands. Cressida knew that her brother's heart was empty of everything but the anguish of leaving Rilla, but his mind was full of details about men's dinners and billets, and whether everything would go as planned, and whether his orders had been comprehensive and correctly carried out. In that he was lucky. To be obliged to think continually sufficiently far ahead to ensure being ready for whatever happened before it happened, meant that the actual moment lost a little of its power to hurt.

At last she had said goodbye with the elaborate unconcern that seemed to produce itself when required, in spite of all misgivings. The twelve miles home had seemed very long, even with the horse eager to reach his stable.

Cressida watched the searchlights on her way to the house. Although they were now as familiar as the stars, she never failed to succumb to their fascination. Tonight the display was more lavish than ever. The great bars of light, waving in an apparently haphazard manner, met and crossed and swept apart again, making a series of swift, clear-cut designs, snatched away too soon to be appreciated, and leaving the sudden darkness deeper. At one moment the whole sky was covered with a lattice of light, in the next a single beam, so close that its blue brilliance hurt the eyes, swept the face of the house, making it leap from the night like a film thrown on a screen. The supreme effect was achieved when a tiny aeroplane, glittering like a toy on a Christmas tree, was magically caught by three lights and followed in silence and with relentless steadiness across the sky, until darkness suddenly wiped off the whole spectacle, leaving the blinking stars in command of the night.

Cressida turned into the house. There was no light in the hall because of the black-out, and the house seemed to be supernaturally silent. Cressida, feeling, as always since lights had become criminal, like a burglar, crept into the house with her torch in her hand. Its beam fell upon a little pile of letters on the hall table. Cressida flicked them over without much interest. Two envelopes at the bottom of the pile slipped apart and lay side by side in the light from the torch. For a moment the writing on the envelopes danced madly, so that it was almost unintelligible. Cressida put down the torch with a little rattle which sounded very loud. She remembered to shut the doors behind her before she switched on the lights. She went back to the table. The two letters still lay there. Cressida stared at them without moving for several seconds. She noticed that her torch was still on, where it stood on the table, beside those letters. She switched off and put it down again. She knew she was doing this as slowly as possible. At last there was nothing to do but pick up the letters. One was addressed in Tori's rather wild but strangely beautiful handwriting. The other was from Charles.

This, Cressida thought, doesn't happen in real life. Her hands ached with weakness.

In a sudden panic she picked up both envelopes and slit them open quickly. She held up the first sheet of paper her fingers managed to unfold.

'If I do not return on Tuesday,' she read, 'you must know that I am grateful for every moment of my life because I love you.'

The words were scrawled in pencil, evidently in a hurry.

There was nothing more, no beginning to the letter, and no signature.

Cressida stared at the few words until her eyes ached. She knew that they had been scribbled down under great emotional stress. She could not have explained how she knew, but she was instantly certain that Tori had been in danger. . . .

But he was in danger all the time . . . the moment he left England . . . this must have been worse danger, something – something must have made him write. He must have written because he could not help himself, because some chance of getting a letter to her had been irresistible. Tori never took risks, except with his own life. But he had taken the risk of sending her a letter. For one moment, for the time it took to scrawl those words . . . .

'If I do not return on Tuesday . . .' '. . . on Tuesday . . .' Casual, as if it referred to a weekend's absence . . . Tori being careful, even when it was his own death he might not return from. . . .

Oh, God, oh, *God*. . . . Cressida could not get any nearer to coherent prayer than that.

His death. Her thoughts had produced the word she would not face. On Tuesday . . . today was Thursday. . . .

'. . . grateful for every moment of my life . . .' For every moment, when there must have been moments, even then perhaps he could see them coming . . . he might be grateful only for . . . only for death. . . .

Death. Tori. Tori who was so alive that in a crowd of a hundred people he would be the one who stood out . . . Tori, who was so alive that Cressida could still see him standing in the middle of the lawns, still see his fragile little figure, so alive . . . 'beauty to remember . . .' 'a picture that I can see always . . .'

Tori. Tuesday . . . Thursday . . . a letter from Charles . . . from *Charles*. . . .

Read it, you fool, she told herself. Do something, anything . . . read the letter from Charles. . . .

She did so.

'. . . I'm in England . . . a job . . . Brede tomorrow . . .' Another little, short, casual letter, saying so little and meaning . . . Meaning? Meaning everything. . . . '. . . to Brede tomorrow . . .'

Tomorrow.

As if no drama was to be spared her that night the grandfather clock behind her struck at that moment. One. One o'clock, tomorrow already. . . .

Charles was coming to Brede today.

Oh, God, I can't, I can't, I can't. . . .

Cressida did not know whether she uttered the words, or whether they spoke themselves only in her brain. She did not know what it was she couldn't do. For a few minutes she knew nothing, and could not even think.

She hurried upstairs, flung off her clothes and got into bed as if she was racing against time to reach some comprehensible safety, some solid place in a rocking world where it would be possible to think.

CHAPTER TWENTY-FIVE

Charles Valery sat in a first-class carriage in a train that was just pulling out of a London station. There were five other people in the carriage, all reading newspapers in which there was an account of a raid by a thousand bombers on Bremen. Great Britain had lost fifty-two aircraft.

'Fifty-two missing . . .' one man muttered to his neighbour, 'that's a lot . . . a lot. . . .'

'A thousand went out, nine hundred and forty-eight came back, look at it that way,' his neighbour replied.

'Still, fifty-two . . .' The first man shook his head heavily. 'Three hundred men . . .'

'Nothing compared to what we lost on the Marne. . . .' His friend shook his newspaper so that it rustled. He folded it into a thick wad and put it in his pocket. He took out a cigarette-case and waved it at his friend, who took a cigarette.

Both men lit up and smoked in silence.

'. . . she said . . . and so I said, well, I said . . . and all she said was . . .'

Little scrappy drifts of conversation, a word here and there audible, the rest a murmur; a ceaseless patter of words, as much part of a railway-carriage as the smell of the smoke and oil, pointless, boring, the little drifts of other people's conversations that had always filled the air of trains.

Out of the window the same rows of dingy houses, the same vile backyards with washing flapping in the dirty air, the same sad cabbages, their once hopeful young greenery varnished with London soot, the same lovely sweep of the river in subtle tones of grey, coming suddenly out of the clutter of chimney-pots and haphazard streets, flowing steadily, deeply romantic. . . .

The same gradual change from the sprawling, dirty, richly human slums to the smug, dingy, neat beginnings of the suburban villas whose back gardens were laid out side by side like a series of messy watercolours arranged for a painting competition; the same huge playing-fields, the same acres of cemeteries. . . .

The fantastic tidyness of a huge nursery garden . . . a smartly painted efficient-looking sewage farm. . . .

All streaming past the train, all a little unreal like a picture being shaken from side to side so that it could not be clearly seen. . . .

Charles told himself many times that this was England. But it was not the fact of its being England that needed emphasising. It could have been nowhere else in the world.

This was England after three years of war. This ordinary, normal, untidy, familiar, sometimes beautiful country, with every railway-station in the usual place and in the usual state of unhurried bustle, where people still filled the trains, still stood about at stations with scrappy luggage and masses of children, still chattered in undertones, still discussed the news with a sort of impersonal gravity, with, one felt, half a mind on its effect upon the stock market. . . .

This was England after the worst the enemy could do in the way of bombing, after three years of what was intended as a strangling submarine blockade.

Charles could not have said in so many words what it was he had expected to find in England. Perhaps he had not quite imagined that the entire countryside would be a blackened ruin, that people would be picking their way nervously between yawning bomb craters and darting into underground holes as soon as daylight began to fade. Perhaps he had not quite expected to see on every face the hard lines of heroism and stark, but controlled, fear.

But England had been for three years described in terms of heroism, in outsize headlines. It had been loudly called the war-torn, the noble, the indomitable, the last outpost of civilisation. Surely it was natural to suppose that all this hyperbole must have a visible cause. But it was certainly difficult to detect in the stolid, well-fed faces of the English people any sign of undue heroism, or any indication that they were making a brave struggle to support life on insufficient food and unremitting hard labour under the constant fear of death.

Here and there, it was true, there were ruined and burnt-out buildings. But there were always burnt-out buildings to be seen from railway-trains, and these ruins looked as if they had quite gently decayed under the slow wear of time rather than been blasted asunder with savage violence in a few seconds. Even the thousands of broken windows merely suggested small boys with stones rather than death-dealing splinters of steel and iron.

And above all, the quietest, most peaceful objects imaginable, the fat, shining barrage balloons drifted comfortably, like enormous children's toys, like a super advertising display got up by some enterprising business company.

The train reached the country. There were aerodromes where only fields had been, but there were still miles of tree and cow-studded fields as well. There were tanks and army vehicles on every road, but there were also thousands of little ten horse-power cars, neat and shiny, looking as though they had been specially built to carry picnic-baskets. There were troops at every railway-station, but they were the same carefree soldiers that had always been typical of the British Army, apparently without a care in the world except to get a cup of tea at over-crowded buffets. They certainly did not look as though they were aware of the fact that they stood between the life and death of civilisation, between the ruin of humanity and its salvation. And yet these were the men who had been defeated by the strongest, most dazzlingly victorious army the world had ever seen, these were the men who had waited, unarmed, for that same all-conquering army to invade their country, which was divided from the onrush by nothing more than a rather larger tank obstacle than most. And there they were, after three years of waiting, still the same cheerful, tea-drinking, comfortably grumbling, placidly obedient and always travelling British soldiers.

The train slid out of one station after another, and with every moment a sense of unreality grew in Charles Valery's mind. At Wichlesbury he left the train. He walked down the platform feeling like a ghost, but not a ghost of the kind to inspire fear, because it was he who was nervous. He was suddenly as shy as a small boy on his own for the first time. It was an effort even to ask a porter for a taxi. It was still more of an effort to decide what to do when he was informed that a taxi was not to be had for the moment. Full of a desire to get away from this newly alarming place where everyone was real except himself, Charles told the porter he would walk and leave his luggage to be fetched at some other time. Later it would, perhaps, be easier to make arrangements, easier to do the normal thing in this normal country, this country whose normality was the one strange thing about it.

Charles walked away through the town, through villages of which he remembered almost every house, across meadows and along field paths as familiar to him as his own name and as strange as a foreign land. Walking took the stiffness out of his knee, and he was unconscious of fatigue, so that the gates of Brede came as a shock. It was hard to realise that he had walked twelve miles.

At the gates he stopped. Surely now, at the gates of his home, he would wake up and see the truth.

He looked at the road winding away from those gates, he saw trees, quiet grassland, a bright glimpse of the river. He saw something of which he remembered every detail, something that went back to the very roots of his life.

At that moment the only real thing in the world was the memory of Harcourt's face, screaming silently, black in death.

So it was this, this peace behind lovely gates, those trees and those smooth acres of grass for which he had come half across the world to fight. This peace, this beauty he had dreamed of until he was full of a murderer's madness. This beauty, which he possessed, had possessed him until he was willing to kill men for it. And it was a dream. Those gates opened on a dream, an unreality almost shocking in the face of the terrible truth.

But if he walked through those gates he would no longer be lost in a normal world, he would find himself in a ghostly one. He would find peace, rest, contentment, personal happiness. He would find enough strength to defend these things against the terrors of hell itself. And he would find himself walking back into a mirage, back into the dream of safety, cut off from mankind, selfishly safe behind the lovely gates that closed against the problems of humanity.

It was at that moment that Cressida saw him. She came round the turn of the drive and saw him, standing just outside the gates, hesitating like a man who had lost his way.

She had decided to walk towards the town until she met him, because it was impossible to stay in the house and wait. But now that he was actually there she felt as if his presence was the most wildly unexpected thing that could possibly be imagined. The sight of his tall familiar figure, leaning back a little so that his weight rested against his walking-stick, could not by the craziest stretch of imagination be made into actual fact.

Cressida stopped automatically for a second or two, but although emotional tension could scarcely have been more acute her sense did not entirely desert her. She walked on. However tense the drama, she and Charles could not stand and look at each other like two dogs working up for a fight from a distance. In spite of everything the absurdity of the idea struck her so that she was smiling with genuine amusement when she arrived at the gates.

She did not know that for Charles her appearance at that moment put the final touch to a vision that held him under a spell. Before she had left the house Cressida had told herself that she was looking haggard and plain. But after the emotions of the night, she decided, it could not be helped. She did not know that emotional strain had given her a strange wild beauty, a sharp, almost exaggerated loveliness which made her face like an artist's vision of it, overaccentuated and startling.

Cressida heard herself saying, 'Hullo, Charles,' in a voice that seemed to belong to some idiotic woman who could think of nothing better to say at a moment for which she had lived for five years.

She heard Charles say, 'Cressida,' and she found herself walking back along the drive with him, telling him quite unnecessarily that she had come out to meet him, and expressing surprise because he had walked from Wichlesbury.

They reached the house and went in. Cressida, sick of the sound, heard her own voice drivelling on about the house being full of strange people, and some of the best chairs being in the attic. She even carried normality to the point of saying she must go and get tea ready while Charles found his way to his room. She escaped to the kitchen, feeling like a Martha who would fuss about food even under the eyes of God.

Charles did find his way to his room. He stood at the window of it, staring out at acres of his own land, buried in peace as deep as the foundations of the world. He turned, and surveyed the room. He looked at his bed, rounded under a creaseless silk cover, at his books in rows against the walls, at the flowers Cressida had put on a walnut tallboy, polished till it was a mirror for the table opposite, at the old, gently-coloured prints in their dim frames, at the delicate pattern of the Chinese silk carpet. As his eyes moved from one loved and lovely object to another, he felt the meshes of the net tighten around him.

With the hurried movements of a man trying to escape he left the room and went downstairs.

The curve of the handrail on the staircase was like silk under his hand. His feet seemed to cling to the thick carpet. The Chippendale chairs which were not in the attic greeted his eyes. The leather sofa seemed to wait for the impress of his body. The ticking of the grandfather clock made him a small boy, peering up to see if it was tea-time. The pewter plates on the mantelpiece glowed like grey moons against the dark panelling. Cressida's flowers lit the room. Sunlight laid a path across the Persian carpets to the foot of the staircase.

Cressida called to him from the kitchen.

Tea was ready.

Cressida introduced him to several people whose presence was odd and unexpected, but who seemed a great deal more at home than he was himself.

'Mrs Yates, this is Mr Valery . . .'

'Mary, you don't know Charles Valery . . .'

Someone asked him about his voyage. Someone said it must be terrible to be in a small boat for fourteen days, and he agreed that it was. Someone else said it was wonderful that people in open boats were found, and he agreed again. He was given slices of new bread and passed jars of honey and jam. Several people offered him cake and tried not to look too closely at his scarred hands. After tea he dried some plates, and someone said it was a shame he should have to wash up on his first day.

He was unaware that Cressida watched him all the time, in a sort of anguish because she felt he might vanish if her eyes let him go for an instant.

When tea was over he found himself in his room again. Suddenly he was too tired to do anything except lie down on the bed, on the immaculate cover, without taking off his shoes.

The rest of the day passed timelessly. After another meal Charles, without knowing how, found himself outside the house, walking with Cressida across the great lawns.

Cressida could never, then or afterwards, have described her feelings at that moment. A child of two, she felt, could not have been less aware of itself, or more at a loss for the next word.

She told herself several times that it was Charles Valery who walked beside her, but it was also a ghost. Or else she had suddenly become a ghost herself, unable to establish contact with the human being whose feet moved in time with hers, but whose mind functioned on another plane.

At the edge of the woods Charles stopped. With an obvious effort he began to speak.

'I oughtn't to have come back, Cressida,' he said. His voice sounded strained, as if he was being forced to speak against his will. 'It was a mistake. I'll have to go away again. I don't know – how to explain to you. . . .'

Cressida's heart contracted out of sheer sympathy for the trouble in his voice.

'Charles, don't,' she said. 'Don't worry.' Worry. Don't worry, the sort of thing one said to a child. 'It's all quite simple,' she went on, driving her thoughts away. 'I mean you – don't have to explain anything to me.' With every word she felt more helpless.

'But I must, Cressida. I must explain. Perhaps not to you but to myself. I – I'm drifting I – It must sound crazy to you, but –'

'Oh, my dear,' Cressida interrupted, 'you mustn't try to say anything tonight. You're – you're tired . . .' Tired. What a word to use of a man who looked like a shadow. '. . . tomorrow, when you've rested . . .'

'That's just it,' Charles broke in, speaking a little more easily, 'I can't rest until I know where I am!' For a second he laughed and the tension was suddenly relaxed. 'You'll have to let me hammer out a lot of words because – well, because you are the only person I can talk to. You see, I –' He paused. This time Cressida did not attempt to fill the gap. 'Years ago I loved you,' Charles went on quietly. 'You knew, didn't you? I loved you when – I went away, and I've loved you ever since.'

It might be me, Cressida thought, talking and not knowing what to say.

'But that – doesn't – that's not the answer, and I've got to make you see why.' Charles went on. 'You've been too important, you're still too important for me to – well, peter out and say no more about it. I love you still. I want you more than anything in the world, more than I want Brede and this – this peace. But – no. Don't say anything, Cressida, please let me go on . . .'

For five years . . . no more waiting. . . .

Cressida's relief because she need not speak was as great as her anxiety about what he would say next.

'You see, I found out something. I had a lot of time to think in that boat. I – got to know myself, because there wasn't anyone else I suppose. And I know now that I'm too – weak-minded to stay here and let myself – love you, and let Brede get a hold on me, and let myself be happy and forget everything else. I can't do it. I can't do it because it would be going back to an old dream that men have dreamed for too long. It is a dream, Cressida, that men can make their own lives, love their own possessions and to hell with the rest of the world. It's not true. It's a dream that's been the curse of the world for so long that it's begun to look real, but it isn't. I began to realise all this when I was floating about in that boat. I tried to decide why I wanted to fight in this war. I couldn't make myself believe in any reason except the old one of keeping the enemy out of my gates! I don't mean I don't agree with – well, with what they call war aims and so on. I do but – but at the back of it all I'm fighting so that the Germans shan't get Brede! It would be easy to fight for that reason. If I stayed here and – took what I want, I could still go and fight, as ferociously as anyone else, but – but it would be for the wrong reason.'

'Oh, Charles. Charles' – Cressida could not prevent herself interrupting this time – 'surely it wouldn't. Surely men have always fought to – to preserve what they love? It can't – be wrong.'

'But it is, Cressida. If it's a good reason, then there'll always be wars. If men are always going to be ready to spring into battle to preserve what they love, war can't end. Don't you see it's a selfish reason? You can wrap it up and call it tradition, or generalise and call it beauty, call it anything you like. But doesn't it simply mean that men are always ready to murder each other in order to keep something they've got that someone else wants? Of course I don't mean that wars are fought by men with only their own petty personal reasons behind them. But every man's petty personal reason can add up to a national cause much more easily than you might imagine. If I stood, literally, at the gates of Brede and fought on my own threshold, I should be fighting for the same basic reason as a man in a tank in the desert, thousands of miles away, a man whose individuality has been incorporated into an army, who doesn't think of himself, who's part of a machine defending an empire. Because it isn't enough to have a great cause put into great words for us, words like the Atlantic Charter. It won't be until every man feels the truth of those words, feels them in his soul, and doesn't just say he believes them, that there'll be a real chance of this war being the last. It's a beginning, of course, it's something to have a reason put into words for us, but it's no use leaving it at that.

Every individual must think it out for himself. Look at what happened after the last war. We were told we were fighting for humanity, for freedom, against aggression, against evil and wickedness and the rest. After four years of blood and heroism and self-sacrifice what happened? What happened to all the war aims and noble causes and fine ideals? Nothing. Simply nothing. Because men went back. They were tired and they went *back*. The moment they could, the lucky ones, who had anything to go back to, went back and wrapped themselves up in as much as they could restore of the comfort of their old lives. They went back to their comfortable houses and safe jobs, and began putting everything neatly back as nearly as it had been before the war as they could manage. They did so little about the less lucky men who had nothing to go back to that unemployment became a national scandal. And even unemployment was wrapped up and labelled as a "problem" and accepted as such, and as the cause of heavy taxes we paid and told ourselves we were doing what we could towards solving the problem. And there were people who sat back and said, Thank God we won the war! Even now, even at this moment, there are people who can say that they would go back to a pre-war life instantly, if they got the chance!' Charles stopped, his voice unsteady with anger.

'That's damnably true,' Cressida said. 'I've even heard people say that the post-war world's going to be so uncomfortable for them that they don't care if they die before it comes true. And they're the ones who talk about fine tradition!'

'It's what's in the minds of millions of the men who are fighting now, Cressida. Not the young ones, not the young ones who have had this war brought on them by the men who "won" the last one. But the men who have had happiness are fighting to get back to it. And it's no good. If men fight to go back it's the end of all hope of peace. We've got to fight to go forward, forward to something as different as possible from the old life, forward to a life for mankind, not back to a life for fortunate individuals. If we exterminated every German on earth, that wouldn't stop war, unless the peace is a peace facing the future and not a peace sinking back with a sigh of relief on the past.'

'We are all involved in mankind,' Cressida murmured. 'Someone, Donne I think it was, said that centuries ago.'

'Yes,' Charles said instantly, 'centuries ago, and we've still taken no notice of the remark. Even longer ago Christ said the same thing over and over again. "Members one of another." He even called us sheep! Sheep, who flock together, whose entire lives consist of mass movement and mass impulse! Well, I don't imagine we're meant to behave like sheep to the extent of moving in flocks and going where the dog drives us, but it's possible to read another meaning into the word. It's possible to imagine the human race becoming sheep-like in a spiritual sense, sheep-like because individuals learn humility, learn that they, as individuals, are not important. Their value exists because they are part of a whole, part of a flock, part of the human race. That doesn't mean they needn't think any more. It means they must think far more deeply. They've got to think for humanity, let their brains be part of a whole too.'

The silence that fell was no longer tense. It was extraordinarily restful. But Cressida broke it.

'Yes, I understand,' she said softly. 'But, Charles, why did you say you were too weak-minded to accept happiness and fight for it? If you believe in what you've just said you wouldn't go back to happiness, you'd go forward to it.'

'I thought you'd say that, Cressida. It's the most difficult part of the whole thing to explain. I don't quite understand it myself yet, but – I've got as far as knowing what I mean, even if I can't say it!'

'I know how that feels,' Cressida said, 'and – if it's too difficult you – needn't go on, Charles. I won't insist on any more explanations!' She ended a little less seriously.

Charles looked at her without speaking for a few seconds. Although he was not more than two yards away from her his eyes were the eyes of a man looking into a very far distance.

'I –' he began at last, 'I'd rather go on, if you'll let me. I'd like to feel I – had finished something! It's too easy to get through life if you never have to bother about who under-stands, or – is hurt by your own inability to think!' He laughed shortly. 'Being – vague,' he added, 'can be a much more active form of cruelty than most people realise.'

'That's – terribly true, Charles,' Cressida said. 'Thank you for saying it.'

'Well,' Charles began again, 'I mean I'm too weak-minded to keep the past and go into the future. I can only do one thing at a time, I suppose that's it really. I'm involved in the past, and unless I – let go of it altogether I'll never get anywhere else. It's like being a drunkard, who's all right as long as there's no whisky in sight! I can go away now and –

face the future. But if I stayed I'd be – well, the man with great possessions.' Suddenly he seemed to forget he was talking to Cressida. He looked into the dim woods, dense with shadows, and went on, like a man in a dream speaking only in his mind. 'I'm a ghost between two worlds. I've got to enter one of them, and it's got to be the new world. I can go forward if there's nothing behind me, and that's what I mean by being weak. A weak man can go forward if he has nothing to leave behind. A man who has no personal happiness can live for the happiness of others. He can give his life to mankind if it isn't – too precious! There are men, or there will be, strong enough to have their own happiness and not lose sight of mankind because of it. But I couldn't do that. I – if I had what I want I – I should forget the existence of mankind! I wish I didn't realise that, I wish I hadn't done so much thinking in that damned boat! But I did and I can't get away from it. I know I can't go back, and if I go on I've got to go alone.' He stopped speaking and then seemed to remember where he was. He added, 'Do you – see, Cressida?' as if he was begging her to agree and let him go free.

Cressida said, 'Yes, Charles. I see.' There was no sign of emotion in her voice.

They began to walk back together towards the house. The summer darkness had not yet come, but the hard outlines of daylight were softening, and the edges of emotion were also, it seemed, less sharp. The house appeared before them, as gracious as ever. But Charles's eyes were cold and distant. His face had become in a few moments curiously calm, almost the face of an ascetic.

'I can't believe in – all this,' he began, very quietly and still, as if he was talking to himself. 'I believe in reality. I believe in the world as it is. I believe in men who have one purpose, men who have forgotten they ever had another life, men who are fighting without a thought of death, suffering without a thought of relief. This – this peace is not a reality. It's a vision that has made men weak. It's something men try to cling to, try to grasp without paying for. And men are being made to pay for it now. The world is full of men who are paying for their visions and their blindness. They're paying for more than that. They are paying for the hope of a future that will not be their future. All over the world men are dying, praying for death, or living in torment, in fear, in despair. Tired old men and women, and even children, are being tortured, driven into madness, starved and abandoned, sometimes to the final mercy of death. And all this doesn't happen by chance. It isn't the result of accidents or mistakes. It's the result of a system, it's brought about by what's been called efficiency! Even cruelty itself is systematic, carefully worked out by men's brains! Probably nothing in the world so far has equalled the efficiency of the German Army. Probably discipline will never be carried to such a pitch of perfection as it has been in Germany. All over the world efficiency has reached a peak, it has become a god. And it is beautiful. That's why it's so dangerous. The beauty of efficiency for its own sake has gone to men's heads. A great army under discipline, ships in convoy, aircraft in formation, machinery in a factory' – Charles paused and then continued – 'you could go on for ever with the list of beautiful, magnificent, successful and efficient results of the art of discipline! And yet it has failed. It has led to the very thing it was invented to avoid. It has led to chaos all over the world! I – I remember ships leaving the States, a convoy of hundreds of ships. One of the most beautiful things I've ever seen. Hundreds of ships under dozens of different flags, ships whose captains and crews could not have exchanged three words with each other in the same language, all sailing together in perfect formation. Every commander knew exactly what to do at all times, every man in every ship knew exactly what he must do all the time. A few flags or a hoot on a siren could alter the course of the whole convoy. One night they met a pack of submarines. Those submarines were under discipline too. They were working together, perfectly disciplined. When they met the ships there was chaos and death. But every man was doing his job, in the worst of the chaos. Every man thought of his job first, and did it if death was the only result. I don't think discipline could achieve more than that. But it has still failed because it hasn't taught men to think! If every man in every one of those ships, and in the submarines too, had known his own mind and obeyed it, there would have been no battle! And it's the same all over the world. We are always being told the German people don't want war, the English don't want war, no one wants war. And yet we have war. We have war because men have been herded, they've been formed into masses, they've been taught to obey without question, to fight and die without hesitation. But men have not been taught to take the advice Christ gave them when He said, "Know thyself."'

Charles's voice ceased, but the sense of his words remained. There was a long silence. Charles himself broke it.

'I've tried to do that,' he said quietly. 'I – discovered myself when I was alone, and because I'm – weak I can only stick to myself if I do it alone.'

They had almost reached the house when Charles stopped.

'I'd like you to know,' he said, 'that – Brede belongs to you now.'

Cressida drew a quick breath, but Charles did not give her time to speak.

'Please, Cressida. Don't let's – argue about it. You see I – I can't let myself cling to – anything. I – couldn't have done what you've done with Brede. You've made it a roof for – some of the homeless and I – couldn't have done that. But I'd rather know it was being done!'

There was another silence. Cressida could not look at Charles, and she certainly could not begin to speak.

I've loved a ghost, she was thinking. A ghost . . . this is a man I don't know . . . someone I can't understand . . . and it's Charles.

Charles began to speak again.

'It's very beautiful,' he said, 'isn't it, Cressida? Ever since I can remember I've thought it the most lovely house in the world. It's been – more than just my home. I've been possessed by it. I tried to break away, when I was quite young. I didn't want to be – owned by anyone or anything. I wanted to own myself. I used to feel that even my parents didn't really own me. When I left school I decided I'd got to get away from Brede. I knew it would be impossible unless I did it at once.

I knew what it was like going back to school. I used to dread leaving the house more than I minded leaving my mother. It was only bearable to go because there were the holidays, always definitely coming, however far away. School was just a series of unreal intervals in my life which was lived here. The first day of every holiday was just the day after the last one of the holiday before. Term was something inbetween that didn't count. When I was about eighteen I – realised what was happening and I tried to make up my mind to get a job that would make me independent. And then – well, then my father – wanted me here. He wanted me to take over the horses. He said he was getting too old. He didn't try to force me, but it didn't need force. I came and – handed myself over to Brede for life.'

For life . . .? Cressida thought.

'And – when I had to go away' – Charles seemed to have leapt the gap in his story with a bare margin of safety – 'I meant that to be for life too. But – well, I don't seem to be able to do the things I meant to!' Charles laughed, a little grimly. 'I ought not to have come back,' he said finally.

'Oh, Charles, you had to,' Cressida spoke without thinking, as if the words had to be uttered. 'You had to come back because –'

Because what? What exactly was the reason for Charles's return being so essential? How on earth explain to Charles, when she hardly understood herself, why it was so urgently necessary for him to have come back?

'I think I know what you mean,' Charles went on evenly. 'You mean that if I hadn't come back I couldn't have – given it up voluntarily? That's true anyway. Last time I – had to go and

252

– there wasn't any choice. But one can't escape having to face a choice in the end.'

Cressida said nothing. She was only just beginning to realise the truth of Charles's words and their application to herself.

Suddenly Charles laughed, and for the first time his laugh held amusement.

'How terribly heroic I've sounded,' he said. 'But I'm not even running away to give my life for my country. I'm going because I want to be free in a free world! If I happen to die in the attempt, at least I shan't have died in defence of private property!'

Even in the fading light Cressida could see that Charles looked different. He looked like a man with life in front of him. Suddenly he turned towards her impulsively. He took her shoulders in his hands. She could no longer see his face and so she did not know that its expression had changed again, swiftly, agonisingly.

'Cressida darling,' he said, and for the first time his voice hurt her. 'Darling. You – must never think this has been – easy, and – I've got to thank you because you – you haven't made it more difficult. If – if you – But I can't explain any more. Please, don't – don't ask me anything, I – Cressida, you've given me something I can't tell you about. You – and Brede. Cressida, I'll be grateful, always – whatever happens. . . .'

Grateful, whatever happens . . .

Grateful for every moment of my life . . .

'Goodnight, Cressida darling.' Charles's voice was so low that she scarcely heard it. His hands were hurting her shoulders. His face was against her hair.

Then he had let her go and walked away into the house.

This time it was Cressida who stood quietly on the lawn alone. She watched Charles enter the house. The house was now just a grave outline in the semi-darkness.

A roof for some of the homeless. . . .

It doesn't matter, she thought, who owns it. It doesn't matter if it's full of strangers, if it's not kept perfectly for its owners. It doesn't matter how valuable the furniture is, or whether the carpets get worn out. It's a home – and not just a possession.

Cressida shook back her wild, fair hair. It's something, she thought. I've done something. It hasn't been a waste, loving Charles all this time. Charles loves me. We've got that for ever. It doesn't matter if we never meet again, because we've got something no time can take away. Memory. Memory is the only thing that lasts for ever. If Charles hadn't come back, I'd have waited for ever, not knowing. . . .

Her eyes roved over the face of the dark house, the house which had meant so much to the man who had just left it for ever. Charles had just walked into the house, but it wasn't his any longer. . . .

It meant too much to him, Cressida thought. I owe it to him not to let that happen to me.

Her eyes came to rest, as always, on the window of the nursery.

Brede will belong to John, she thought. He will be one of the men of the new world, strong enough to be part of mankind and a whole man as well, strong enough to own his life and give it to humanity. Or at least, she went on with a little crooked grin at the exalted level of her thoughts, he will if I'm a success as a mother!

CHAPTER TWENTY-SIX

Charles Valery left Brede very early in the morning, before anyone else was awake. He walked away from the house without looking back, a free man with his eyes on the future, without even the incubus of a suitcase to interfere with his new freedom.

He left the lovely gates of Brede behind him and walked down the quiet grey road on which the sun did not yet shine. His mind was empty and at peace. There was time now to rest his mind before continuing with the thoughts he had only begun to understand and work out. There was all of time to make these new thoughts clear, these thoughts he had tried to put into words, perhaps a little too soon, before they were properly formed in his mind. He did not try to think about the future in detail. He looked at it more as a state of mind than as an existence in which action would have a part. He did not wonder what sort of job he would be able to get, or whether he would actually fight, or whether he would fly. He did not dwell upon imaginary and thrilling combats, or picture himself handling new and magnificent aeroplanes. He knew that it did not matter whether his future was exciting and dangerous, whether he died spectacularly in a moment of exaltation, or whether he sat in an office and filled up forms. He knew that none of these things mattered because he had already won the initial victory without which the battle could not even begin. He had won the victory over his own mind, and was free because he had defeated himself. If his life was to last twenty years or a week he would never again lose this freedom.

'Man, self-conquered, shall by man unconquerable be . . .'

He could not remember the source of the quotation that ran in his mind, and did not try to. Nothing but the truth of it mattered.

Behind him, in the house he had left, life proceeded as if that strange, swift visit of his had never taken place. Cressida got out of bed at a quarter to seven, went down to the kitchen in her pyjamas and opened the boiler, put the porridge in the oven, riddled the Aga and opened the kitchen windows, actions which took less than ten minutes and were as natural to her now as the routine of putting on her clothes. So natural were they that she often found herself listening in genuine amazement when people said what a bore the boiler was, and, of course, cooking breakfast . . . ! She could not have been more surprised if someone had complained that it was a bore having to clean one's teeth.

When she was dressed Cressida went back to the kitchen, where old Northeast was by now coming and going on his large, deliberate feet, taking away ashes and bringing in filled scuttles, saying good morning to Cressida in the same words every day, words in which only the adjective qualifying the weather varied, words which ended always with the familiar inquiry about the vegetables to be brought in that morning. This inquiry had a routine of its own.

'Well, madam,' the old man would say, precisely at the moment when he stood on the doorstep brushing coal-dust off his hands, 'what is it today?'

'Well, Northeast, what do you think we ought to finish?' Cressida would reply, taking her cue unfailingly. According to season she might vary her words as far as saying 'begin' instead of 'finish'.

For the sake of appearances Northeast would wrap himself in what seemed to be deep thought.

'The purple sprouting's drying up this weather, look,' he might then remark, or 'Them birds be getting at the peas.'

'All right, Northeast. We'll have them in.'

And old Northeast would depart, ostensibly under orders, to bring in the vegetables he had already decided to bring in.

This morning the fate of the vegetables was arranged as usual, and then Northeast paused.

'The master's back then,' he remarked.

'He's gone away again, Northeast,' Cressida said. 'He –' How difficult, she thought, to explain Charles's sudden departure. 'I think he – found he couldn't stay, you know.' How feeble, she thought. I shall have to do better than that.

But it was enough for Northeast, it seemed.

'Ar,' the old man said calmly. 'When I seen him yesterday,' he went on after a moment, 'I thought to myself he hadn't properly come back, not rightly come home like. Time enough for that, I thinks, when the war's over.'

'I don't think he'll come back – even then,' Cressida said. 'He said that – that people came back too soon after the last war, that if everyone comes back there won't be any end to war.'

'Ar,' Northeast said again, 'and that's true enough. There's some,' he went on, 'as won't give nothing up till it's took from them. The master never was one o' them, look.'

With which profoundly true remarks the old man plodded away to fetch his cabbages.

Some as won't give nothing up till it's took from them, Cressida thought. So old Northeast sees that too. Well, why shouldn't he? It's a very simple truth.

And perhaps that very simple truth was the reason that the English people were not, even yet, in what was known as a state of total war. Millions of people, almost everyone probably, had volunteered their services to the country in some form or other, but among those millions there were thousands who would not give up anything that was not actually taken from them. People would not give up small personal comforts, they would not give up the privacy of their homes, they would not give up their amusements, their games, their use of the car when a bus travelled the same road, they would not give up their servants, they would not even give up making toast by electricity until these things were taken from them by force of law. Most of Europe and a great part of Asia had had everything, even life, taken from them by force alone. The totality of their state of war had been violently thrust upon them. The English, by the mercy of God and the miraculous gallantry of a few young men, had been saved from the same fate by the skin of their teeth. But still,

still they remained, those people who wouldn't 'give nothing up till it was took from them'.

Breakfast began and was finished and washed up, and it was time to think about something for lunch, and then there would be the boiler to stoke and tea, and something for supper to be concocted out of an empty-looking larder.

The post came without a letter for Mary Handley, who still did not know what had happened to her husband in Tobruk. The Rimmington-Clarkes received news that the Colonel was to leave England in a week's time, for an unspecified destination. Mrs Yates hurried upstairs to bath the baby after seeing her husband off on his motor-cycle.

The day proceeded as all other days, as if yesterday had been imagined, as if Charles Valery had never come back.

And it was Friday, and on Tuesday Tori had not returned.

And that's how life goes on, Cressida thought. Life goes on and on. The cabbages stand in rows, and somewhere men are clutching at wreckage in wild seas with oil burning on the water. The trains are full of men reading their newspapers, and somewhere old men and women are being driven in herds away from their homes, sleeping in the cold under trees, hiding in cellars and jungles. Some people are living gloriously, knowing the terrible joy that has fear only just ahead of it. For some the fear has come and gone, leaving desolation behind it. For some the fear walks with them doggedly, steadily at their side. Men are fighting, perhaps happy in the excitement of action. Men are working in deadly boredom in safe offices. Men are flying in close combat with death in the lonely sky, waiting in the deadly cold for unseen danger on the endless sea, marching in quiet country lanes, driving lorries through English villages or through the ruins of other villages in other countries, standing by silent guns in English fields, sweating by guns red-hot with the fury of rapid fire, poring over maps in deep, warm rooms that are never lit by daylight, handling steel and iron under arc-lights that burn day and night and look down on the ceaseless racket of machinery and the ceaseless drip and smell of oil, filling up forms in offices where the rattle of typewriters never ceases, and plodding out into gardens to fetch the cabbages.

And women are doing most of these things too, she thought. Some of them are living new lives with more intensity than they could have imagined, some are more bored than they could have believed possible. Women are not all doing new things. Women are cooking, bathing their babies, standing in queues for fish, waiting for letters that do not come, opening telegrams, putting washers on taps, patching leaky roofs with bits of felt and plasticine, stoking boilers, carrying things that are too heavy for them, coalscuttles, cases of ammunition in factories, suitcases in trains, or just shopping baskets filled too full.

And children are playing in complete unconcern in fields and in the streets, making sandcastles with the contents of rotted sandbags, throwing stones and sticks into static water belonging to the fire services, spotting aeroplanes as a game, looking for caterpillars and birds' eggs, and scarcely turning their heads to watch the tanks that clatter past in the lane behind them. Children are going to school and playing cricket and football, learning Latin and arithmetic and obedience.

Are they, she thought, are they learning to grow up into the new world?

Is anyone learning that?

Is anyone, in this vast universal effort to defeat an enemy, learning how to defeat the worst enemy?

Tori's words, 'the worst enemy . . .'

The words Tori had written, '. . . grateful for every moment of my life because I love you.' Grateful for every moment. . . . Not grateful for anything he had got out of life, not grateful for any gift, but grateful because he had been able to give. . . .

And Charles, 'I'll be grateful always, whatever happens . . .'

Both the men who loved her were grateful because they had been able to give her something.

Cressida turned away from the kitchen window. She took a saucepan over to the Aga. Perhaps her somewhat high-flown thoughts had given her a heightened view of the commoner things of life, but the Aga looked to her symbolic at that moment. It seemed cleaner, squarer, more solid than usual, like a fortress for the simple, sane things of life; comfort, good food, warmth, friendliness. . . .

She stood there, stirring the contents of the saucepan very carefully.

I know now, she thought, what Tori means.

If you have enjoyed this Persephone book why not telephone or write to us for a free copy of the Persephone Catalogue and the current Persephone Biannually? All Persephone books ordered from us cost £10 or three for £27 plus £2 postage per book.

PERSEPHONE BOOKS LTD
59 Lamb's Conduit Street
London WC1N 3NB

Telephone: 020 7242 9292
sales@persephonebooks.co.uk
www.persephonebooks.co.uk